Frontier
of Fear

Frontier of Fear

A Novel

Michael Hartland

Walker and Company
New York

Originally published in Great Britain.

First published in the United States of America in 1992
by Walker Publishing Company, Inc.

Library of Congress Cataloging-in-Publication Data
Hartland, Michael.
Frontier of fear: a novel / Michael Hartland.
p.   cm.
"Originally published in Great Britain" —Verso t.p.
ISBN 0-8027-1202-9
I. Title.
PR6058.A69496F76   1992
823'.914—dc20   92-10152
CIP

Printed in the United States of America
2 4 6 8 10 9 7 5 3 1

For Maria,
with love

The road to Paris and London lies through the towns of Afghanistan, the Punjab and Bengal.

Leon Trotsky
1879–1940

PROLOGUE

The Province of Sind – Pakistan

The gallows had been erected overnight, a makeshift structure of metal scaffolding in the centre of the market place. It creaked in the hot desert wind, dust lashing the eyes of spectators who stood in silence, gaping at the three ropes dangling from the cross-beam.

Soldiers in steel helmets crouched on roofs around the square, sweeping it with machine-pistols as the crowd parted to admit a rusty army lorry. Standing on its back were six more soldiers and a mullah chanting from the Koran, for this was dawn on Friday, the day of prayer, the day of retribution. Three figures swayed above the tailgate, two young men and a girl. They wore grey prison clothes, arms tied behind them, fetters on their ankles, bodies already broken by the weeks of beating and starvation.

The truck stopped under the crossbeam and the crowd murmured as a man in a sports shirt looped a noose around the neck of each prisoner, positioning the metal eye that had replaced a knot under each left ear. For a few minutes the three victims stood outlined against a crimson sky; then the hush was broken as the engine coughed back into life. There was a grinding of gears and the vehicle moved forward slowly.

One of the men leapt from the back of the truck, plunging down with a shout of defiance. The other two cowered back, shackled feet fighting to grip the rocking metal platform until they were dragged off, the boy first with the scream of a terrified child. The drop was too short and none of the prisoners was killed outright. The three bodies twisted at the end of their ropes, coughing and choking as they gasped for air. The girl was the lightest and took longest to die, slim hips writhing obscenely for ten minutes as her face turned black.

'Jesus,' muttered the American journalist at the back of the crowd, turning to a veiled woman beside him. 'What was their crime?' he asked in Urdu.

9

The woman's eyes above her *chador* remained fixed on the gallows, enjoying every detail. 'Traitors,' she spat into the dust. 'Spies.'

PART ONE

1

Vienna

Three thousand miles away, Sarah Cable felt a less fatal tightening of the throat as she locked her car door. Six weeks of planning, but this was the moment when it could all go wrong.

She strode across the car park, leaning into an icy wind from the Danube, and took the escalator up to the rotunda. In the cloakroom she pulled off the overcoat of heavy green loden and gave her appearance a final check in the mirror. Straight fair hair hung loose on her shoulders and the blue dress matched her eyes. Very demure, very English. Pity she was twenty-six, nearly six feet tall and skinny – he probably preferred them plump and fifteen – but at least her neckline was flattering. To steady her nerves, she browsed at the newspaper stall for a few minutes, then walked quickly to the lift.

The building was a squat, concrete cylinder, with curving walls of glass that looked out over the spires and tenements of Vienna. Outside, the United Nations flag flapped mournfully, frayed at the edge like the organisation it represented. Inside, groups of diplomats glided about the long room with expressions of bored superiority, snatching at the trays of glasses carried by waitresses in dirndls. It was the usual watery gin and Campari.

There were at least a hundred people at the reception and the chatter was deafening. Ross Aitken from the Canadian Embassy emerged from the crowd, grinning at her. 'Okay? Ready?' She nodded and picked up a glass of orange juice as Ross gave a dry account of his disastrous ski weekend in the Salzkammergut, making her giggle but not relax.

Her target stood in the corner, deep in conversation with an earnest Swede and a fellow with wild eyes and a tie covered in soup stains. That must be Labovic, the new Yugoslav counsellor. She tried to avoid staring at the man on Labovic's right. He was quite tall, perhaps an inch or two shorter than Sarah, with a face full of character and a mass of wavy black hair. Usually she thought moustaches ridiculous, but his looked bold and inevitable for he had the rugged appearance of a mountain man, a Pathan from the North-West Frontier. She could imagine him with luxuriant whiskers, turban and bandolier, fighting against the Russians in Afghanistan.

Now they were close. 'Hi, Nazim.' Ross introduced her casually. 'Do you know Sarah Cable? She just started work here in Safeguards.'

He shook her hand regally. 'Nazim Rashid Khan. How nice to meet you.' His eyes were arrogant and intelligent. They said that he had noticed she was pretty, but there was nothing unduly interested or, unfortunately, predatory in them.

She smiled back. 'And to meet *you*, Dr Khan.' *Just flutter your eyelashes*, Nairn had said. *He can't resist the company of beautiful women, so long as they appear to be worshipping him.* 'Where are you from?'

'The Pakistan Embassy. How long have you been here, Miss Cable?'

'Nearly a year, but I've been away a lot on training courses.'

'And what do you do in Safeguards? Are you a secretary?' The question was distant, patronising, but his gaze kept falling to her breasts. Ross had drifted off. Things were starting to go according to plan.

'No, I'm an inspector.' She smiled. 'Rather a junior one.'

'Forgive me.' He suddenly came alive. 'But there are very few women on the scientific staff here.'

She laughed. 'Don't worry – I'm quite used to it. Everyone thinks I type for a living.' She sipped the orange and looked at him coyly over the top of the glass. 'Is your wife here tonight?'

'No. My family has gone home for the winter – they find it too cold here.' He spoke with only a slight Pakistani intonation.

Or your government likes to have them back as hostages, just in case you get ideas about jumping ship with all those wicked little secrets. 'It must be lonely for you without them.'

'Not really. I am very busy, you know – ours is only a small mission and there is a lot to do.'

And you're an arrogant bastard who probably wouldn't notice if you never saw them again. C'mon, she willed him, wishing she did not feel so edgy and scared inside, *you're off the leash and I'm available.* He was still speaking to her.

'Have you been to my country for the agency yet?'

Momentarily she thought of his hideous country – not the mountains, but the hot plains and the squalor, the harsh mullahs and the stoning and the whipping-frames. But it was best to forget all that. 'No, I haven't been outside the Euratom countries, but I should

14

prefer to work in Pakistan and India – it would be far more interesting.'

'Then we must have lunch together, Miss Cable; I can tell you something about our nuclear programme and you can teach me the work of an inspector.'

'That would be very kind. I should be honoured!' It was hard to give a simpering, girlish smile when you were looking down at the man. For the first time she noticed his suit: there was a silver thread in the light grey, almost flashy.

'And are you finding your way about Vienna?'

'I've been away so much I still feel like a tourist.'

'Really? Perhaps I could help a little there too?' It was something to do with his clipped way of speaking and his aristocratic bearing – he made picking her up sound almost condescending, the master addressing the pupil. 'You need to know where to shop, cafés, bars, that kind of thing – although of course as a Muslim I do not drink.' He raised one eyebrow and smiled for the first time, as if to suggest that might not be entirely true.

'Thank you, if you have the time.'

'Not at all. It would be a pleasure. Do you have a phone number?' She wondered whether giving him the number guaranteed you a call – or did he collect them all week and select the most promising at the weekend?

'Yes.' She fumbled with her handbag. 'I have a place in the Thirteenth.' He took the used U-bahn ticket with her number scribbled on the back. 'Or you could always ring me at the office.'

'But of course.' He pocketed the phone number briskly. The great man was moving on. 'It was good to meet you, Miss Cable.' He gave a slight bow and turned away; moments later Sarah saw him shaking hands with Georg Menzel from the American Embassy.

A mile up the river, two Austrian police were struggling to haul a body out of the current. Their baggy green overcoats dragged in the mud as they laid it flat in the headlights of their car, blue light still flashing on its roof. The corpse was that of a middle-aged woman, naked, greenish-white and puffy after immersion in the icy water. It had been battered in the steel gates of a sluice, but one of the officers crouched and pointed to the pattern of smaller lesions on the scrawny thighs and stomach. 'Cigarette burns?'

The other man nodded. 'And not easy to establish identity.'

The head and hands had been hacked off before the body was thrown in the river, but the kneeling policeman lifted the left arm to reveal a tattooed mauve number still legible after forty years, the unmistakable brand of a concentration camp. The Wiesenthal centre

15

had records that might put a name to her, and it was only a phone call away in the First District.

It was ten o'clock when Sarah unlocked the door of her small apartment. A note lay on the coffee table, the same one she had left for Johan. *Sorry, darling. Tried to get you on the phone all day. Something has come up. Can't make it this evening, but will be back about nine. Love you. S.*

He must have found it when he let himself in – she had given him a key – and his reply was curt. *I'm sorry too. Johan. 9.30.* It was the second time in a week that her other life had made her stand him up and she really *liked* the guy, this kind, Swedish giant with the blond beard. He worked in another part of the agency and it was a nice uncomplicated relationship, a delightful change to find a man so strong and gentle that he made her feel small and fragile again. He might have bloody well waited – but why should he, after shelling out for two theatre tickets and not knowing whether she would be out all night? Oh, stuff it. Damn. *Damn.*

She was still fuming when the phone rang. It was Mr Munster from the Embassy.

'Hello, Sarah?' He never said his name. 'Are you alone?'

'Yes, it's okay to talk.'

'Was the meeting with our overseas client satisfactory?'

'I hope so. I made the bait pretty obvious. Let's see if he swallows it.'

'You're sure you can go through with it?'

'Quite sure.' It wasn't true, but it was too late to tell him that she was scared as hell.

'Fine. Your country needs you and all that. Good luck.'

She snorted. 'Good *night*.'

'By the way . . .' His tone had changed, he sounded shifty.

'Yes?'

'Gerda seems to have vanished.' Sarah felt a cold fist clench in her stomach. Gerda was the Austrian typist Munster had wormed into the Pakistan Embassy, nearly sixty, a Mauthausen survivor, indestructible. 'I expect she's pushed off ski-ing without telling me.' He didn't believe it, any more than Sarah did. 'No need to worry – I just thought you should know.'

Sarah's mind was spinning. Pouring herself a whisky with a shaky hand, double-locking the front door, for the first time she sensed real danger. Suddenly she felt terrified and painfully alone.

2

Washington

It had all started six weeks before, not by the Danube but the Potomac. Three men were crowded into the basement office, looking out on a wintry corner of the garden. Nairn had never been in the White House before and, the way the briefing was going, he wasn't likely to be invited again. Ed Yagubian leant back with his feet on the desk, thumbs hitched behind red braces which he pulled out like bowstrings. 'Your Prime Minister speaks well of you, Sir David, that is why I agreed to this meeting when Georg here said you'd be in town. But I find your analysis profoundly depressing.'

The other two moved uneasily on their chairs, studying a back-lit map display on the whitewashed wall until Nairn stood up and swept his hand along the red line separating Pakistan and Afghanistan at its centre. He was tall and gaunt, dressed in a shabby suit that badly needed pressing. 'The North-West Frontier has always been a troublesome region, professor.'

'I read Kipling as a boy, Nairn. But I was hopeful that the threat of the last few years was over. Secretary Gorbachev claims he is withdrawing the Red Army from Afghanistan.'

The third man spoke for the first time. With thick-lensed spectacles and a check jacket, Georg Menzel looked like the American academic he had once been. Now the vulpine eyes belied the scholar's stoop. 'If so, he's doin' it darn slowly.'

'If that man stays in power, the President believes he intends to keep his word.'

Nairn thought of the old man hunched in the Oval Office upstairs, tired, frail, vague. 'Gorbachev's military establishment would disagree.' Nairn stayed standing by the map. 'They cannot be seen to be defeated by a bunch of Third World guerillas.'

'As we were in Vietnam.'

'Indeed, professor. Gorbachev is a statesman who can take a long view – if he lasts. But the war continues and the Red Army is simply being replaced by stronger Afghan forces with Soviet "advisers".

17

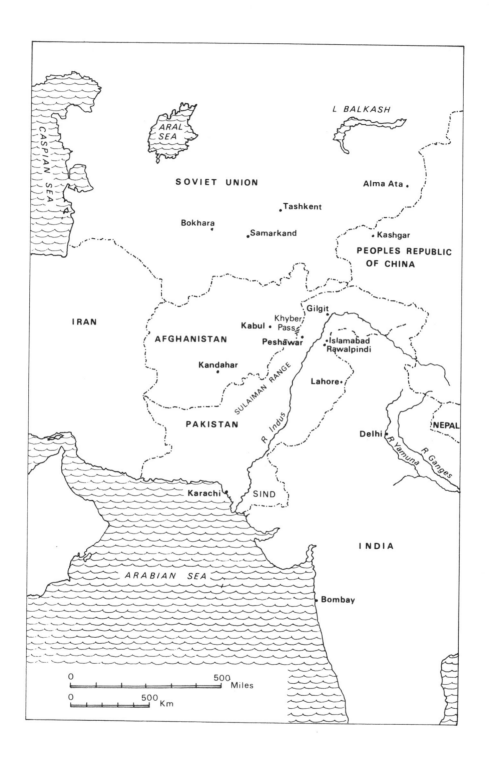

Gorbachev's generals would still like to pour in more firepower and crush the Mujahedin.' He moved his hand southwards, into northern Pakistan. 'A third of the Afghan population has left the country. About three million are in refugee camps here, camps which also harbour the guerillas.'

'And that sonofabitch Zia would like to see the back of them, smuggling drugs and arms, wrecking his economy.'

'He has enough problems of his own,' Nairn countered quietly. 'There are plenty of left-wing groups that would like to hang him from a lamp-post and there are leaders more extreme than Benazir Bhutto. Pakistan could easily see a coup.'

'And that would mean a government sympathetic to Moscow.' Menzel had a voice that grated like a chainsaw. 'A modern version of the old warm water port policy. No need for anythin' so crude as an invasion any more. With a socialist regime in Islamabad, the Soviet navy could use the Indian Ocean harbours, the Afghan army could cross the North-West frontier and take out the Mujahedin.'

'We couldn't allow that to happen.' Yagubian fiddled absently with a paperknife, staring away from the others into a corner, as if talking to himself. 'If Zia falls and the Russkis or their friends cross that line, even for a few days, decent freedom-loving hicks from Maine to San Diego will be rooting for a war. This country has been caught with its pants down too often . . .'

'No doubt we could find a political solution.' Nairn sat down again. 'But it would be a dangerous moment, too hot for comfort.'

'A political solution? Can *you* think of one, Nairn? Damn me, I can't. We avoid conflict by keeping a balance. Pakistan belongs to the West – it used to be in your goddam Empire – and the President will not let the Soviets have it, gentlemen, not even by proxy. If the scenario you envisage comes to pass, we should have no alternative but to use force.'

God, thought Nairn, *does he actually believe his own rhetoric?* 'Our Empire is long dead, professor, and Pakistan's an Islamic tyranny – don't be taken in by a few rich young men playing cricket. The use of force in a region that is so unstable would be too dangerous to contemplate, unthinkable.'

'Nothing is unthinkable, Nairn, in the defence of freedom.' The serious part of the discussion was plainly over.

'I guess Sir David and I need to talk further, sir.' Menzel rose abruptly as if anxious to get out of the room.

Nairn and Menzel left the White House in a long black Lincoln sedan, the glass partition behind the chauffeur firmly closed. 'You reckon this thing is serious, Dave?'

Nairn winced; no one had called him Dave since he was eleven.
'Very.'

'Uh-huh.' Menzel pulled down a jump seat and put his feet
up. 'Gout playin' up again. It's all too far off for the average
Congressman, y'know. All that matters here is when those missiles
come whistlin' over Alaska.'

'They just might, if there's too much sabre-rattling about the
defence of freedom. Who the devil is he trying to convince? Himself?'

'No, he believes it already, that's the problem.' Menzel stared out
of the tinted car window as they glided past the Bureau of Indian
Affairs. 'I agree it's dangerous, Dave, but I got you a personal
interview with the security adviser to the President of the U-nited
States himself and he heard you out. For Christ's sake, what more
can I do?' He lit a small cigar and inhaled deeply. 'You made a lot
of Zia's toy bomb – what's the truth of that?'

'You know as much as us, probably more. You've withdrawn
aid from Pakistan until he guarantees there's no secret nuclear
programme, but all the evidence points to it.'

The car crossed the Roosevelt bridge and joined the expressway
to Langley. 'Sure, we have intercepts, satellite photographs. We
know about the research and the underground purchases of fissile
material in Khartoum. But has it produced usable weapons yet? I'd
like to know that. I'd like to know that very much – way things are,
it could just be the joker in the pack.'

Nairn nodded. 'We did have an agent in their research centre at
Kahuta.'

'The guy they arrested? What happened to him?'

'They sentenced him to death, along with two students he'd used
as couriers – one was a girl of eighteen. They haven't hanged them
yet, but they will when they've got everything out of him.'

'Yeah. They got some pretty heavy interrogation techniques.'

Nairn's jaw tightened, but he said nothing.

'You still got that typist in their Vienna Embassy?'

'She's just starting to be useful.'

'Vienna *has* to be their base for buyin' in the equipment and
expertise, with half the nuclear industry in and out of that benighted
agency. Eisenhower must have been out of his skull when he set the
bloody place up.'

Nairn nodded agreement. 'What's our programme now?'

'Back to Langley for a seance with the Director. Then I'm takin'
you to the Market Inn for dinner. Alaskan King Crab. But time is
short, Dave. This operation is goin' too slow. Afghanistan, Pakistan,
Iran – all Mickey Mouse countries with worse human rights records
than Attila the Hun and armed opposition movements that want to

cut the present government to pieces.' He breathed out a ring of blue smoke and jerked a contemptuous finger back towards the White House. 'And whatever my commander-in-chief may want to believe, the Russians *are* still hangin' on in Afghanistan.'

'I agree it's a flashpoint.'

'Flashpoint? It's more than a fuckin' flashpoint – what the hell are those dumb Pakis goin' to do if the Russkis cross that border and take out the Mujahedin? What the hell are *we* goin' to do?'

It was late when they left the Market Inn, two ageing men, incongruous in their office clothes, followed at a discreet distance by the two young agents who had dined at an adjoining table, their hands never far from the revolvers scarcely concealed beneath their suits. The Lincoln was waiting under a yellow street light. 'Ali Baba is the answer,' growled Menzel, the chainsaw voice mellowed by Californian red. 'Has to be.'

Nairn had drunk little and glanced around nervously as the car door opened, to make sure they were not overheard. 'We can't talk in the open, Georg.'

'Balls,' growled Menzel, but he snapped an order to the driver and they sat in uneasy silence for twenty minutes, crossing the river again and winding up into the darkness of Arlington. The minders followed in another Lincoln. When they stopped, Menzel led them into an avenue of gravestones. Nairn followed, towering over the other man, clutching his overcoat around him. 'It's bloody cold, Georg. I hope this won't take too long.' The two figures set out briskly, footsteps echoing in the frost, the others thirty feet behind, until they came to a clearing among the tombs, looking down on the floodlit centre, the obelisk of the Washington monument and the white marble columns of Lincoln's. 'Very pretty, Georg.' Nairn was shivering. 'But I preferred the inn. Could we go back to the hotel now?'

Menzel rounded on him in the blackness. 'When we've got a few things straight. An hour ago I offered you a valuable asset. Nazim Khan is highly placed; he can give us precise detail on their weapons programme – and become a powerful agent of influence in the long run.'

'Did you really have to give him the codename Ali Baba?' Nairn started to light his pipe, as if it might warm him against the bitter cold. 'And you want us to run him?'

'Pakistan is in your sector, Dave. We respect that.'

Nairn gave a snort of disbelief. 'But you haven't actually *recruited* him yet! He's done no more than talk to your man in Vienna in terms that suggest he might be interested in help to leave his government's service and settle in America. Who're you kidding, Georg? Is that any more than a request for asylum?'

Menzel gestured in the dark, away from the floodlights to the dark shapes around them. A glimmer of moon showed a line of conifers swaying in the wind. 'Dave, this is a cemetery, right?'

'Right.'

'I brought you here because a lot of people in this town would like to bury you. Right?'

'I'm sorry to hear that.' Nairn seemed unmoved.

'David, I'm deadly serious. You Brits are the junior partners and down there are men who will never let you forget it. They didn't want you as Chief, they can't understand you, they still mistrust you because you protected Bill Cable when he was compromised in Nam.'

'Cable confessed – I didn't see why he should be crucified after coming clean.'

'It went down real bad here. They're offerin' you Ali Baba because Pakistan and Afghanistan matter. But it's also a test. A test of your good faith.'

'Why are you telling me this, Georg? Can't you wait to see the inside of Sing Sing?'

'For fuck's sake, I've known you thirty years. Do I need a better reason? But you *must* get Ali Baba on your payroll, you *must* bust the Paki bomb programme. He's a valuable asset and if you screw this, they'll screw you. I'm warnin' you as a friend, Dave.'

'And how exactly am I supposed to screw him?'

'Put pressure on the sonofabitch.'

'Is he susceptible to money?'

Menzel shook his head in the dark. 'No. Compromise the bastard. Get some houri layin' him. Get photographs of them on the job.'

'I'd prefer to win his trust.'

'There isn't time for that hearts and minds crap, just nail him by the balls.'

'Even if I agreed with you, Georg, we've been conspicuously unlucky so far. One agent due to be hanged, the other producing nothing conclusive. To do what you're suggesting, we'd have to use someone expendable. Life is cheap to these people – one mistake and she'd be finished. Even if we persuaded Khan to co-operate, he could easily be caught himself.'

'So they torture the bastard and string him up. So what, if we've got what we need?'

'If we've provided him with a woman, they'd do the same to her.'

'Ali Baba is stationed at their Embassy in *Vienna*, friend. With luck you could finish the whole thing without your agent ever goin' near Pakistan. If Khan survives long enough to become an agent of influence in Islamabad, that's a different ball game.'

'He wouldn't survive. We'd be lucky to discover the truth about the nuclear thing and even that could cost us . . . maybe it's worth it, but where do I find the girl?'

'You got a whole service to choose from.'

'How can I use someone already in the service? Half of their names are in the Diplomatic List and most of them must be known to the opposition. She'd be blown in days.'

'Then find a new face from outside.'

'All the possible stringers in Vienna are as well known to the Pakistanis – or the Russians – as to us.'

Menzel sighed, then coughed as a blast of pipe smoke blew in his face. 'You force me to spell it out, David. You know perfectly well that you have just the girl already on your books.' He sensed the sudden tension as Nairn's body stiffened. 'For Christ's sake, she grew up in Vienna, she's gone back there to work, she's attractive, she's intelligence trained but not currently in your outfit.'

There was a long silence as Nairn stared down at the floodlit Capitol, then he spoke almost inaudibly. 'I can't do that.'

'Her family owes us, David.'

'I can't do it. It's not an option.'

'Why the hell not? We've been keeping an eye on young Sarah these last few years.'

'You bastards.'

'Dave – we've discussed it at Langley and it's the obvious solution, the *only* solution. It's right for the job and right for you. The father dropped you in it, now use the daughter in a successful operation and you come up smelling of roses.'

'This isn't the Middle Ages, Georg.' Suddenly Nairn sounded angry – and rattled.

'Just do it, friend. If you don't, your fans will think you lost your grip or you're screwin' the kid yourself. Your enemies will bring up the whole damn Cable thing again – they'll shaft you, David, and this time they'll do it with a red-hot poker.'

3

Vienna

Sarah Cable was feeling pleased with herself. She had just woken to find Johan stretched out under the duvet with his arms around her. Enjoying the warmth and closeness, she lay there studying his face in the grey light that filtered through cracks in the shutters. Whenever they were together he made her feel comfortable, secure, and she liked him being even taller than she was and equally vigorous in bed. She would miss him on the trip back to England.

Sarah had grown up in Vienna, where her father had been a minor diplomat at the British Embassy. When she was eight her younger sister had been killed in a car accident and Sarah's world collapsed in ruins; unable to cope with the grief, her mother had a breakdown and walked out, so Sarah and her father had grown very close. Although he later resigned after a failed intelligence operation* Sarah had followed him into the service, but there had still been too many reminders of the past so five years ago she had decided to break free.

She had chosen physics as a degree subject that might get her a job, found a place at Liverpool University and then worked on the production line in a nuclear fuel plant for a year before going back to Vienna, the city which she still regarded as home. Arriving with three hundred pounds scraped together and nowhere to live, she had found work in one of the United Nations agencies located in the city after the war – not a grand diplomatic number, but a mundane technical job. The apartment was one of five in a solid villa in Larochegasse, built in the palmy days when there was still a Habsburg Empire, before Vienna was brutalized by the Nazis and the Red Army in succession. It was in the basement, only two rooms with a tiny kitchen and bathroom, but the first home Sarah had made for herself.

She rested on her elbows and kissed Johan's closed eyelids, then

* See *Seven Steps to Treason*

slid out, shivering as the cold air hit her, wrapped herself in her dressing gown and turned up the heating. She was running a shower when Johan woke up and shouted to her. Turning off the water, she blinked in the steam and stuck her head round the door.

'Are we late, Sarah – already it is time for me to take you to the airport?' He was sitting up in bed, the ice-blue eyes grave above his fair beard, as if the question were of deep significance.

She laughed. 'Not yet, darling. My plane isn't till eleven – I'm flying via Frankfurt, remember?'

'You still haven't told me why you're going? I shall miss you.'

She returned to the bedroom. 'I told you last night, lover – it's only for five days and I *am* coming back. They're just sending me on a course about reprocessing and it happens to be in Liverpool. It'll be terrific – a chance to look up old friends. I'm sorry they aren't sending you too.'

Sarah smiled at him as he reached up and opened the front of the dressing-gown, then found herself in his arms as he stood and kissed her. 'We needn't go to Schwechat for at least an hour,' she murmured, wriggling with pleasure as he slipped the robe from her shoulders.

Nairn landed at Heathrow twenty-four hours later. An immigration officer met him at the door of the British Airways 747 and ushered him down a stairway and back to the tarmac, where his car was waiting. Chris, who had been his driver for ten years now, handed him a black despatch box of urgent papers and Nairn opened it with the small key in his pocket. It was nine in the morning, but he was going home before travelling on to the Cut.

The dark blue Rover did not join the crowded motorway, but followed the old Great West Road, reaching Chiswick in forty-five minutes. Alison was waiting in the flat by the river where he had lived alone for many years as a widower; she was twenty years younger than Nairn, growing plumper but retaining the vivid auburn hair that had first attracted him. He had wanted to sell the flat when they married, but she had seen that he would never settle anywhere else and instead quietly transformed it. Tactfully she had left traces of his past – the sagging leather armchair by the window, the ugly little bureau that had belonged to his mother – content that the weekend cottage they had bought in Dorset would be entirely her creation.

She kissed him as he picked up their baby daughter, playing on the kitchen floor. 'Bacon and eggs, love?'

'No thanks, they gave us something on the plane, but I'd like some coffee.'

'Okay.' She filled a kettle and continued in the same even tone. 'What's wrong, David?'

'Wrong? Nothing.'

'Don't try and con me. You can't.' She turned and put her arms round his neck, meeting his eyes gravely. 'You look *awful*, darling. Either it was a most ghastly flight or you've got something dreadful on your mind.'

'I can't talk about it.'

'I'm sorry.' Alison understood about his strange life and never pried, although sometimes he told her secrets that she knew he shouldn't and she was careful to forget them. She poured the hot water over coffee in a filter. 'Is it firing someone or putting them at risk?' It was usually one or the other.

'The second. It's a filthy job and she's the obvious choice, but I just can't face it.'

'If there's only one choice, you must do whatever you'd expect from someone further down the line. I married you because I respect your toughness, Nairn, as well as loving that nice, gentle side. So stop agonising and get that coffee inside you.' She kissed him again, then met his eyes sternly. 'She, you said? Is it someone young? Do I know her?'

He looked away awkwardly. 'Yes, you do.'

Alison's soft mouth hardened. 'Then just get on with it, or they'll all think you're a complete fool.'

4

Liverpool

As a student Sarah Cable had lived in Birkenhead, crossing the Mersey by ferry every day into Liverpool, so nostalgically she had chosen to stay in a Birkenhead hotel for the few days of the course. The third evening she went to a pub near the university with some friends, then swung off for the quay with her long stride. It was still early – just nine o'clock – so she was in plenty of time for the last boat to Woodside. She waited in one of the cabins on the floating pier, painted by Mersey Ferries in garish red and blue in a desperate attempt to compensate for the litter swirling in gusts from the estuary and the smell of greasy chips from the twenty-four-hour caff. A group of punks swaggered by, one swinging a studded belt, ready for a punch-up.

They looked Sarah over as she turned up the collar of her white trenchcoat against the cold, but walked on, recognising a young woman who could take care of herself. When she first met Nairn, nineteen-year-old Sarah's face had been fresh and trusting. Seven years later her hair was still long and fair, but she had changed greatly: high cheekbones stood out in a face that was striking, angular but with a wide sensitive mouth and amused grey eyes that could swiftly become fierce. Her body was still slim, but held with the physical confidence of a woman who had become an accomplished fencer, a girl's softness long since replaced by arm and leg muscles that were hard and powerful. With all that and five feet ten tall, Sarah drew admiring glances even when she was slopping around in faded jeans and a headscarf – though there was such strength of character in her bearing that many men retreated as fast as the punks. Happily Johan had not.

The ferry tied up, bouncing against rubber tyres dangling on the slimy wooden piles, and a deckhand let down the gangway with a crash. The boat was empty except for a couple of swaying drunks and a bus driver going home with his bike. Sarah hurried past the squalid buffet counter, up the companionway to the shelter on the boat deck. Its steel bulkheads were painted prison green, but she liked the old-fashioned seats of slatted wood and there was a tang of salt above the oily waters. The view alone was worth the fare – the two cathedrals floodlit on their hills, Scott's massive Anglican Gothic tower disdaining the modern cone of Paddy's Wigwam that served the Catholic community – and it was a good place to do your thinking.

When she got her degree, Nairn had come to Liverpool and, leaning on the rail of this ferry, invited her to rejoin the service, but she had said no; with hindsight she knew that she had meant 'not yet'. As the boat rocked and the screws went astern, Sarah smiled to herself. She was going to enjoy Vienna, but sooner or later there was one thing above all else that beckoned in her life. Sarah Cable had decided to become a top intelligence officer, to succeed where her luckless father had failed. She owed it to herself and she owed it to him.

The Birkenhead pier was modern, all orange metal tube and glass, like something hijacked from an airport. She had just dropped her thirty pence in the machine when the man fell into step beside her. He seemed to appear from nowhere, a nondescript face looking up at her, horrible scurf on his shoulders. 'Miss Cable?'

'No.' She pulled her coat closer around her. 'Piss off or I'll call the police.'

'I *am* the police, Miss.' He displayed a warrant card in a plastic cover.

She strode on towards the car park, making him scurry to keep up. 'Just assuming I believed you, what do you want?'

'Could we have a word, Miss? You *are* Sarah Cable, aren't you?'

'Who the hell are *you*?

'Detective Sergeant Holman, Liverpool Special Branch.'

She snorted and gestured toward the lights of the Woodside Hotel. 'I'm staying there. If you want to talk to me, we'll go in and I'll phone police headquarters to check you're genuine. Okay? Or would you prefer to try some other sucker?'

'No, please do that, Miss. It's most urgent that I talk to you.'

Nairn was waiting in a seedy guest house on the other side of the Wirral. It huddled under wet trees at the end of a lane, a clapboard building with bare light bulbs shining out into the dark from a glassed-in verandah. Sarah picked her way through the mud, tripped on the rotting wood of the steps and opened the door with an expression of distaste. He was sitting at a table with a stained formica top, sipping a tumbler of beer and rearranging the sauce and ketchup bottles into a pattern of alternate red and brown.

'I expect it's nicer in the summer.' The gaunt face cracked into a grin. 'Bit bleak at this time of year.'

Crossly she sat down opposite him, hearing the unmarked police car drive away. 'Was all that drama really necessary – couldn't you have just rung up or sent me a train ticket to London?'

'Security, my girl.' He looked her up and down severely. 'Would you like a drink?'

'Since I'm here, yes.' She knew she sounded off-hand and aggressive, but couldn't help it; he still made her feel nervous. Nairn stood up and stuck his head through a doorway. 'Two more beers please, Grace.' It was difficult to imagine this tall, shabby figure, with its slight Scots accent and proletarian habits, as the head of the intelligence service of a banana republic, let alone the United Kingdom. 'Is beer okay? It's all there is.'

'Terrific, David. I've never met anyone else who knows so many utterly revolting places in every corner of Europe.'

'I know quite a few in Brazil and the Far East, too. Grace and Ella worked for us in Mozambique, you know. I think they're dykes. They bought this place when they retired.' A plump woman with a broad smile brought in two glasses of lager and a packet of nuts. She did not look in the least like a lesbian – but how could you tell? 'Thank you, Grace, that's very kind. Now then, Sarah, how the devil *are* you? You don't look over pleased to see me.'

She smiled and gave him a chaste kiss. 'Of course I am, David. It was just a surprise after nearly two years.'

'Job going well?'

'Yes, it's fine. How are Alison and the baby?' Nairn had been a widower when she first met him and at first Sarah had dismissed the new Lady Nairn as an unliberated sex traitor with fabulous legs for nearly forty and an IQ of about three; she was also more than a little jealous. But soon there had been a baby daughter and Nairn looked fitter and ten years younger. He recovered the energy old friends – and enemies – remembered from years before. She had to admit that there was a certain depth to Alison, though her sheer bloody niceness still got on Sarah's nerves.

'They're fine too.' There was an awkward silence – with Nairn there often was – until he looked up abruptly. 'Thought any more about coming back into the racket?'

Sarah felt a twinge of wariness. Perhaps he'd come himself because he knew she was half in love with him and once he could twist her round his little finger? She shook her head.

'Still plenty of time.' He fiddled with the sauce bottles again casually, too casually. 'Look, Sarah, a small job's come up that you could do for us in Vienna. Since you're already there, I thought you might be willing to help out – and it might, well, help you decide about the future?' He watched her jaw stiffen and added hastily, 'It wouldn't interfere with your work at the agency – and it would help me a great deal.'

Sarah looked away from his face and studied the red and white check curtains. 'The agency would sack me if they found out.'

'Your career doesn't lie with the agency.'

'Doesn't it?'

Nairn stood up deliberately and went out, coming back with two more bottles of lager. She felt uncomfortable as he looked searchingly into her face, eyes piercing under spiky black brows. 'Perhaps I've got it wrong, Sarah, but I've always felt that sooner or later you would want to go on where Bill left off?' Sarah met his gaze in defensive silence; Nairn had a frightening capacity to know your mind better than you knew it yourself, but did he see through to the bitter hatred for those who had destroyed her father, distorted her own life? Surely he wouldn't be sitting there now if he did? Nairn gave a hard smile. 'And you're tougher than Bill, you know – you could be an even better intelligence officer, if that's what you want.'

Sarah was not going to admit how close he had come to the truth. She could not help being intrigued, but listened in silence. 'You could rejoin the service afterwards if you want – with a good posting as a First Secretary.' Skipping a grade or two, it was an out-and-out bribe. 'Or stay in Vienna with our grateful thanks and a modest payment into a Swiss bank. I believe your course finishes tomorrow?'

Sarah nodded uncomfortably – she was already certain that he'd engineered her return to Liverpool from the start. 'I'm confused, David. Maybe you're right and I *shall* want to come back after a few years in Vienna, but I'm not ready yet – and I'd imagined being posted to an Embassy, not working under cover, pretending to be something I'm not. I'm not sure I could cope with being an illegal.'

'You could cope all right.'

She poured more lager. 'Just supposing . . . just what would you want me to do?'

'You know I can't tell you that here.'

She shrugged. 'You will if you're serious.'

He grinned conspiratorially. 'If you'd like to know more, postpone your return flight by forty-eight hours – it's the weekend, so you won't be missed until Monday – and get the 9.10 train on Friday from Lime Street to Bristol Temple Meads. There'll be a Ford Granada waiting for you outside the station.' He was already pulling on his overcoat. 'You can always back out afterwards.'

5

Clevedon

Next morning the whole episode seemed unreal. Sarah pushed Nairn to the back of her mind and caught the ferry to the university, but she had lost interest in reprocessing and by the end of the day curiosity overcame caution and she made the phone call to Vienna. The following day she caught the train south to Bristol. A dark blue Granada was waiting under the glass canopy outside the station and ten minutes later they had skirted Cumberland Basin and crossed the Avon, driving west through farmland and scattered villages in driving rain. The safe house was in Clevedon, looking out over black shingle and mud flats to the Bristol Channel. It was Victorian, detached, standing in a row of similar buildings, all of weatherbeaten grey stone, and the car drove straight into a garage at its side.

A man of indeterminate age ushered Sarah through a narrow door into the kitchen, then up to a room facing the sea, furnished with two wooden desks and a circle of tatty armchairs that were plainly PSA issue. 'I'm Herron.' He had a curious, nasal accent. 'From the Embassy in Vienna – Sir David has asked me to brief you.'

'You do know I haven't taken the job yet?'

'Yes – if it all falls apart, we trust you to forget everything I tell you. Okay?' She nodded. 'Fine. Then you won't mind signing the usual declaration under the Act.' He thrust a scruffy piece of paper at her.

Sarah started. The familiar printed sheet suddenly faced her with the reality of what she was getting into, but she signed it with a bold *Sarah J. Cable* and watched it go into a steel cupboard with a combination lock. There was something odd about this Herron. He was prematurely grey over a smooth round face and spoke with exaggerated jollity, as if he felt ill at ease. Was that something to do with her, or a permanent condition? He seemed like an NCO masquerading as an officer: *God, you're a snob, Cable,* she thought to herself. He told her to call him Tom, but she was to find out later that insensitive parents had given him the names Philip Ronald

31

Andrew Thomson, with inevitable results in the juvenile milieus he had so far chosen for his life: minor public school, the army, the service.

They sat side by side at one of the desks and he spread out papers, lecturing her briskly. 'Operation Forty Thieves. One of my main purposes in Vienna is to gather intelligence on the near-nuclears, the eight or so countries that are close to producing atomic weapons. In some cases like Israel, they already have, of course.'

'Is there any point – we can't do much about it, can we?'

Prat Herron looked affronted. 'Of course there is,' he said severely. 'We may not be able to *stop* them, but we need to be warned just how many of the great unwashed are making bombs that could blow us all to kingdom come. They're all in hot spots like the Middle East – we could be dragged in.'

Sarah nodded and stifled a yawn; she turned to stare out across the grey sea rolling in from South Wales, then back to the old-fashioned sea-front. It reminded her of childhood holidays: the cast-iron balustrade along the esplanade, a park with threadbare trees and octagonal bandstand, holding her divorced father's hand, so proud of him despite her increasing knowledge of his failure and disgrace.

'That brings us to our prospect Dr Khan, codename Ali Baba.' Herron produced a grainy photograph and handed it to Sarah. It had been taken from some distance and from above: by someone in a window when he was walking along a street perhaps?

'How old is he?'

'Forty-two.'

'At least he's not bad-looking. Even dishier than Imran Khan.'

'Not my type, Sarah.' That exaggerated jollity again. 'But convenient if he's yours. Interesting chap. Poor background. Brought up in an orphanage in Singapore, but got adopted by a wealthy Muslim family, who sent him to a decent school and Karachi University. Then did his doctorate at Stanford in California. Brilliant scientist. He's been working for their Atomic Energy Commission for about twenty years.'

'Doing what?'

'That's one of the many things we don't know, but we assume he's been involved in their work on weapons. In Vienna his front is nuclear attaché at the Pakistan Embassy. He represents them at the agency where you work. Perhaps you've met him?'

'No.' She shook her head. 'I don't see much of diplomats. I just trog round power stations checking the material that's supposed to be there hasn't been wheeled away by the military. And it's taken me a year to qualify to do even that.'

'He goes to all the Vienna meetings trumpeting about Pakistan's peaceful intentions, but we think his real job is to get hold of the materials and equipment they need for their bomb factory.'

'How certain are we that there actually *is* a bomb factory?'

Herron's glare said that such scepticism was not to be tolerated. 'Not one hundred per cent – that's one of the things we want to find out.'

'Just what am *I* supposed to do? If you're working round to an invitation to go and catch AIDS from him, you can forget it.'

'Good Lord no, nothing so crude. He's already made an approach to a friendly Embassy.'

'Who did he approach?'

Herron hesitated. 'The Australians. They passed it to the Americans and it found its way back to us.'

'Why don't you just get on with it?'

'He seems to have got cold feet since, which is hardly surprising – his people could be pretty nasty if they found out. But we suspect he's out of tune with his masters and might still co-operate if he could vanish in the West afterwards.'

'Why should he take the risk?'

'Conscience? More likely he sees that it's an unstable country and if there was a coup he'd lose everything, so he'd like to get out with a sackful of our money.'

'And me?'

'We'd like you to get close to him, help us be certain he's genuine, pilot him through a difficult time if he's serious.' Herron smiled for the first time. 'If he isn't, you'd have compromised him and we could screw him anyway.'

The day passed slowly until six when Sarah escaped and walked down to the sea in the dusk, pulling her anorak over the sensible blouse and dark skirt she'd been wearing all day to impress Prat Herron, who hadn't even noticed. She had a drink by herself in the Royal Pier Hotel, sitting in the window and staring at the dark patch of sea where the pier had been before it collapsed in a storm. All that remained was the latticed steel island that had stood at its end – now lashed by grey waves a hundred yards from the shore, looking as lonely as Sarah felt.

She spent a sleepless night, torn between the security of the life she had invented for herself in Vienna – the cosy apartment, the undemanding job, Johan – and the frisson of danger offered by Nairn. Shortly after dawn she pulled on her tracksuit and ran along the front. The bulbs of fairy lights hung from wires stretched between the cast-iron lamp-posts, waiting to be switched on again next summer. As her feet pounded the pavement, she continued to push the decision away – there would be plenty of time to think on the journey back to Vienna. Outside the Express Café, now boarded up for winter, salt-stained bunting flapped over a tantalising notice offering English breakfast for ninety-nine pence.

PART TWO

6

Kabul

Kirov was woken by the first explosion. She had been dozing in the armchair in the corner of her bedroom, fallen asleep over a report from Peshawar. Instinctively she picked up the revolver that always lay on her bedside table at night, switched off the light and cautiously drew back the curtains.

It was cold on the balcony, but there was a view over the city, its stinking alleys and jerry-built concrete blocks now in darkness. How she hated this Godawful place. A fire was blazing about a mile away, near the Arg, and the rattle of automatic fire was punctuated by heavy explosions. Somewhere below, a tank clattered along the dirt track that passed for a road. Stepping back inside, she checked the time: it was two in the morning. She picked up the phone. As she expected, it was dead, but Nikolai appeared within seconds of her pressing the bell. He wore a camouflage flak-jacket and carried a machine-pistol. 'What the hell's going on? Is it the Mujahedin?'

'I can't find out, General, both our telephone lines have been cut. The guards are deployed around the villa and I have ordered them to shoot any intruder on sight.'

'You've tried the radio?'

'Yes, but there's no response from military headquarters.'

'That's impossible. Let me try.' They hurried downstairs to the communications room and she pressed the red panic button that gave instant contact with the barracks. It lit up and buzzed, but there was no response. 'What the blazes is Grigorenko playing at?'

The ADC stood by impassively, waiting for instructions. 'Get the car,' snapped Kirov. 'And six of the guard to escort in the jeep. We're going to find out what's happening.'

'Are you sure that's safe?'

'It's a bloody sight better than waiting here to be cut to pieces.'

The jeep bumped down the track from the villa, its occupants hidden by raised steel sides, a heavy machine-gun bolted to the scuttle beside the driver. The big Zil followed, armour-plating and soft suspension making it yaw over the potholes, and the two vehicles picked up speed along the stretch of tarmac road into the city. They drove without lights, gliding in the grey moonlight past darkened buildings and streets emptied by the curfew. Military headquarters was only fifteen minutes away, but they were halted at the gates by soldiers in full combat dress with steel helmets.

A sergeant poked the barrel of his Kalashnikov into the car as soon as Nikolai lowered the window. 'Who are you? What do you want?'

'This is Major-General Kirov, Minister Counsellor at our Embassy. The Minister wishes to see General Grigorenko at once.'

'Impossible. There is an emergency. Come back tomorrow.'

The sergeant's face was lit by a sudden blaze of flame about a hundred yards away, followed by the crash of an explosion. The cascade of red sparks was like a firework display, but the ground shook. 'We are Soviet officials,' shouted Nikolai. 'Do you really want us to stay out here and be killed?' The sergeant faltered, then gestured for them to wait and spoke into a portable radio. It crackled back and after a long silence crackled again. The gates opened and the two vehicles drove in.

Colonel-General Konstantin Grigorenko was holding court in his underground command post and kept them waiting in the building above for half an hour. Kirov fumed, but remained aloof, refusing vodka – which was supposed to be banned from military establishments these days – but accepting a glass of tea from the orderlies who stared at her curiously. They had never glimpsed the woman spymaster who had come to the Embassy three months before and was rumoured to be close to the General Secretary himself. She was not GRU – so could safely be ignored – but she wore a military uniform with breeches tucked into leather boots and used the masculine form of her surname, instead of the feminine *Kirova*. Some sort of loony feminist. They all knew what she needed – and what other use was there for a woman in this man's bloodstained country?

Eventually a young major ordered Kirov's ADC and guards to wait while he ushered her down the concrete steps, through a steel blast-door, into a room full of soldiers operating radio consoles, maps of the country around the walls. Grigorenko was a weather-beaten man in his forties, with a straight brow of coal-black hair above the equally black lines of his eyebrows and moustache. He was unsmiling under the sickly green lights. 'Sorry to keep you waiting, Nadia Alexandrovna. It would have been safer to stay at your house.'

Kirov bit back her fury. His offhand tone said that he had made her wait as a deliberate snub – and the patronising bastard was using her first name and patronymic to emphasise his superiority, two ranks higher than her, if ten years younger. 'Exactly what is going on?' she asked coldly. 'There appears to be a battle around the presidential palace and part of the commercial quarter is on fire.'

'Everything is under control and I am about to report to the Ambassador.' A crooked smile. 'Your boss.' He emphasised the put down. 'But I can tell you it is not the Mujahedin. It appears that our PDPA comrades are engaged in another of their squalid power struggles and I am reliably informed that in a few hours the radio station will announce that Quazi Islamuddin is the new Party Secretary.'

'What about Habidullah?'

'I suppose he will retire through ill health.'

'Bullet wounds? Like Taraki in seventy-nine?'

Grigorenko shrugged. 'I neither know nor care. My duty is to maintain the safety and effectiveness of our forces.'

'Which you are doing by letting a coup, a *change of government*, take place without lifting a finger to interfere?'

'My orders are to leave these niggers to settle things among themselves.'

Kirov drew a deep breath; even his thick Ukrainian accent was irritating. 'This is all very odd. May I use your radio link – it would save me driving on to the Embassy?'

'I regret not. I am ordered to suspend radio communications for twenty-four hours – you will find the Embassy is cut off as well.'

'Whose orders are these, General?'

He met her eyes sharply. 'My orders as supreme commander of all Soviet forces remaining in the Democratic Republic of Afghanistan.'

'Your orders from where, the Politburo?'

He shrugged. 'From Moscow. I am not at liberty to say more.'

'Your orders from *where*, General?'

Grigorenko turned away without replying.

It was still pitch dark at five in the morning, and the moonlight had gone, when a column of T-72 tanks advanced on the Arg, followed by several armoured troop carriers. The procession halted at the portico and a cohort of Red Army soldiers entered the palace, cautiously gripping their Kalashnikovs. They returned ten minutes later and the lieutenant saluted as Kirov and Grigorenko joined him on the marble steps. 'It is quite safe, comrade General,' he said to Grigorenko. 'Allow me to guide you.'

The two Generals followed him down a long corridor, studiously ignoring each other and led by a group of twenty troopers, heavy boots clattering on the marble. The building was a shambles, scars of bullets white along the panelling, delicate furniture smashed, rugs torn from the walls. Men lay in pools of blood where they had fallen, some in uniform, some in dull brown *petous*, like rough blankets. In several cases the trousers had been ripped off and the bodies mutilated.

In an anteroom, a young Afghan asked them to wait and turned on a radio set. A voice announced the appointment of Quazi Islamuddin as General Secretary and President of the Revolutionary Council, first in Dari, then in Pashto, the two main languages of the country. Nothing was said about the fate of his predecessor and a scratched record played the Internationale.

As the broadcast ended Nikolai opened the double doors to the cabinet room, but stopped on the threshold. It looked as if a bomb had gone off in there. No, plainly a bomb *had* gone off – the floor was ankle deep in plaster and jagged stonework, the ceiling was missing and bodies with burns lay twisted in the ruins. Kirov rounded on Grigorenko. 'Do they always make this much mess when there's a change in leadership? Your orders were not to intervene? I don't understand it.'

'Nor do I, Nadia Alexandrovna, but those are my orders.' He gave a superior smile. 'It seems Comrade Blackarse Islamuddin has friends in high places.'

As they continued to wait for the new leader, there was a burst of automatic fire from outside and the two Russians walked to a window. The yellow headlights of army lorries lit the yard. Objects wrapped in blankets were being tossed into the back of a truck as a group of four men and two women were urged from a door, clubbed by soldiers with the butts of their AK-47s. One man and a woman were naked, as if they had been caught in bed, the woman vainly trying to cover her pale body with her hands. They stood confused, slithering on bloodstained cobbles and blinking in the glare, until a machine-gun raked across them and they collapsed like bundles of rags. The woman was left standing and, after a moment of hesitation, started to run away. Another volley pinned her, jerking, to the wall until her body jack-knifed over, almost cut in half.

Kirov stared at the scene helplessly. Something was terribly wrong and she recognised one of the men in the yard as a *Spetsnaz* officer from Grigorenko's headquarters. Habidullah had been a trained doctor, almost civilised, but Islamuddin was young, Maoist, mad – this coup was unreal. Someone from outside had engineered it, someone who gave Grigorenko orders, but told her and the Ambassador nothing.

7

Vienna

The morning after the reception, Nazim Khan drove down the autobahn to Linz, where he turned north on winding roads leading out of Austria. At times he followed the Danube, passing little towns of steep-roofed houses clustered around their church with an onion tower, plunging down into the fast-flowing river. Eventually he joined the German autobahn and sped on to Regensburg, where he stayed the night in a hotel near the cathedral. It was an old-fashioned place with dark oak furniture and tapestries on the wall. The bed had been turned down and a piece of chocolate in the shape of a pear, wrapped in silver paper, left on the pillow, along with a card from the management inviting him to put his shoes out for cleaning during the night.

While Khan slept, Herron who had checked in as Herr Schneider, toiled in his room down the corridor. First he polished the Pakistani's expensive brown brogues until they shone, then slid the tiny bug between the sole and welt. The thing looked too small to withstand the vibration and still transmit, but Technical insisted that it would function for long enough. Then he went down to the hotel garage and placed another, magnetised, transmitter under the petrol tank of the Mercedes. It was as well that he had both devices, for the car did not leave the garage next day. Khan quit the hotel at eight o'clock and hired a Volkswagen Passat from a Europcar agency two streets away.

They picked him up again outside Nuremberg and Herron in the lead car tracked him to the Volkspark. The Nazi stadium was still there, but a road ran through it, separating the high stone grandstand – built behind the podium where Hitler had ranted against a backdrop of scarlet swastikas – from the three lower stands that made up the square. The US Army had turned that into a football field. Once its torchlit ceremonies had terrorised a continent; now the whole place was quietly crumbling away, lichen on the stone terraces, bronze doors turning green, lithe fair-haired teenagers practising tennis strokes against the walls.

41

Khan parked in a row of cars close to the lake and walked away, past a steaming sausage stand, towards a *Gasthaus* at the edge of the park. Herron drew up just as the Pakistani reached the door with its Budweiser sign and menu chalked on a blackboard. The bug was working well and Herron was able to make notes, although the tape turning on the back seat would record everything. Deep in concentration, he did not see the shadows outside. When the car door was wrenched open, he turned with startled eyes and felt a blinding pain as the long stiletto drove into his chest, the wet pad on his face stifling his attempt to scream. When the back-up car arrived fifteen minutes later, the tape and notes were gone, but Herron had been left for them to clear up. His corpse lolled forward over the steering wheel, blood still oozing from the wound to soak his shirt and jacket, but none of the passers-by had noticed. The *Gasthaus* was empty except for two Japanese tourists.

Nazim Khan did not ring Sarah on the Saturday after the reception. Half-disappointed, half-relieved, she phoned Johan but there was no reply. On Saturday afternoon she went by herself for a swim at Hohe Warte, the new sports centre with its sybaritically warm pools bordered by café, bar, sun-beds and plump Viennese scoffing *Wurst* and chips. She punished her body with thirty fast lengths of the main pool, mindless effort designed to make her forget Johan. Afterwards she dressed and had a coffee in the bar. She was so used to spending weekends with him that she felt quite at a loose end. Ridiculous, she told herself sharply, are you completely without resources, Cable? Tomorrow she would take herself for a long walk in the forest above Klosterneuburg, in the bend of the Danube, tonight she would catch up on her reading.

Out in the car park, she picked her way through the crowd of teenagers and young mothers with children. As she unlocked her Volkswagen, a dusty Mercedes was parking a hundred yards away. A tall man climbed out, followed by a girl in her early twenties. She was petite, delicately made, with wild red hair; the man was Johan. Grimly Sarah gripped the steering wheel of the Golf and started the engine. *The bastard.*

Next morning she had more or less recovered her equilibrium. The flat had a glass door to a tiny patio, slightly sunk below the level of the garden. It was too cold to sit out there in October, but Sarah opened the door and lolled in an armchair with her feet on the radiator, breakfasting on black bread and redcurrant jelly. Perhaps she would drive past the airport at three in the afternoon, by which time the English Sunday papers should have arrived on the plane from London.

He rang at exactly ten o'clock. 'Hello – Sarah?' She did not recognise his voice at first, but something in its tone made her freeze.

'Yes. Who is that?'

'Nazim Khan. I wondered if you would be free to have dinner with me this evening?'

8

Vienna

Sarah recovered quickly. 'Dr Khan? How nice of you to ring. How are you?' What absurdities came out when you were caught unexpectedly.

'I'm fine, thanks – and hoping to enjoy a little more of your company.'

'This evening, did you say?'

'Yes, I hope it's not too short notice?'

'I think I'm free.' Mustn't sound too eager, she flicked the empty pages of her diary. 'Yes. I'd love to.'

'Perhaps I could pick you up about six?'

'Okay. Do you know where I live?'

'You did tell me – in the Thirteenth, Larochegasse 23.'

'Yes. There are four bells on the gate – you ring the one marked Cable. See you tonight.'

Sarah went for the walk she had planned in the hills, but gave the Sunday papers a miss. She had too much else to think about. For one thing she was scared stiff. Gerda's murder had been discussed in horrifying detail in the down-market *Kurier* and thereafter in every bar in Vienna. Sarah had no doubt that her targets were to blame – and how much did Khan know about it? Could he even have been *there* when they tormented her? The thought did not make her look forward to the touch of his hands. And then, although Sarah had not got to the age of twenty-six without her share of affairs – some torrid, some feeble – she had never before actually set out to get a man nearly twenty years older into bed. Perhaps she would find him repulsive. Perhaps he would have kinky tastes. Perhaps she was worrying too much . . .

In the afternoon she took a long bath and put on scanty black underwear. She wrinkled her nose at the figure in the mirror – she looked like a female wrestler masquerading as a tart, pubic hair curling through the lace of her pants. She added a sexy perfume Johan had given her and pulled the little black dress over her head.

It showed off her long legs and wide brown shoulders; with her fair hair flicked over one shoulder she would stun him.

When he rang the bell, she pulled on her coat and went out to the locked wrought-iron gate from the street. He seemed unpretentious in a grey sports jacket and black trousers: middle-aged clothes, but younger in manner than before. She would not ask him in now, perhaps later. He whisked her into his car and sped off. It was a white Mercedes with expensive soft leather seats in light brown leather, appalling taste but beautifully comfortable. As they bounced over the railway crossing towards the city, Sarah lay back and tried to relax.

Nazim Khan knew his Vienna. The Mercedes joined the Ring opposite the Opera, weaved between the trams and turned off through the arch into the massive bastions of the Hofburg. He parked in a square at the heart of the Imperial Palace and they crossed the Michaelerplatz on foot, into the old town. He had booked a table at *Le Salut*, a small French restaurant with scrubbed wooden tables and red and white checked napkins, a place she knew her father had used when he worked in the Embassy. They dined in a corner by candlelight, exchanging sanitised versions of their life histories. Khan spoke lightly, when she pressed him, of childhood poverty in Singapore, until he was adopted from the orphanage by a prosperous Muslim family from Lahore. Sarah had a feeling that he was suppressing a great deal of pain but concealing less of his past than she – and it was a good dinner, both of them warily drinking little.

Afterwards they walked through the narrow alleys, footsteps echoing in the dark, until they emerged unexpectedly from an archway into the courtyard where he had left the car. He asked her back for coffee, almost shyly, not as she expected from the great womaniser, and drove up the hill into Grinzing.

His apartment was in a modern two-storey block, one of hundreds built in the sixties and seventies to provide expensive accommodation for the diplomatic community accredited to the UN agencies in the city. It was typical: a large living/dining room, with a terrace outside patio doors, a kitchen, bathroom and two smallish bedrooms. It was furnished with the owner's pretentious Viennese furniture, giving the main room the feel of a museum. 'It's a lovely flat,' said Sarah, peering out at the terrace.

'Do you like it? It's suitable for entertaining, which is part of the job, but not much of a home. Would you like a drink? I have a good port locked away where my fellow Muslims cannot see it.'

They sat at opposite ends of a long blue sofa, sipping the dry red liquid. Sarah studied the photographs in cheap plastic frames that were the only personal touch in the room, picking up one that was brown and faded. 'She is very beautiful.'

'That is my mother. She was sent from a poor home in Karachi to be a house-girl in Malaya, where she had relatives. I was born there, not in Pakistan.'

'What was your father doing in Malaya?'

'I don't know.' He gave a distant smile, amused rather than embarrassed. 'I don't know who my father was. No doubt my mother would have told me, but she was killed by terrorists in the Emergency. She was working for an English family on a rubber plantation; they killed them all and burnt the house.'

'How old were you, Nazim?'

'I was eight.'

'It must have been awful – how did you survive?'

'I was hidden in the jungle with some of the Malay workers. When the killing was over, we trekked south to Singapore and I was put into an orphanage.'

'You mean you walked there? Through the jungle? How far was it?'

He laughed. 'A hell of a long way – I think about two hundred miles – but it was a long time ago.'

Sarah suspected that she was probing too deep and picked up another photograph. 'She is very beautiful, too.'

'Beautiful women are important to me.' His eyes smiled as he poured more port. 'That is Farah, my wife,' but there was no affection in his voice. 'These are my children, Mahmoud and Noor.' Sarah smiled at the young faces, a boy of about seven with the serious look of his father and a chubby little girl with a huge smile. 'I miss them a great deal when they go back to Pakistan.' This time he spoke with unaffected love. So the children mattered to him; that could be a complication later.

'Does Farah like it here?'

'Not much, but she is dutiful. She likes to return home for several months a year – she is still very close to her parents. You look surprised. Why? I know the image of Pakistan is not a good one in the West but, believe me, for people like Farah's family,' – Sarah noticed that he did not say 'people like us' – 'it is comfortable enough.'

'Did I look surprised? It's just that your children must miss you – your wife too,' Sarah added hastily.

'Certainly I miss *them*. But you must understand that Farah and I do not find separation too bad.' He hesitated. 'Ours is an arranged marriage, you know – a long betrothal, but we met only a few days before the ceremony. Still we rub along well enough.' He said it casually, quickly, but Sarah again sensed the suppression of passion and pain; she moved closer. So far he had shown none of the predatory characteristics for which he was so well known; on the contrary he had been a charming, civilised companion. He still radiated a charismatic masculinity and the instinctive, animal side of her would find it all too natural to be taken by him, but tonight she had an uneasy feeling she would have to make the running – that did not seem to be his objective. She followed him into the kitchen, where he made the coffee he had promised an hour ago and kissed her gently on the mouth. 'You are a good listener, Sarah, that is what we old men need.'

'You're not old, Nazim, just a little jaded, perhaps? I'd like to do something about that – when you show me all over Vienna, as you promised.'

He took her shoulders and held her at arm's length, intelligent brown eyes searching her face. Was there a brief hint of suspicion? Just for a few seconds? Then he laughed. 'That is a most excellent idea, Sarah. A little North-South co-operation with a beautiful blonde ice-maiden – I should be privileged.'

'I'm no ice-maiden, Nazim.'

'No, I don't believe you are. How about Wednesday evening?'

'Wednesday sounds fine.'

'I will ring you.' He poured the coffee. 'By the way, I think it would be better if neither of us mentioned this evening to anyone else.' For a second there was a trace of anxiety in his voice. 'My Ambassador would not like it.'

Ten minutes later they stood in the cul-de-sac outside. 'Rudolf Kassnergasse is quiet,' he chuckled. 'Always quiet as the grave. They hate the children and I suspect they are all watching behind their curtains now, wondering who is the elegant white woman that Paki is seducing.' He started the engine. 'One day I must find out who the hell was this Rudolf Kassner who gives his name to such a bleak place.'

Sarah stared out of the window as they drove through Grinzing, where the last revellers were leaving the *Heurigen* and the smell of wine fumes hung in the street. Unbelievably he hadn't made the expected pass. His reputation had to be a pose, a front like the arrogance. Later she lay awake for hours, mystified, intrigued despite herself with this unexpectedly attractive man whose sexual interest in her seemed to have evaporated.

9

Azerbaijan

The Antonov landed at a military airfield south of Baku shortly before midnight. Grigorenko had held up Kirov's departure from Kabul, asking for repeated weather reports with a concern for her safety he had never shown before, then insisting that she use his personal aircraft, which naturally required a mechanical check. He need not have bothered – there were high winds and electrical storms over the mountains which delayed the flight anyway. After three hours of bucking up and down, the captain appeared in the cabin, clinging to the doorway for support, and shouted to Kirov above the din of the gale. 'I'm sorry, General, but it is unsafe to go on. May I land?'

The airfield was in a valley near the Caspian Sea. Kirov's face was lashed by the wind as she struggled down the steps to a waiting jeep and there was enough moonlight, slanting through scudding clouds, to show the cluster of huts and a row of silver Mig-21s. She was shown into a bare office, furnished with wooden chairs and a steel desk. It stank of cigarette smoke, as did the air force major who joined her, still buttoning up his tunic. He was about fifty, with the forlorn eyes of a no-hoper. 'Welcome to Stepankoran, comrade General. We don't get many high-ranking visitors here, so I apologise for the lack of comfort.' He gestured at the lightning flashes outside. 'And for the weather.'

'How long do you expect it to last?'

'Twenty-four hours, possibly longer. Your captain is bound for Moscow, I believe?'

'Yes.'

'You might do better if we drive to Baku so you can take the train.'

Kirov stared through the rattling window. The Antonov was being refuelled by a tanker. 'How long would it take to get to Moscow that way?'

'I had in mind that you might go to somewhere just north of the

Caucasus – maybe Rostov – where you could get another plane. Would you like me to see what I can arrange?'

Before Kirov could reply an enormous explosion rolled across the airfield. She threw herself to the floor as the Antonov split in two and vanished in a ball of orange fire, the window blew in, splintered glass filled the air and the light went out. Within seconds the blaze spread to the tanker and a second explosion shot flames high in the air. Cautiously getting back to her knees she felt the heat on her skin, even though the inferno was a quarter of a mile away.

An alarm bell was ringing and a fire tender shot past the window. The major stared at her aghast, pressing a dirty rag over a cut on his hand, his face lit by the flickering yellow flames. 'That must have been a *bomb*. My God, you've been lucky – I didn't know the Mujahedin were so sophisticated.'

Kirov studied the burning aircraft. 'Not the Mujahedin.' But she spoke so quietly that he did not hear.

Fifteen hundred miles to the south-east, across the frontier with Pakistan, the ice-capped peaks of the Hindu Kush gave way to the brown Sulaiman hills. As the sun rose, two men lay in the chilly mouth of a cave, surveying the road below. It wound along the floor of a deep valley, a strip of shiny black tarmac, incongruously new against the weathered boulders. Soon the sun would be blazing down and the surface of the tarmac turn sticky, as it had been last night when they burrowed the mines into it. The valley was empty, for this was a closed area leading up to the secret place where caves honeycombed the rock of the mountain, the entrance guarded by soldiers with fierce dogs, behind a fence of steel staves and electrified wire.

The two men knew nothing of events in the Afghan capital, although their task was related to them. They had walked for two days, over the pass from Mina Bazar, and watched the convoy of cars drive up to the site yesterday. Now they were ready, the Soviet-made rocket launcher loaded and pointing downwards. There was nothing left to do but crouch on the cold rock and hope they might escape after the attack.

By the time that the first car appeared, the sun was higher, but the valley floor still in shadow. It was a white Mercedes, the first of three, driving at about fifty miles an hour – much faster than they had expected. The younger man focused his binoculars on the cairn of stones he had fashioned in the dark: the moment a flash of white metal appeared in front of it, he would press the button on the small radio transmitter. He held his breath. As the cars raced nearer, Ahmed shifted beside him, adjusting the RPG-7 against his shoulder, splaying his legs to avoid dislocation by the violent recoil, lips moving in silent prayer. The mine detonated right under the first car, hurling it into the air in a silent burst of rock and flame, followed by the rumble of the explosion reverberating between the valley walls. A chain of smaller explosions erupted down the centre of the road and the second car ploughed into the wreckage of the first. The third slewed sideways and two figures leapt out. '*Borou bekheir*,' growled Ahmed with a chuckle, firing the first rocket. It whooshed down too high and burst harmlessly on the hillside, but the second struck the undamaged car, piercing the armour-plated door and flinging it violently on its side, crackling with orange flame.

Ahmed's calm fingers continued to reload until he had propelled the whole box of six rockets into the blazing cars, now rapidly fusing into a single mass of twisted metal in the inferno. After one blast, a figure detached itself and ran towards them with clothes alight. It was cut down by a burst from the younger man's Armalite and the spray of bullets stopped two others as they tried to run for cover.

For a few minutes the scene was silent, apart from the roar of the fire, and a column of oily black smoke rose against the vivid blue of the sky. The two men descended the hillside cautiously, slithering on loose pebbles. The heat kept them back from the wreckage, but it was plain that there were no survivors. Only three people had got out of the burning vehicles and they were all dead. One lay apart, the remains of his suit still smouldering; it was made of a grey material, lightweight and expensive. Ahmed turned the body over. The face was unmarked, about fifty, intelligent despite the eyes staring wide in death.

'Is it he?' The younger man whispered, although there was no one near to overhear.

Ahmed gave a wicked grin. 'It is the *kafir*, delivered to our hands.' He drew the knife from his belt and knelt to slash the dead man's throat, watching the blood flow over the blade until he straightened and wiped it. Neither of them heard the Land-Rover approaching until it was a few hundred yards away.

Ahmed jerked upright. 'They must have radioed to the site for help.' He watched impassively as the soldiers ran towards them, firing erratically. Without hesitation he reached into the leather pouch on his chest, then spread his arms and embraced the other man tightly. 'Remember, little brother, it is better to die in a *Jihad* than to live under a tyrant!' His cry of '*Allah Akbar*' was lost as the grenade burst between them.

It took Kirov more than twenty-four hours to reach Moscow after the interminable drive to Baku, a filthy train and another bumpy flight to a military airfield. She huddled into the back seat of the waiting Zil and watched the pine forest flash past in the headlights, through eyes half-closed with exhaustion. There was no radio-telephone in the car – she should have expected that – so she could do nothing until they reached the familiar apartment block on the Lenin Hills, near the university, the two hundred square metres of uneven wood-block flooring that was her reward for a lifetime in the service of the state. But twenty years ago the reward might have been exile to a camp or a bullet in the back of the neck. Maybe that could still happen, for the Zil was being followed by a series of nondescript cars as it drove into the city and there was a man sweeping the street outside the block, another weeding the flower-beds – unheard of in Moscow at six in the morning.

The caretaker acknowledged her vaguely when she stepped out of the car, as if it were a few hours rather than three months since she had last been there, and Kirov took the lift to the top floor. The heat was off and the apartment cold in October; condensation on the windows had frozen into patches of wafer-thin ice. Her furniture was covered in dust sheets while she was stationed in Kabul, but she dragged one off and settled into an armchair, still wrapped in her overcoat. The flat's one good feature was a wide window looking down the hillside to the river; she gazed at the view for a long time, uncertain what to do next.

The phone was probably tapped, but she had prepared for that when she moved in years ago. Hidden between the walls of the kitchen and bedroom was a small space, lined with lead and hopefully still secure from eavesdropping. She swung back the bookcase, moving easily on tiny casters, and turned the dials on the steel plate set in the wall. Worked one way, a small door opened to reveal the cavity of a safe. Worked the other, a slab of wall five feet high hinged outwards, giving access to the secret room. She switched on the light and swung the door shut behind her.

The battery of radio and telecommunications equipment stood on metal shelves. She dialled the special number and within seconds began to see through the confusion. No, said Martia, she could not speak to Mikhail Sergeyevitch because he had a heart attack six days ago. Where? In Estonia – he and Raisa were taking a weekend off privately at a spa hotel by the sea in Tallinn . . .

Kirov closed her eyes as if suddenly in pain. 'Is he going to die?'

'They say it is not too serious, but I'm not sure – he is still in intensive care.'

'Why the devil wasn't I informed?'

'It was his instruction, comrade General – he said *no one* must know. There will be no announcement until he is back at work.'

Kirov ground her teeth in frustration – she had been Mikhail Sergeyevitch's friend and confidante since she worked with him as director of security in Stavropol twenty years ago, one of the few to recognise his potential when he was still an obscure provincial official. He would have sent her a message if he had been firing on all cylinders. How else could she be expected to watch his back in Kabul, where he faced open revolt from the military? 'You mean no one knows, no one at all?'

'Well, just a few members of the Politburo, of course.'

It got worse by the second. 'And exactly where is he?'

'In the clinic at Kuntsevo.' The special clinic for the Politburo and Ministers – every one of his enemies would know that the General Secretary was ill and vulnerable. The vultures would be gathering.

'I must see him later today.'

'That may be difficult, comrade General.'

'Don't be ridiculous, Martia – it's absolutely vital that I talk to him.' For the first time Kirov noticed the quiet at the other end of the line. There was none of the usual clatter of electronic typewriters and buzz of conversation; Martia was alone in that huge office overlooking the Kremlin gardens.

'Marshal Malinovsky said I should allow no one but senior members of the Politburo . . .' The woman sounded frightened; perhaps she already saw the writing on the wall.

'Do as I say, Martia. I shall see that no harm comes to you.' Kirov wished that she felt as confident as she sounded. 'Ring now on another phone.'

'I can't. I'm sorry, but I tried to phone a few minutes ago and they told me I must go through Malinovsky.' She was almost in tears. 'He is taking care of everything.'

10

Vienna

On Wednesday Sarah met Nazim at the Café Museum, near the market, and he took her to a performance of modern ballet by a Dutch company at the Theater an der Wien. Plainly he had thought she would enjoy it, but she was bored stiff – and holding hands in the dark gave them no opportunity to talk.

Afterwards they had a quick supper at Smutny's, close to the theatre, and he drove her home. She asked him in for coffee; he drank two cups and left with a chaste kiss just before midnight. That was it. She had learnt a little more about his past life, but nothing useful about his work. He seemed to find her amusing and attractive company, but nothing more. She had worn the same black lacy bra and pants, but he hadn't even clapped eyes on them yet. Crossly she hurled the silly things into the linen basket.

Mr Munster had set up a safe house for the operation, an apartment in an old block near the Stadtpark. It was built round a quadrangle, with entrances from the street in two opposite sides. From the apartment it was easy to see whether Sarah was followed; if she was, a window would be opened and her instructions were to walk straight through and out the other side. Then she would take the U-bahn from Stadtpark station for a few stops and go home.

Early on Thursday morning, still burning with frustration, Sarah dialled the emergency number she had been given. A woman answered, 'Argosy Travel.'

'Do you have a charter flight for Paris tomorrow?'

'No, but we have one this afternoon at four o'clock.'

Add three and a half hours. 'That may do. Are seats available?'

'Yes, there are plenty of seats.'

'I'll ring back to confirm.' The meeting was arranged at the safe house, for seven thirty that evening.

Before her first encounter with Nazim, she had met Nairn in Linz and expressed her lack of confidence in Prat Herron. 'He's a wally,

53

David. If he's my back-up I'll be terrified all the time.' A week later, a phone call had summoned her to take a train from the Franz Josefs Bahnhof to Tulln, a small town about twenty miles up the Danube. A man had joined her in the empty compartment when they stopped at Klosterneuburg. He was tall, with a strange flat top to his head and a face like an Identikit picture that had gone wrong, a real-life Frankenstein creation. He immediately became Mr Munster and she wanted to giggle every time she saw there was no bolt through his neck. In fact he was called Ken Payling and she had grown to trust him as her controller. He was plainly senior to Herron, possibly the head of station at the Embassy. He never told her and she knew better than to ask.

She walked up the broad flight of stairs, pausing at each landing to check that she was still alone; her footsteps echoed noisily against the stone walls and the silence was reassuring. Munster opened the heavy door as she reached it. He must have been watching her through the brass spy-hole. They sat in the bare living room, drinking Typhoo tea in chipped mugs. 'It's not going right, Ken. Probably he's doing everything you suspect, but he's also a very nice bloke, not the neo-rapist you thought. He's got this lousy arranged marriage and can't stand his wife, that's all. I think she comes from a richer and classier background – remember he was once a street urchin, until someone adopted him – and maybe she reminds him of that too much.'

'He's been seen out with a lot of women over the past year.'

'Well – his wife spends most of her time in Pakistan and he's not queer. Most men in their forties would take other women out. It's not against the law and God knows there are enough available here.'

'Why do you think he picked you up in the first place?'

'I made it bloody obvious that I fancied him and was available. Most men of his age would go for a bit of crumpet in her twenties if she just lay on her back and waved it at him.'

Munster looked slightly shocked. 'But he's a gentleman?'

'Something like that. All I know is that I'm not learning much and I'm not compromising him. I wish I'd never taken the job on.'

'But you're forming a relationship?'

'I suppose so. But it could take *years* at this rate, Ken – and we haven't got years, have we?'

'No, but we'll give it a month or two. Just go on winning his confidence. One way or another we'll nail him as a source, better still as an agent of influence.' Munster reached into his briefcase and produced a faded green book. 'Put this on your shelves and ask him round to dinner. *Tête-à-tête*. Candles. A screw if he wants it.'

Sarah skimmed the pages. '*Swallows and Amazons*? It's a kids' story – what am I supposed to do with that?'

'I believe he's very fond of it. I'm told it was one of the first books he ever owned, in that orphanage in Singapore – it may be a way of getting closer. He had a rough time as a kid, bloody awful, it must still hurt.'

'How on earth do you know so much about him?'

'I have my sources. Singapore was a colony when he was a child and the local Special Branch were remarkably on the ball. They kept tabs on everything, even the orphanage . . .'

'Okay, guv.' Sarah made for the door. 'By the way, what happened to that idiot Herron? The fellow who briefed me in Clevedon?'

'Prat Herron?' Munster hesitated, but made a quick recovery. 'He's not with us any more, Sarah. Went to a new post a couple of weeks ago.'

Sarah phoned Nazim at his apartment early on Friday evening. Most diplomatic entertaining was confined to the four evenings from Monday to Thursday, leaving weekends free, so she expected him to be at home. He was not. Nor was he at the Embassy when she rang there.

He telephoned her at half past ten. 'Hi, Sarah, it's me, Nazim.'

'Hi, handsome. Where are you?'

'At the apartment. Are you going away for the weekend?'

Sarah smiled to herself. Diplomats could afford to go away for weekends, to ski or to the lakes, but for less well-paid UN officials it was a rare event. 'No, I'll be here. Would you like to come round for supper tomorrow?'

'I'd love to, but tomorrow I have to work with some visitors from Islamabad.'

'Sunday, then?'

'That would be great.'

'Can you come early – about four – so we can go for a walk in the Wienerwald while there's still daylight?'

'Of course. At four – I look forward to it.'

''Bye, Nazzie.'

'Cheerio, Sarah.' For all his good points, Nazim could sometimes sound like Peter Sellers masquerading as an Indian, the idioms of his British-style boarding school near Lahore slipping out. Sarah waited a few seconds and then deliberately dialled Nazim's number. She let the phone ring for at least three minutes, but there was no answer. Why had he lied to her?

Suddenly the black shapes in the garden seemed to move threateningly and she was terrified to be alone. She seized her coat and rushed out, hands trembling as she unlocked the gate, leaving it swinging open as she hurried down the street. There was a *Heurigen* not far away, where she could be surrounded by normal people for the price of a *Viertel* of wine. Larochegasse was empty under the dim yellow lamps and she glanced over her shoulder at the sound of footsteps. She thought she saw a figure slipping into the shadows and started to walk faster, then to run, panting, eyes wide with fear as she rounded the corner.

11

Moscow

Kirov turned on the heating in the dusty apartment. Waiting for the water to heat for a shower to wash away the painful journey, she phoned the office on the ring road and asked for a car. At least she still carried some weight there; twenty minutes later she saw a Zil park down in the street.

Standing naked in the cascade of hot water, she went on puzzling. Her phone calls had yielded nothing but doubts. She had intended to report to her chairman, but he was mysteriously out of town for a few days; and in fact she had always doubted his commitment to the new man at the top. It would be dangerous to talk to anyone else in her own service until she was clearer just what was going on – and even riskier to confide in anyone outside it. She had left some clothes in the apartment when she was sent to Kabul, so she dressed in a blue tweed suit against the cold and took the lift down to the entrance, feeling unpleasantly alone.

The gardener and the street-sweeper had moved, but they were still there. Much good would it do whoever controlled them. A frisson of danger made her adrenalin run faster as a driver she did not know opened the car door, but she told him firmly to take her to the office.

Her old set of rooms had been reallocated when she was posted abroad, but they had let her keep a small office on the first floor, just above the cafeteria and the glass lobby with its bust of Dzerzhinsky. By the time she arrived the door had been unlocked and a young secretary, who had been arranging papers on the desk, turned as it opened. The girl saw a handsome grey-haired woman in her fifties. Once that face had been beautiful; it was still attractive, but with more of a grandmotherly roundness. '*Dobraye utra*, comrade General,' she said warily.

'I see you have been busy. *Spasiba.*'

'*Pazhalsta.*' The girl stood with downcast eyes, as if uncertain how to react to someone so senior.

Kirov gave her a reassuring smile. 'I shall be most grateful for your help for a few days, until I return to Afghanistan. What's your name?'

'Tania, comrade General.'

'Well, Tania, did you get all the documents I asked for?'

'Most of them. The secret ones are in the locked box on the table – they said you have a key for it – as I'm not allowed to see them.'

Kirov opened the steel container and thumbed through its contents. 'The minutes of Foreign Affairs Committee G don't seem to be here.'

'Aren't they, General? I did ask for them.'

'Don't worry. Would you like to fetch some tea while I read all this?'

By early afternoon it was clear that there were puzzling gaps in the classified papers relating to Afghanistan, Iran and Pakistan. At three o'clock she finished another glass of tea, fingering the metal holder thoughtfully, and set out for Kuntsevo. She did not telephone first, for she was certain that her request for a visit would be refused. It was a sunny autumn day and her feeling of impending doom lifted as the car sped down the express-way. When she reached the steel gates, they were closed, but half a dozen guards in grey overcoats stood on duty. An officer hurried to the car as it stopped and Kirov pressed the button to lower the electrically controlled window.

He looked at her questioningly and she displayed her Kremlin pass. 'I am Major-General Kirov. I am here to visit the clinic.'

'I apologise, General. My instructions are to admit no one.'

'I have come to see the General Secretary.'

His eyes looked puzzled under the grey fur hat, then he turned and marched to the small concrete guardroom. While she waited, Kirov stared at the driveway, winding away between rows of gloomy firs on the other side of the double gates. There was no sign of life in there. Then the young officer was back, saluting in deference to her rank. 'The General Secretary is not here. I cannot admit you and must ask you to leave at once.'

Kirov nodded. There was no point in arguing. She sat back in the leather seat as the car turned round, with a renewed sense of foreboding.

Anatoly Levshin did not live in a luxury apartment on the Lenin Hills. Since his return from Wrangel's Island he had been allocated a one-room flat in a new development south of the city, beyond the last station on the Metro. It stood in a rough clearing in the forest, a five-storey tenement surrounded by mud; the concrete block walls had not been rendered and inside the electricity and water worked only intermittently. He slept on a soft bed for the first time in thirty years, but it was almost as cold as the camp.

He had spent the day at the Writers' Union and the gossip had been interesting, just about worth the long trek back to his horrible new home. After the Metro he had caught the crowded bus, which wound between trees for a second hour, full of the smell of sweat and garlic. Alighting by the roadmakers' shack, he picked his way in the dark between heaps of gravel and the silent road-roller, using a torch to find the path of duckboards to the apartments. It was the lack of made-up roads that saved him – the two Volgas should have been hidden behind the block, but they had been forced to park right in front, shining in the moonlight, the only cars on the site, for none of the residents owned one.

Levshin hurriedly switched off the torch. Those were not militia cars, after some petty criminal; they had no markings or blue lights. It had to be him. The bastards – he'd only been out three months. *Glasnost*? Bollocks. Or perhaps the rumours he had been hearing all day were true. Counting the windows, he identified the two which served his apartment on the fourth floor. There seemed to be a dim glow behind them, hardly showing against the white light from the flat next door. So they were waiting. The deeply lined face grimaced in the dark – they would have to wait a long time. He turned and crept into the trees.

He did not see the ditch, but he felt the rough concrete of the sewer pipe when he crashed down onto it, grazing both his knees, a flint flying up to cut his cheek. He was still scrambling out when they came running, two dark figures with flapping overcoats. They were shouting for him to stop, using his name. 'Levshin! We know it's you. Stand still! We want to talk to you.' Why did they think it was him? He could be an innocent passer-by. More shouts. A shot, the noise of splintering bark when it ricocheted, another shot. His ears were singing and he could smell the cordite, but he went on weaving through the trees, running as fast as his ancient legs could carry him.

Suddenly his boots were almost silent, on a path of moss, and he realised that the other footsteps had stopped. He leant against a tree, his lungs red hot, and gulped for air like an athlete at the end of a marathon. The bastards had lost him, at least for a few hours, but it was bitterly cold, well below zero, and he had nowhere to shelter. Blood was trickling down his face and his clothes were torn from the fall, so to make matters worse he looked conspicuous. Then he had an idea, rather a clever idea, and set off towards the road.

12

Vienna

On Sunday Nazim turned up in jeans and a Stanford University sweat shirt. 'You old phoney,' laughed Sarah, kissing him at the gate.

'Old? Phoney?' He glared at her with mock sternness. 'I did my Ph.D. at Stanford. After all, I'm not actually *black* so it wasn't too hard to get in.' They drove around the Höhenstrasse and walked up a steep path through the forest. It was cold, but they emerged on a bluff under a clear autumn sky. Far below was the city, surrounded by wooded hills on three sides, by the broad muddy sweep of the Danube on the fourth. In the distance Sarah could see the big wheel turning on the Prater. She felt Nazim's arm round her waist. 'It's a good place, Vienna,' he said. 'Stable. People have enough to eat. You Europeans are very lucky.'

'Better than Pakistan, Nazim?'

'Pakistan had potential, but many problems. There could be great violence before we can settle down to making the economy work.'

'What sort of violence?'

He shrugged. 'Every sort. There could be a rising against Zia, you can't hold people down by force for ever. On top of that, the Indians hate us and the Russians have had an eye on our warm-water ports for centuries. Isn't that enough?'

'You aren't supposed to say things like that – what would the Ambassador think?'

'He'd probably agree – nobody in their right mind would want to be in Pakistan at the moment – but neither of us can speak freely.' He put his hands to her shoulders and held her at arm's length, studying her face thoughtfully. It was a gesture to which she would become accustomed. 'But I trust you, Cable. I think I shall call you Cable in future. Sarah is a garden party name, Earl Grey tea on green lawns. A cable is something secure.'

'If that's meant to be a compliment, thanks.' She nuzzled his neck gently. 'It's also nearly the first thing you've said in the last hour. What's wrong?'

For a few seconds his eyes looked furtive. 'Nothing, Cable. Everything is fine.' Suddenly he gestured at the clustered spires below. 'Oh bugger it. But for God's sake keep this to yourself. I was just wondering how much longer I'll be here.'

'Why, Nazim?'

'A man has been assassinated back home, someone senior to me in the Commission. They may be ordering me back, to take his place. That's all.'

'Would it be a promotion?'

'Sure, a big one – he's number three in the whole set-up – but I don't *want* to go back yet. I sometimes question whether I want to go back at all.'

Later, much later, Sarah lay beside him on her bed, feeling strong arms around her. *Swallows and Amazons* had half worked. He had talked a little more about life as a street urchin in Singapore, joking about the privations of the orphanage. She knew that he was hiding deep wounds, but when pressed he just smiled and distanced himself from it. 'It was a long time ago, Cable, some of it was unpleasant, but I survived. Now tell me about you . . .'

It was frustrating because she wanted to understand him, to know about the small boy he had once been. And she wanted to know, she had to admit, because in other circumstances, whatever the danger, she could have fallen for him in a big way. She felt increasingly uncomfortable at the deception, but then the warm closeness blocked out all other sensations. She fondled his penis, which was like a piece of thick tarred rope, feeling it swell in her hand, and sighed dreamily as he stroked her back and buttocks, then her breasts and the sensitive space between her thighs. They did not make love and once again he left with a shy kiss soon after midnight; but she sensed for the first time that there was something real between them.

Munster was ecstatic when she reported to him. 'To have him in a top spot back in Pakistan would be even more use to us. I'll find out who the dead guy was – I haven't heard anything about an assassination.'

'He isn't too keen to go back.'

'Perhaps he thinks they'll bump him off, too?'

'No, it's deeper than that. He really hates the place.'

'That's not how it seems to me.'

'He's pretty mixed up behind that façade, Ken. He still feels close to the poor, wants to do his bit to improve things, but he hates the Islamic fundamentalism and its cruelty – and the snobbishness. Some wealthy Singapore merchant paid for him to go to a posh school near Lahore and he's felt an outsider ever since. He makes jokes about how the ruling class let him in because he was good at sums, even gave him one of its daughters, but doesn't really accept him. He makes light of it, but he feels it very deeply.'

'My heart bleeds. For Christ's sake, Sarah, at least two people have been *killed* to protect this bastard.'

Sarah looked up sharply. 'Two?'

Munster coloured slightly. 'You know about Gerda – the other was before your time.'

'Someone might have bloody well told me before.'

'Perhaps, but the point is I'm not losing any sleep about Ali Baba. If they put him at the top table long enough to help us, I don't give a toss what happens afterwards.'

'No. No, I suppose not.' Sarah pushed away the tiresome feeling that she found something desperately attractive in Nazim's mixture of confident power lightened by flashes of vulnerability, but vulnerability faced with courage . . . it was a strong aphrodisiac. She concentrated on what Munster was saying.

'. . . I believe he's going to Frankfurt shortly. Is there any chance of your going with him?'

'I shouldn't think so – why's he going?'

'According to intercepts, he's going to a meeting at a company called Akron Industries.'

'So?'

'We believe Akron is a shell company set up by Pakistan – it provides cover for purchase of machinery and materials, for their weapons programme.'

'If it is, they aren't going to let me in, even if I do string along.'

'No, but if he's troubled, as he seems to be, he might confide in you afterwards. In bed,' Munster added, unsmiling. He had no sense of humour.

But there was to be no trip to Frankfurt for Sarah. Back in the apartment she turned on the late television news; the last item comprised shaky film of a large student demonstration in Karachi, broken up by police and soldiers with brutal force. She watched tear-gas canisters exploding on the ground, followed by figures in blue helmets, gas-masks and plastic visors tearing into the crowd with whips and staves. She was not surprised to hear that Nazim Khan had left town for a few days.

It was a wet evening in Cheltenham. In an asbestos hut at the back of the rambling complex of buildings in Priors Road, a young clerk was taking a bundle of flimsies from the vacuum tube that had delivered them, like the tubes once used to carry cash to a central desk in department stores. 'Got a bit more on the Pakis,' he said to his section head, who was taking down an illegal poster urging GCHQ staff to renewed industrial action whilst peering over his shoulder in the hope that no one would see him.

'Bully for you.' Luther turned away down the corridor to his small glass-partitioned office. 'Stick it in the tray.'

'No, Cal, could be urgent. Remember one of our friends from Century was asking for anything on the wog bomb factory?'

Luther winced. He had felt shifty about his name from schooldays – insensitive Evangelical parents having christened him Calvin – and resented the boy's familiarity, as he disliked the frivolity of denying the Pakistan Atomic Energy Commission its proper name. 'So?' He eyed the nineteen-year-old AO's shoulder-length hair with distaste.

'Remember you stuck in a lot of new keywords to try to flush anything out?'

'Of course I do, Darren.'

'Well, I think we done it. Look.' Darren waved the sheets of flimsy, following his boss into the office where they were laid on the grey metal desk. Each sheet was headed TOP SECRET UMBRA and covered in computer text. Luther ran his finger along the hieroglyphics above the intercepted material. 'Picked up in Hong Kong, eh, telegram from Russian Embassy in Islamabad to Bonn – I guess that's just an indirect route to Moscow, to confuse us – but using a bum code, oh dear, silly, *silly* darlings.' He read rapidly through the text which was pitted with gaps where words had not been picked up or not decoded: but there was enough.

'So our *Russian* friends have got a source in there, have they? But he failed to get himself promoted when the late and unlamented Dr Syed got the chop . . . pipped at the post by someone called Khan, whom he accuses of being mixed up with us? But his control orders him to keep quiet and denounce Khan at a more opportune moment. Strewth, *won't* they just have the knives out in Islamabad, blood everywhere.' But he would still put the whippersnapper in his place. 'It's too incomplete, Darren. You really must learn that we can't put up things that don't make a little more sense – send it back to linguistics, tell them to try and fill in some more gaps.'

The boy looked crestfallen. 'Immediate, Cal?'

'Routine will do quite well, lad.'

13

Moscow

On the Lenin Hills, Nadia Alexandrovna Kirov woke with a start and reached instinctively for the lamp by her bed. The digital clock said two in the morning. The scraping came again, outside on the balcony; she always tried to have a bedroom with a balcony – the early morning sun was almost the only luxury she had time to enjoy. She switched the light off again, padded to the glass door, revolver in hand, and peered through the crack in the curtains.

Another eye met hers, a wild eye rolling in a ravaged face, and she recoiled, gripping the gun tighter. Gingerly she peered through the gap again. There was a man out there, scraping at the glass. He must have climbed down the fire ladder from the roof, a burglar, a rapist, a madman? She was about to telephone the janitor, when some instinct made her pause. There was something distantly familiar about the angle of his head and neck, an image from long in the past. She cocked the revolver and opened the glass door a few inches: the chain would stop it going further. 'Stand still!' she ordered, levelling the gun at his chest. 'You have no right to be here and I am armed. Put your hands on your head.'

She felt a wave of fury radiating towards her and thought he was about to become violent, but then the dark figure obeyed. As he moved, the rags of his coat flapped against the night sky and she smelt his sweat. Whoever he was he needed a bath. 'So sorry, excellency, you see I have nowhere else to sleep.' The voice was bitter, sneering, familiar.

'Keep your hands there and come closer, turn your face towards the light from the street.' She peered at him. A gaunt man with a harrowed face that told of torture and starvation, eyes luminous and full of hate. 'Good God,' she breathed. 'What are *you* doing here?'

'Did you think I was dead?' The same sneering laugh. 'Just because you put me in a camp?'

'I put you in no camp, Levshin; the courts did that.'

He leaned forward and spat in her face. She stepped back sharply. 'You bloody fool, I nearly shot you.'

His face twisted against the glass of the door and his speech slurred. 'What – no bullet in the stomach for an enemy of the s-shtate? Don't tell me little Nadia Alexandrovna's found a soft heart in her old age?'

Kirov decided against calling the janitor; it would be embarrassing and hard to explain that she knew the intruder. 'You're pissed – what the hell do you want?'

'Just to talk to you, darling.' She recoiled from his breath, which stank of raw alcohol and the bitter smoke of cheap cigarettes. 'Can I come in?'

'I suppose you'd better, but don't try anything or I'll put a bullet through you – and I mean it, Anatoly, by God I mean it.' She slipped the chain on the doors and switched on the light as he stepped into the room. His face was full of suffering and bitterness, unrecognisable from the young man with whom she had dug trenches in frozen earth during the siege of Leningrad. 'Sit down there.' She gestured with the gun, switching on the baffler against electronic eavesdropping; every room of the apartment had one, turning like a metal fan under the ceiling, though she knew they were ineffective against the latest bugs. 'How the hell did you get in?'

'Fire escape, then I found your balcony. I came here before, you know, a long time ago.'

'I remember: you got disgustingly drunk. I'll give you five minutes, then out. What do you want?'

'Five minutes, eh? The Major-General is too generous.' He let the sarcasm hang in the air and belched; Kirov wondered just how drunk he was – not badly if he had climbed the fire escape to the roof and then found her balcony and dropped down into it. 'I've been waiting thirty years to tell you what I think of you, Nadia Alexandrovna, it may take a little longer than five minutes.'

Kirov suppressed her anger – after half a lifetime in the camps the poor bastard was entitled to let off steam – but she did want to get him out of the building as soon as possible. 'I don't give a damn what you think, Anatoly. You behaved like a bloody fool and I could do nothing to save you.'

Levshin's eyes narrowed. 'Save *me*? Sonya and I saved *you*. We all misjudged the temperature after Stalin died. You encouraged me to write the articles they condemned as treason – and Sonya to complain about the chaos in her hospital. When they expelled us from the Party and put us on trial, we kept our mouths shut and you survived.'

'I have not forgotten that either. I tried to help you both after you

65

were sentenced , but *you* made it impossible with your protests and hunger strikes. Your sister had more sense and I got her out after fifteen years, with a permit to leave the country.'

'Fifteen years! Was that the best you could do? They say Sonya died of cancer, somewhere in England?' Kirov stared at him with pain in her eyes and he looked away. 'I suppose it was better than dying of cancer while still being booted to work in the mines.' His mouth curled in a sneer. 'But not much.'

'What do you want, Anatoly?'

'I used to fuck you, d'you remember? In the siege, you kept your figure better than most despite the lack of food. Good fuck, you were, up against the side of the trench or in the hut, covered in sacks, nice firm thighs. Still firm, are they?'

Kirov's mouth tightened and she kept the revolver trained on him. 'I have good memories of that time as well, there's no need to cheapen them. You can be as coarse as you like – it doesn't shock me, it just makes me sad – but our paths separated a long time ago.' Her face hardened. 'For the sake of the past I let you in here, Anatoly – if you were a stranger you would be in a cell at the militia post by now – but you are becoming irritating. Why have you come?'

'They let me out three months back. Now they're trying to arrest me again. I'm on the run – I need somewhere to hide.' He gave a contemptuous laugh. 'I thought this place would be ideal, then I'll go on keeping quiet about what happened thirty years ago . . .'

Kirov ignored the threat. 'Why are they after you, what have you done?'

'Nothing, nothing at all. Exemplary character, living in concrete shit-house kindly supplied by state, down in swamp south of city. Spend so much time waiting for the bus I couldn't get up to anything even if I wanted.'

'Then I don't understand.'

'Don't you?' He stared at her with watery eyes, lip curling. 'You know, I don't think you *do*, and there I was thinking little Nadia Alexandrovna's so important these days, knows everything, pulls the strings . . . where've you been these last few months?'

'In Afghanistan.'

'Ah.' He wagged a finger at her triumphantly. 'That explains it. You haven't heard the gossip?'

'What gossip? For God's sake come to the point, it's the middle of the night and I need some sleep.'

He shook his head. 'Then I can stay?'

'No.'

'No hospitality, no gossip.'

'You can sleep it off for a few hours, but you'll have to leave before morning.'

He seemed to shrivel inside the ragged coat, the aggression suddenly gone, and she thought he was going to weep. 'I'll tell you anyway,' he mumbled. 'For old times' sake.'

He was no longer dangerous, but Kirov was still anxious about eavesdroppers. She met his gaze and put her finger to her lips, pointing meaningfully at the walls. 'You must go now,' she said loudly, gesturing to the door into the hallway with her revolver. He understood and walked in front of her to the outer door, where she pulled on an overcoat over her nightdress. Out in the lobby she unlocked the door to the emergency stairs and he climbed up them, through a second locked door to the roof. It was cold in the open air, but they squatted side by side on a large warm flue pipe, sheltered from the wind by the parapet.

'Tell me what you've heard – just facts, please, leave out the self-pity.'

'It was at the Writers' Union, mostly.' His speech was still slurred, but he was trying to be businesslike. 'They say Gorbachev is ill, a heart attack. Some say he's dead. Some that he isn't ill at all, but under arrest.' Kirov sat in silence, pulling her coat tighter against the cold. 'Well – what do *you* think?'

'I don't know, just go on.'

'They say Malinovsky's after the throne.'

'Do they?'

'Has been for years, hasn't he? Was in the running when Andropov died.'

'He's a barbarian,' muttered Kirov.

'They say you're for the chop. That's the other reason I'm here – you tried to help Sonya and I owe you. Right at the top of Malinovsky's little list, they say you are.'

'Anything else?'

'They say Gorbachev was too keen to get out of Afghanistan. Malinovsky and the military couldn't stomach that – they want to use more napalm, heavier bombs, chemicals, really smash the Mujahedin. Maybe promote a rising in Pakistan as well, get a friendly government and a naval base on the Indian Ocean.'

'That's absurd. The Muslim fundamentalists in Iran would join in, so might the Americans – we'd have a war on our hands. Maybe a rebellion in our own Muslim states. It would be a disaster.'

Levshin grinned in the dark. 'You important people fuck up everything. It's the old Tsarist policy. Nothing changes.'

'Just *who* is saying all this?'

'People. Everyone.' He was speaking rationally now, staring out over the city, dark at the centre except for the red stars still floodlit on the spires of the Kremlin. 'Well *is* it absurd? If so, where the bloody hell is your pal Mikhail Sergeyevitch? He hasn't been seen in public for weeks.'

'I think he may be ill. I don't believe the rest of it.' Kirov smiled wryly at the irony: Major-General and ex-convict shivering together in the cold, just as they had nearly forty-five years ago under German shelling, the bare roof the only place they could talk safely. 'But I need time to think. You can sleep in the spare room and have a bath – you smell as if you need one. We'll talk again in the morning.'

14

London

It was nine in the morning when the short man arrived at Heathrow Airport on a Pan Am flight from Washington. Although Menzel was met by a Second Secretary from his Embassy at the plane door, and ushered away from the crowded corridors of Terminal 3, through a series of doors unlocked by immigration officials, his expression remained one of distaste. Georg Menzel had long forgotten the ruins of Hamburg where he played as a hungry child. Ten years a CIA station chief, he appreciated the all-American virtues of efficiency, air-conditioning and political isolation. Barbarians started at Heathrow, never mind their quaint pretensions to a special relationship.

He stepped fastidiously over the litter outside the Terminal, ignoring the polite 'Good morning, sah' from the turbanned Sikh who was sweeping it into a barrow. The Chevrolet had tinted windows and curtains, so he was spared the sight of further examples of British decline as it swept round the perimeter road. The car stopped after twenty minutes on Bedfont Green only a mile south of the airport. The house was Georgian, standing by a pretty Norman church with yew trees arched over its door. The ground shook as Boeings roared overhead every two minutes.

In the drawing room double-glazing kept out the aircraft noise and the high windows gave on to a garden enclosed by red-brick walls, covered in wistaria, that hid the modern warehouses and battery-hen housing. This was the England of which Menzel approved, classical simplicity matched by the pin-striped suit of the figure that shook his hand and pointed to a pair of leather club armchairs. 'Nice to see you, Georg, thanks for stopping by.'

'No problem, Gerry. Good of you to come out here – but I thought Nairn was handlin' Ali Baba himself?'

'Nairn is abroad, Georg.' Menzel looked visibly relieved. He didn't like Gerald Clayton, the head of Nairn's South and East Asia Division, but he was only thirty-eight, thrusting, more brutal in his thinking. It was easier to deal with Clayton. Anyway they might be confronting him as Chief before long.

The two men faced each other warily while a woman in a blue overall served coffee, then Menzel came straight to the point. 'Seems Cable is doin' well? No sign Ali Baba suspects her?'

'None. He seems to have accepted her completely. No reason why he shouldn't. She's a pretty girl and her background is genuine – she'd been in that job for over a year before they met, with no intelligence connection. And he approached the Australians, not us.'

'And now he's goin' back to the key job in Pakistan?'

'So it seems. Presumably it was a Marxist group who assassinated Syed – didn't know how much they were helping us, did they?'

Menzel smiled inscrutably. 'This could be one hell of a successful operation. Can you complete the circle by gettin' Cable moved to inspect the reactors in Pakistan? Keep the relationship goin', use her as a courier, really compromise the bastard?'

'I've asked our mission in Vienna to speak to the agency and get her a change of duties. We can't tell them why, of course, but I'd expect them to co-operate – we provide a significant part of their budget.'

'She must be under a hell of a lot of pressure. Suppose she cracks?'

'We take that risk. If she cracks in Vienna, we whip her back to London. If she cracks in Pakistan –' Clayton shrugged – 'we disown her.'

Menzel nodded. Nairn would have jibbed at putting Sarah more at risk, but Clayton took every opportunity to cross swords with him. He would get the succession by thrusting Nairn aside, not being recommended by him. It was distasteful, but convenient. 'It makes sense, Gerry. We need them in place just long enough to be sure there *is* a programme, and if so how many warheads and where they're stored. The key questions. We can take it from there. That girl's won his confidence – she must be good, a damn sight better than that wimp of a father.'

'A promising young officer.' Clayton's elegant silver hair surely had to be dyed to make him look more distinguished. 'There's bound to be an element of danger when she's in Pakistan, but we've no alternative.'

Menzel felt uncomfortable. There would be more than 'an element of danger'. In his briefcase was the series of intercepts culminating in Zia's order for an investigation to trace the leaks from Kahuta. It had finally been sparked off by newspaper articles in Britain and America, and Menzel was sure Khan had nothing to do with them, but an intelligence alert could easily focus on him. If it did he'd be finished in days. 'How long will Nairn be away?'

'At least a couple of weeks.'

Menzel seemed about to speak, but instead fumbled in his pocket for matches and lit a cigar. Hell, the bastard Paki was expendable; so was the girl. In the last analysis so was Nairn. Clayton wasn't going to mention the intercepts and Menzel left his case closed.

In Vienna, Nazim Khan sat in the agency boardroom, occupying one of a half-circle of thirty-five desks, not unlike the ones he had used at school, facing a low platform where the chairman sat with two members of staff taking notes. The wall behind the chairman was disfigured by a white plastic symbol of an atom surrounded by olive branches. The room was crowded. Over forty countries had sent large delegations to the meeting, which was about technical aid to the Third World and pre-ordained to achieve nothing. Nazim had lost count of the hours he had spent in this room with its hideous orange carpet and no windows; he had yet to hear anything take place there that he could honestly describe as useful.

They broke up at five and drifted out into the curved reception area where he had first met Sarah. The building was round and everything in it followed the curve of the walls. It was already dark outside, the lights of the city gleaming across the dark line of the Danube. He smiled vaguely at one or two diplomats who greeted him and hurried to one of the telephone kiosks. '*Nein*,' said the whining voice at the garage. '*Leide*, the car is not ready. I must the fuel pump replace and the part does not arrive.'

'Damn. When will it be done?'

'Not before lunchtime tomorrow, *Herr Botschafter*.'

'I'm not the Ambassador, Klaus, just one of his staff. Can I pick up the car in the afternoon?'

'I do my best, *Herr Doktor*.'

'Thanks.'

'Very good, *Herr Doktor*.'

Nazim took the lift down to the rotunda, already empty as diplomats scattered to comfortable apartments all over the city, out into the cobbled plaza in front of the building. He thought of taking the U-bahn from the station immediately outside the gates, but instead walked down the steps to Wagramerstrasse. Trams were clanking along their rails on each side of the road, but there was also a taxi rank. A cab flashed its lights as he approached and drove the few yards to where he stood. He opened the rear door and flopped into the seat. 'Rudolf Kassnergasse, Grinzing, *bitte*.'

The driver nodded behind his glass screen and accelerated into the traffic crossing the long bridge. On the other side he turned right and followed the embankment by the Danube. Nazim looked back at the familiar shape of the UN complex, outlined by the lights of its towers like a dinosaur brooding in the dark wasteland across the river.

By the time they passed Friedrich Engels Platz, he had almost dozed off: the air-conditioning in the UN building always made him drowsy, even though it was only half past five, but he would soon come to with a drink at home. They would be there in ten minutes: a left turn at the Nordbrücke and up past the *Pam-Pam* supermarket into Grinzing.

When the taxi did not turn left, but sped up a ramp and onto the bridge, he sat upright in surprise and leant forward to tell the driver he was going the wrong way. But the glass screen was shut tight and there was no response to his rapping on it. He tried to claw it open, but it would not shift. In sudden panic, he reached for the door handle, thinking he could jump out at the traffic lights on the other side. There were no door handles on the inside of the car and his panic turned to a wave of fear. He was not going home. He was in trouble.

Across the river, the car accelerated through a shopping centre, out into dark countryside. Without warning it left the road and bumped down a track into a farm. Nazim tensed ready to defend himself, if possible to kick aside whoever opened the door and make a run for it. But they stopped in a barn, dimly lit by yellow bulbs dangling from the rafters. The right-hand door of the car opened and a thickset man in a black balaclava levelled a revolver at him. 'Don't try to move, Khan, we don't want to hurt you unnecessarily.'

Nazim resisted an urge to take a chance and hurl himself at his kidnapper, but he was holding that gun in a businesslike way and the hammer was drawn back: the slightest move and it would fire. He got in beside Nazim and crouched in the corner, resting the revolver on his knee. Nazim felt another man get in on the other side. 'Who the hell *are* you?' he roared at them. 'You can't get away with this. Take me back into town before the police pick us up.' He was relieved that his voice sounded furious, masking his inner terror, but the car was already back on the road.

'Shut up.' The accent was muffled and he could not place it, possibly East European or Arab? From his own country? Nazim's terror increased. 'Or we put sticking plaster over your mouth.'

'I said who the devil are you? And where are we going?'

There was no reply. They were travelling at high speed now, headlights raking across rows of lime trees on each side of the road.

72

The muffled voice growled again. 'Do you have any engagements this evening?'

'Of course. I shall be missed within half an hour.'

'If that's true, when we stop you will give me the phone number wherever you were going and I'll make your apologies.'

'Go to hell!'

'Just do it, Khan. We don't want to use force, but we will if necessary.' He yawned noisily. 'Now shut up. We have a long way to go.'

After half an hour, the car stopped in a field where a small aircraft was waiting. 'Kneel on the floor and put your hands behind your back.' Nazim snorted, then felt a thump in the kidneys. Half on his knees, he felt his wrists seized and handcuffed behind him. The metal bit into his wrists sharply. 'I want that phone number now.' A hand seized his hair and twisted his head round, the pulling on his scalp surprisingly painful.

Two hard eyes searched Nazim's. 'You weren't going anywhere tonight, were you?' A handful of hair was pulled out. 'I don't want to hurt you, Khan, but it's a kick in the balls next.' The voice lowered menacingly. 'I said you weren't going anywhere, were you?' Hands gripped his arms and a foot swung back deliberately.

'No, I wasn't.'

'Good boy, that's much more sensible.' They put a blanket over his head and hustled him across rough stubble and into the cabin of the plane, the door slammed shut and he was still lying on the floor when it tilted and they were airborne. He felt a prick in the arm and lost consciousness.

15

Moscow

Anatoly Levshin spent the day huddled in the lift machinery room, just below roof level in Kirov's apartment block. She had been surprised to find him awake at six thirty in the morning, washed and shaved with the men's razor she kept for occasional use by her visitors. She would have been even more surprised to know that the old derelict had got up an hour before, a habit from years in the Gulag, and made a thorough search of her apartment. He had pocketed tins of sardines, caviare and a tin-opener from the kitchen, adding the spare set of door keys he found in a littered drawer of her desk, surprised that a pro like Kirov should leave them there.

At seven he thanked her, wished her luck and left, not using the lift but the emergency stairs that led to the basement; she had waved him goodbye, standing at the apartment door in her dressing-gown. But he did not go down the dusty concrete steps – he climbed upwards until he found the low door to the lift room. It smelt strongly of oil and carbon brushes, but there was space for him to sit on the floor and the electric motors gave off a little heat.

At intervals during the day Levshin consumed a can each of caviar and sardines, washed down with water from a fire bucket hanging on the stairs. Kirov had told him she would be back at seven in the evening, but he was not to return to the apartment. In the quiet of the afternoon, he crept back down the stairs and turned the two keys in her lock, terrified that the other front door on her landing might open; but he entered unobserved. Kirov was a senior intelligence officer, so he moved as quietly as he could, assuming that the place would be bugged. There might also be intruder alarms set off by movement, although he could see no sign of hidden cameras.

He was angry with Kirov. She could have helped him to leave the capital – or the country – had she wished. She had sheltered him for the night, fed him and let him use her bathroom, but that was not much from one's teenage sweetheart, for bonds of affection forged in the trenches facing the Nazis. But no anger showed in the care with which he examined her study. Last night the desk had been bare – there had been no papers to be seen anywhere, only a feminine jumble of keys, tissues, lipsticks and paperclips in one unlocked drawer. The single steel filing cabinet had been closed, a security bar padlocked down its front.

There were still no papers to be seen. Levshin peered through the Venetian blind. Outside he could see the ugly Stalinist skyscraper of the university at the top of the hill, the long grass slope to the river and the Metro station on the bridge across it. Apart from the firs, the trees were leafless as winter set in, but a few figures in red and blue parkas were strolling among them. He was breathing deeply to steady his nerves, knowing that as soon as he opened one of the secure containers he might be triggering an alarm.

But last night he had decided what to do and he had to take the risk. There was no point fiddling with the safe he had found behind a picture in the living room: it had a complicated combination lock that he could never open. Equally it probably took so long to operate that Kirov might not bother to use it for documents in her possession for only a day or two. In that case where would she shove them? The most likely place would be that filing cabinet. If only he could find a key.

Levshin tried every key in her desk, but none of them fitted. He went into her bedroom, with its plain beige carpet and wide double bed. He wondered who shared it these days, for he could not imagine Nadia Alexandrovna being completely celibate. The room was a curious mixture of the military and the feminine. A big wardrobe contained dresses and well-made tweed suits, with several dark-blue uniforms. There was a dressing-table with a round mirror and pretty silver-backed hairbrushes. He opened the drawers one by one, but found no keys.

After riffling through every drawer he could find, it was plain that the only way he could open the cabinet was by force, so he went into the kitchen to search for suitable tools, returning to the study with a collection of meat skewers, kitchen knives and a mallet for tenderising steak. The brass padlock was small, with a keyhole in its base. He guessed that the half-circle of metal that went through the hasp on the filing cabinet would be of toughened steel, but the body of the lock did not look unduly strong. Carefully Levshin held it in one hand and rammed a skewer into the keyhole. He brought the mallet down on the skewer, at first with a sharp tap, then several times with all his strength, hoping to God that no one would hear the noise. The skewer crunched into the lock mechanism, then bent, and he twisted it about until pieces of the lock started to trickle out. The padlock fell open.

The cabinet contained three drawers of hanging files with neat typed labels. The fourth drawer, at the top, was empty except for several thin files stamped with a Top Secret classification. Levshin glanced through them – they were the minutes of some intelligence committee dealing with the region centred on Afghanistan, Pakistan and Iran. He fingered the hanging files, extracting documents where they looked interesting, but many concerned Kirov's financial and property affairs, bank statements and papers related to her villa on the Black Sea. Plainly little Nadia did not suffer from financial problems like those that had bedevilled Levshin ever since his return from Wrangel's Island.

He assembled the classified files into a small parcel and wrapped it in a black garbage bag from the kitchen. Finally he sat in the living room and thumbed through an old photograph album until he found a snap of Nadia Alexandrovna at the age of about twenty, in army uniform but strikingly pretty. He extracted it and put it into his pocket. Letting himself out of the apartment he descended to the basement, where he emerged cautiously into the garage. Several black cars were parked in a row, but there were no people. The whole block would be occupied by fat cats from the *Nomenklatura* and they would be at their offices, their wives shopping in the special shops, their children at the privileged schools. As he dropped the remains of the padlock into a drain, he spat in contempt, then froze as a car drove down the ramp from the street. Hidden behind a concrete pillar, he watched two men get out and walk to the lift. They had the unmistakable look of the KGB in plain clothes.

A side door led to a small yard at the back of the block, accommodating four large, wheeled garbage containers. The newly clean Levshin wrinkled his nose at the smell of rotting cabbage, but strode past briskly into the service road, on into the street, down towards the Metro. On a corner he paused to use a pay phone, making a short call to the American Embassy, using guarded phrases.

Sarah walked slowly from the U-bahn station back to Larochegasse. It had been raining and the street lights reflected on wet pavements under the trees. She was not looking forward to the evening. It was bad enough feeling in constant danger, as she had ever since the operation started; finding that she liked Nazim, was deeply attracted by him, was a complication that made it very much worse. Pretending to fall for a man she couldn't stand would have been difficult, but more straightforward and less painful.

She felt unable to talk to Munster about it and had asked for an air ticket to London and an appointment with Nairn. Munster told her that this would be an impossible breach of security – and anyway

Nairn was away from London. Today Munster had met her at a lonely spot by the Danube during her lunch hour, reported that Nazim had returned from his visit to Akron in Frankfurt and ordered her to meet him again as soon as possible, in the hope that he might let something slip.

She unlocked her front door, turned on the heating and settled down by the phone: no point putting it off. Nazim was not at the Embassy but the girl who answered said he had left a meeting at the agency and should be at home, so Sarah dialled the apartment. The phone rang for five minutes but there was no reply. Suspicious, she put her coat on again and drove the Volkswagen round the Höhenstrasse, through the Vienna Woods looking down on the lights of the city, to Grinzing. It took forty minutes to reach Nazim's apartment. There was no answer to the bell and the lights were out. It was odd that he'd been back a day without making contact – and now he'd vanished again. Puzzled and edgy, she spent the whole journey back to her apartment trying to figure out why.

16

Moscow

The Lenin Museum was crowded with schoolchildren, brought by the coaches parked in the Square to visit one of the dullest collections in the world. Most of the exhibits were letters or old photographs in glass cases. Levshin had hidden his black bundle behind the cistern in a nearby public lavatory and walked in confidently, pausing to look up at the world map showing the spread of Marxist-Leninism in coloured lights. Up the escalator he found his contact waiting by Lenin's Rolls-Royce. She was a girl of about twenty-five, lacy white blouse crisp beneath her red topcoat. She had a neat, unremarkable face, showing even white teeth when she smiled.

'Odd sort of car for the workers' leader?' She gestured at the magnificent leatherwork and brass headlamps. She spoke Russian uncertainly, with a Deep South accent, reminding him of Scarlett O'Hara in *Gone With the Wind*, which he had once seen in English with sub-titles.

Levshin nodded, feeling in his pocket for the sample papers he had chosen: his heart started to race, for he had no way of knowing whether she was really an American diplomat or a KGB agent planted after his call had been tapped. He walked with her to an alcove where they could not be seen and handed over the two files he had selected as samples. She rolled them up and pushed them into her handbag. 'I'll need to check this stuff,' she whispered. 'But it shouldn't take too long. I'll meet you back on Red Square in two hours, between St Basil's and the Place of the Skull.'

Nazim Khan woke up when the plane landed. He could see the lights of a building through the window, but had no idea how long he had been unconscious, or where they were. His throat felt dry as sandpaper – that would be the drug – and they had freed his hands, but his right wrist was handcuffed to one of the guards before the aircraft door was opened. They led him across grass to what looked like the clubhouse of a flying club, but there were no signs to indicate what country it was in. Inside he sat in a comfortable armchair, a guard to each side, facing two lamps angled towards him. They dazzled his eyes and he could not see the face of the figure behind them.

'I'm sorry about all this drama, Dr Khan, but it seemed the most secure way of arranging for us to meet.' The voice told him nothing, although it sounded vaguely Scottish. 'May we offer you a drink? Beer? Fruit juice?'

Nazim thrust his head forward aggressively. 'You won't get away with this, you bastards. Who the bloody hell are you?'

'Please relax, Dr Khan. We honestly mean you no harm.'

Nazim felt a glass placed by his free hand and picked it up awkwardly. It was orange juice and he swallowed the whole tumbler. 'I said who the bloody hell are you?'

'We are men of honour, as I believe you are.'

'More like a collection of gangsters! You bribe my garage, pick me off the street, beat me up, kidnap me, then talk about honour?' He was shouting partly to conceal his fear, but the fury was genuine enough. 'Honour? Crap! I warn you – you are committing a very serious crime and I demand to be returned to Vienna at once.'

'Don't worry – you'll be back in Vienna by morning. We just want to follow up a conversation you had with my colleague Mr Mallaband of the Australian Embassy a few weeks ago.'

Nazim felt a further wave of anger and apprehension. 'I don't know what you're talking about.'

'I think you do, Dr Khan. This is not a trap – we are nothing to do with your own government. I am an officer of the intelligence service of a Western country.'

'Of Australia?'

The question was ignored. 'We are told by Mallaband that you are not in sympathy with the present government of Pakistan, that you might be willing to help us. Is that true?' Nazim stared into the patch of blackness, saying nothing. 'If it is true, Dr Khan' – the man's tone softened – 'you would be doing something that could only have beneficial results for your countrymen, who live every day in danger of violence, revolution, possibly even war.' He paused, but Nazim still said nothing.

This time the silence lasted several minutes, until the soft voice broke it again, showing no stress or irritation. It was a friendly voice, too damned friendly, thought Nazim. 'We understand that you would be doing this for reasons of conscience, but if we could help you in any practical way, we should of course be privileged to do so.'

Nazim jerked in his chair. 'I don't want your bloody money – you can't buy me! If you think I'm accepting a bundle of filthy notes while you take photographs to blackmail me, you've got the wrong man.' He made to stand up, but hands pressed down on his shoulders and the handcuff sliced into his wrist sharply.

'My dear Dr Khan, we wouldn't dream of anything so crude. As I said at the beginning, we see you as a man of honour.'

Nazim bridled, blinking angrily into the lights. 'Then why did you bring me here by force? Call off these thugs and tell me what you want without threats.'

There was another long silence as if the man were considering how to respond. 'Dr Khan, we understand you are going back to a senior job in your government's service, where you will have full knowledge of their nuclear programme.'

'What of it?'

'If, as some allege, that programme includes the production of nuclear weapons, you will have full knowledge of that too. I thought that was why you approached Mallaband?' Nazim did not reply. 'Unless I have misunderstood, you are offering us your co-operation? You will be a man of influence, who can help us to devise policies which will avoid your country going up in flames.'

'And if I'm caught I would be executed – we are talking of my country's most closely guarded military secret!'

'But you *offered* your help, Dr Khan. Didn't you?'

'I did, but I've had second thoughts. Yes, I *am* troubled about my country's policies and thought a private line of communication might be helpful. But the danger has increased – you are now asking me to commit high treason in a country close to revolution. I prefer to remain alive.'

'Ah, but I think you overestimate the danger, Dr Khan. You would not be caught! You are too senior, too powerful. We should watch your back and if ever you were in danger, we should do our best to spirit you away to a new life in the West, a new identity, a new country.'

'I have a wife and two children – in Islamabad.'

'We should rescue them as well.'

Nazim snorted. 'It would not be so easy – and for someone who is asking me to join his band of brothers and risk my neck, you seem unduly coy. These lamps are blinding me and I am still shackled to this gorilla on my right. If you want me to trust you, show me your face, tell me who you represent, then I might start to listen.'

'Would you start to listen seriously, Dr Khan?'

'How the hell should *I* know? There would be a lot to discuss.'

Abruptly Nazim felt the steel unlocked from his wrist and heard a series of clicks. The piercing lights went out, leaving him blinking and astonished as the room emptied. He was alone with the tall, gaunt man who was moving to an armchair near him, about to light a pipe. 'Okay, Dr Khan? Here I am. We are alone and there are no bugs. If you don't want to do business, just say so and we'll return you to Vienna. No reprisals.' He smiled with eyes that were wise and penetrating. Plainly he knew a great deal about his quarry – Nazim wondered just how much.

'It is all so sudden.'

'I don't want to press you, but we haven't got all night. So what's it to be, Dr Khan? Yes or no?' Nazim was still rubbing his eyes and blinking. 'Perhaps it would help to talk a little of the past? Of things that happened in California in 1968?' The voice hardened. 'Or even before that, in Pakistan?'

The school outside Lahore was still called St George's, but its religion was Islam. Nazim stayed there in the holidays as well as the terms, except for one summer visit back to the Khans in Singapore. His adoption meant little more than payment of his school fees and lack of spending money made him a perpetual outsider. But he found one good friend in Hamid Ibrahim. Ibrahim had everything: handsome features, an easy, languid charm, brilliance on the cricket pitch, a father who was a senior government official with inherited money. In the rigid atmosphere of St George's, poor academic work was rewarded with a beating, so Ibrahim was glad to accept advice – or ready-made essays – from Nazim, who had no problems in that direction. In return, Nazim was sometimes invited to the Ibrahim family home in Karachi in the vacations.

Afterwards it was natural for them both to go on to Karachi University; and the Khans made no difficulty about the fees. Nazim made a second visit back to Singapore, feeling grateful and dutiful, but his adoptive father was dying of cancer and Mrs Khan not overjoyed to see him. On the advice of Ibrahim's father the two young men read maths and physics in Karachi and applied for jobs with the government in their final year. Both joined the new Atomic Energy Commission and were sent on, almost immediately, to complete their studies in America. Thus 1968 found two young Pakistanis arriving at Stanford University, south of San Francisco.

Even for the sophisticated Ibrahim, California was overpowering: the climate pleasantly warm, not burning like Karachi, the beach-life, the big ranch-style houses that they had previously seen only on films, the wondrous supply of liquor, above all the freedom and lack of poverty. And the American girls. On the whole, the green campus by the Pacific was not the most intelligent place to send two young men in their twenties, suddenly liberated from the restraints of a strict Islamic society.

Nazim met Robin at a lecture in one of the cool Spanish-style buildings grouped around the university tower. She was short, with pretty features in a round face, dark curly hair and an open, companionable manner. Like Nazim, she was a foreigner – from Australia – and working for her doctorate. He asked her out that same evening. The Pakistan government had thoughtfully provided their two students with a shared car and a generous living allowance, so they drove into San Francisco. He took Robin to a shell-fish restaurant on Fisherman's Wharf and she took him to a disco afterwards.

Apart from Ibrahim, Robin was the first person with whom Nazim had really felt comfortable in the whole of his life. As a scientist he was accepted because he was plainly brilliant; at St George's and in Karachi he had been a passable cricketer. He attracted respect, but not affection. Perhaps the cause was the self-sufficiency he had developed to survive as a boy, for both the lonely trek to Singapore and the orphanage had taken a deal of surviving; whatever the reason, there was a barrier. Now he did not care what the reason had been, for in Robin's arms the barrier had gone. For fourteen years he had guarded a faded brown photograph of his mother in his wallet. No one had seen it, but now he shared it without embarrassment or the aggressive pride he sometimes felt in his poor origins. Robin replied with boxes of snaps of a vast family spread around New South Wales. When they made love for the first time it was evident that she had far more experience, and he was afraid he would disappoint her, but there was soon an easy intimacy between them. After two months they moved into a small apartment together, over a general store in Palo Alto, a few miles from the campus. Nazim had finally rejected the constraints of Islam and found himself.

Ibrahim gave them a brotherly blessing and went on screwing around, smoking marijuana and spending his father's money. He knew he would never get any kind of degree, but believed – rightly – that his father would protect him from the wrath of the government that was investing more than the annual cost of a two-teacher village school in his son. Nazim and Robin lived together for nearly two years. By the time he completed the thesis for his doctorate he had given some painful thought to the future. In March of the last year, they borrowed a tent and camped for a week in the dunes behind a beach near Monterey.

The third evening they barbecued fish over a driftwood fire, drank a little white wine, made love and walked in the moonlight. With the surf booming in the background, Nazim took her hand. 'In three months we shall leave Stanford,' he said deliberately. 'I dread it, Robin. Can we stay together? It is what I want most in the world.'

She gripped his hand tighter. 'Is that some kind of a proposal, Nazim?'

'That's exactly what it is.'

She threw her arms around his neck. 'That's the nicest thing anybody ever said to me, but . . .'

He looked into her face gravely. 'But what?'

'But I love you, hulk, but I'd like to spent the rest of my life with you, but what about the practicalities?'

'You mean I am brown and you are white?'

'No, that's one of the excitements. But you're supposed to be going back to Pakistan to build power stations. I'm supposed to be going back to Australia to teach maths. Have you forgotten?'

'No. We just have to make a choice.'

'Do you mean you want me to come and live with you in Pakistan?'

They were walking barefoot through the surf and he splashed a few paces before replying. 'That's one choice. They did send me here and I'd like to go back and do something useful.'

'But I'm not a Muslim, I'm not an anything, and how would they take to a plump white woman going about in shorts?'

'They wouldn't. The rest wouldn't be impossible, but I can't promise that you'd like it. The alternative would be for me to get a permit to work in Australia, or here? They both need nuclear scientists.'

'Do you *want* to do that?'

'I would prefer to pay them back by working in Pakistan – but you do come first, Robbie.' The long shape of an oil tanker was passing out to sea, its green starboard navigation light gleaming on the water. 'There's something else, too.'

'What's that, love?'

'I have no time for the powerful people who sent me here – and I don't believe I'll be allowed to do much that will benefit the poor. Sooner or later they will want me to design weapons, not power stations.'

She shivered. 'God, this sea's cold – and you make me feel frightened.'

'Frightened?'

'Two years ago I didn't want to love anyone, I didn't want anyone to love me. I didn't want the burden of someone else's pain. You never tumbled to that, you big dope, and now I'm so happy you didn't.' She kissed him. 'But won't they be furious with you?'

'I would pay back my government the cost of sending me here, every last rupee. I would offer to do some postgraduate teaching in

Pakistan, if I can find a job that would allow it. I have thought hard about it all. I don't belong anywhere – Malaya, Singapore, Lahore, Karachi, Stanford – I don't want any more one-night stands.' He kissed her. 'I just want to share a patch of earth with you, Robin, and I don't give a damn where it is.'

PART THREE

17

Teremangal

The small town lay in a wide valley near the Afghan frontier, just a few miles inside Pakistan. For centuries it had been a peaceful farming community, but then the refugees started to arrive. After eight years, their tents and ramshackle corrugated-iron huts dominated the place. There were more Afghans than Pakistanis – gun-running, drug-smuggling, resting and regrouping for the war over the border. That morning, a group of Mujahedin was squatting in the shadow of a *chaikhane*, sipping their bowls of sweet tea and watching the caravans of donkeys and camels churn up the mud in the alleys. Their weapons were close at hand – American Armalites, Russian Kalashnikovs, old British Lee-Enfields – as they talked to the two Americans with cine-cameras. One guerilla had been to New York and spoke some English. 'When I was in your land I lived with Mr and Mrs Grodzinski in Queens. Do you know them, travellers?'

'America is a big place, Selim Mansour.'

'Sometimes Mr Grodzinski offered me beer in the evening, and I was very tempted, but to drink is against my religion.'

'Did you ever have an American girlfriend, Selim Mansour?'

'No, traveller, American women are not like ours. They are too forward. Once one I did not know kissed me – on the *lips*.' He lowered his eyes meaningfully. 'In a bar.'

The American switched to Dari and changed the subject. 'Do you ever see Russians over here, Selim Mansour?'

'Russian girls, traveller?'

'No, just Russians.'

'They bomb the villages just across the border, to make travelling difficult and frighten us.'

'But do they send in agents, spies?'

'*Insh'allah.*' The Afghan shrugged. 'It is possible, but if we caught one he would pray for death long before it came.'

While they had been speaking a dull rumble, like thunder, had been growing in the distance. Now they looked up as it crashed overhead, followed by a sporadic rattle of machine-gun fire as the big jets swept down the valley. '*Shuravi!*' cried Mansour. 'But they have never attacked us here before.'

The bombs fell slowly, turning in the sky, as the men dived for shelter in the shadow of mud walls and an open drain. Explosions crashed between the hills. Flames leapt into the air where wooden houses collapsed and caught fire, terrified men and women raced past in panic, stumbling through the mud of the alleys. The raid was over in minutes, with columns of smoke rising all over the town and the refugee camp, the crackle of burning and screams of the injured filling the air. Mansour pulled the American back to his feet. 'See how the *Shuravi* slaughter women and children, traveller. The Mujahedin training camps are concealed in the hills, and they must know it. Our men will be terrified for their families down here, when they see the raid, but they are safe and this will just make them hate the *kafirs* more.'

'Smash them,' growled the Marshal at the head of the table. 'That's what we have to do now.'

The meeting of Foreign Affairs Committee G was in a conference room on the third floor of the Council of Ministers building, looking out over the Kremlin gardens to the river. Only three members were present, with a secretariat of four young men from the Foreign Ministry. Malinovsky had assumed the chair after announcing that the General Secretary was still in hospital. He dominated the room by sheer size, a great bear of a man with a head that had long been completely bald; even in his well-cut suit, he was plainly a soldier and he rushed through the business with military efficiency. Committees were a pain, but one had to follow the formalities of collective decision-making. He concluded the discussion on the last item. 'It is regrettable that still no formula has been found to allow us to complete a dignified withdrawal from Afghanistan, but no doubt our admirable diplomatic service will continue their efforts. In the meantime we in defence will ensure that the military situation is contained.'

As he closed the loose-leaf file and stood up, one of the double doors from the corridor opened. A woman in a blue dress came in and he stared at her with a puzzled expression. 'Why, Nadia Alexandrovna, how nice to see you. I thought you were still in Kabul.'

Kirov's jaw tightened, but she gave him full marks for downright cheek. Still in Kabul? The bastard had been watching her ever since she returned. 'I'd like a word, Marshal. In private.'

'By all means, my dear. Let's talk here when the others have gone. Incidentally, you missed a useful session – you *are* still a member of this committee, aren't you?'

'I thought so, but mysteriously no one told me your meeting was taking place.'

'How regrettable – but no doubt they thought you were still in Kabul?'

'I came back yesterday and phoned the secretary to ask the date of the next meeting. He said he didn't know.' She walked stiffly to the window and watched a crocodile of children passing the great bronze statue of Lenin; they were in Pioneers uniform, red scarves knotted round their necks. Kirov did not wish to be seen chatting as a friend with Malinovsky. She felt his eyes on her back and wondered whether he was mentally undressing her or imagining her with a bullet hole in the back of the neck. Probably the second, although once, in the long imperial decline under Brezhnev, he had seized her passionately at a drunken party in a *dacha* out at Zhukovka, explaining in graphic detail how old soldiers preferred the comfortable flesh of a mature woman, not the skinny young gymnasts and ballet dancers usually favoured by Party bosses.

'You're a handsome girl, Nadia Alexandrovna,' he had belched, eyes watery from the vodka, trying to steer her towards a summer-house by the small lake.

She had tried to decline coquettishly, 'Yuri! I'm fat and fifty – and flattered of course, but not here, *please*.'

Then he had become angry and shaken her roughly by the shoulders. 'My girl corporals don't bloody well refuse me, you stuck-up bitch. You let one try – I'd take a cartridge belt to her arse and post her to the Arctic.'

At that point Kirov had slapped his face and made a cutting remark about brewer's droop. She knew he had never forgiven her – and from such trivia a vendetta could start. She heard the doors close and turned sharply.

'Now, what can I do for you, Nadia?' He gave a superior smile, knowing that he could needle her more by being nice than by shouting.

'I want to know what's going on, Marshal.'

'Going on? I don't understand?'

'Oh yes you do. Where's Mikhail Sergeyevitch, for a start?'

'The poor fellow had a mild heart attack and is recovering in hospital.'

'Which hospital?'

'Why, the clinic at Kuntsevo, of course.'

'Then why was I not allowed to see him when I went there yesterday?'

'He is resting, Nadia Alexandrovna, he doesn't want to see anybody yet.'

'I insist on talking to him. Today.'

'But my dear, we must listen to the doctors. He mustn't be troubled with state business – not until he is better.'

Kirov's eyes narrowed. 'We'll see about that. Secondly, what the hell are you playing at in Afghanistan? Grigorenko has permitted a change of government that can only make it harder for us to withdraw. I hear that we've bombed the Mujahedin in camps across the border in Pakistan. What are you trying to do – start a war?'

'Afghanistan is an independent country. If their Party decides on changes, it is not for us to stop them.'

'Why the devil not? Without our support their Party would be out of power and hanging from the gates of Kabul. Now Habidullah, a moderate, has been shot and that madman Islamuddin is in charge. It was insane to allow it.'

Malinovsky shrugged and sat down at the table, gesturing her to a chair opposite.

She continued to stand. 'I'm not being fobbed off, Marshal. The military have been putting forward contingency plans for short, sharp moves against the Muslim states to the south for years. That's how we got into this mess in Afghanistan. If you've got some bright idea about invading Pakistan or Iran as well, forget it. It would be lunacy and the Politburo would stop you.'

'Don't be absurd, my dear.' Kirov winced. 'There's no question of anything like that. Of course, if our comrades in those countries rise against oppression, we should no doubt give them moral support.'

'You mean you're trying to foment a rising against Zia? Or the mad Ayatollah? Moral support? Like guns and explosives and money?'

'No, no, nothing so crude.'

'I don't think I believe you, Marshal. This sounds too much like all those madcap schemes – Plan Darius or whatever the last one was called – that others of us have been opposing for years.'

'Nonsense. Even if some crisis were to arise, nothing will be done in haste.'

'You mean you'll send the tanks in slowly? I came here because I've heard some ugly rumours, Marshal, and I hoped they were untrue.'

He flushed dangerously. 'Nadia Alexandrovna, you are overwrought, otherwise I might be deeply annoyed. Here we are at a time of crisis when your intelligence effort is vital, yet you have deserted your post in Kabul.'

'I have deserted nothing – I returned to Moscow because I was confused by what was going on.'

'Confused? Perhaps you are finding it too much of a strain and could do with a rest? Somewhere quiet by the Black Sea for a few weeks?'

'I am not overwrought, strained or tired. I am asking you questions about matters within my competence and you are refusing to answer them.'

Malinovsky stood up, his face dark and menacing. He said nothing, gathered up his papers, and walked to the door.

'Wait a minute,' she shouted. 'You can't just walk out on me – I haven't finished.'

He turned abruptly, hand on the brass doorhandle. 'Well *I* have.' Then he was marching off down the corridor with his half-dozen uniformed staff officers, who had been waiting outside, falling into step behind him. Kirov followed, half expecting a tap on the shoulder from a Kremlin guard as she descended to the front door. But the sentry saluted as usual and her Zil was still there on the square of yellow gravel, not a van waiting to take her to a psychiatric prison. She sighed in relief as the car passed through the gate under the Spassky Tower and picked up speed across the Square, tyres drumming on the cobbles. She was still at liberty, but for how long?

Kirov would have been even more concerned if she could have seen the column of T-72 tanks grinding its way south through Uzbekistan; and the five hundred Spetsnaz troops landing from Antonov Cub transports in Kabul. She would have been positively terrified had she known of the six Spetsnaz who would arrive in Karachi that evening, travelling in civilian clothes on false Danish passports.

Anatoly Levshin passed the two hours nervously. He walked down to the river, past the small crowd at the eternal flame commemorating the Great Patriotic War of 1941-45, then along the embankment by the outer wall of the Kremlin. He sat on the grass slope for a long time, watching the boats on the river, then strolled on and turned left again, up the slope to the Square.

She was there as promised, the same wholesome young woman but in different clothes. She greeted him with a smile. 'Do you think you're being followed?'

'No. If they knew where I was, they'd pick me up.'

'Okay.' He loved her Deep South Russian. Plainly he was not dealing with anyone very senior. 'Let's stroll a bit. This is a good crowded place to hide.' They mingled with the groups of tourists. 'You material was interesting. Do you see such papers regularly?'

Levshin clutched his thin overcoat round him. 'I'm afraid not.'

'You're not an official?'

'I'm a poet.'

'Really?' She looked sceptical. 'But you have more than the sample?'

'At least a dozen such files.'

'Then I don't understand. Where do they come from?'

'From a senior officer of the Committee for State Security.'

She glanced at him curiously. 'I understand your desire to be discreet, but I must have his name.'

Levshin hesitated. 'Is that really necessary?'

'If you want us to buy the stuff, we have to be certain it's genuine.'

'It comes from Major General N. A. Kirova.'

'Kirova? And is she offering to continue the supply?'

'She has no idea I have the files. I stole them from her apartment.'

'You stole them from the home of a senior intelligence officer?' The young American's eyes narrowed. 'I find that hard to believe. How did you get in?'

'We know each other from long ago.'

'But you cannot maintain the supply?'

'Look, this is one-off. I want to leave the country. If you want to trade, get on with it. If you don't, I'll go to someone else.'

'No, we want to trade, but I need more stuff to evaluate.'

'I haven't time for that."

She sighed. 'Just what do you want?'

'I want a passport in a false name, but genuine and with permits to leave the country. I want five thousand roubles in used notes and one hundred thousand US dollars deposited in a Spanish bank.'

'A *Spanish* bank?'

'Yes – I'll tell you which one.' They were strolling along parallel to the Kremlin wall, passing the dwarf fir trees and young couples having photographs taken in their wedding clothes. 'That's all I want. Nothing else.'

'That's quite a lot – I need to get authority to conclude a deal like that.'

'How long do you need? I'm in a hurry.'

'Meet me at eleven tomorrow with six more files and I'll have the passport and the roubles. I'll be on the sidewalk between Novodevichy cemetery and the Metro. If we're satisfied with the material, we'll exchange the bank passbook for the rest three days later. Would that suit you?'

'I don't have much choice, do I? I want the dollars deposited in the Banco Hispano-Americano, Barcelona.'

'You seem to have it all worked out.'

'I had nearly thirty years in a camp to think about it.' There was no point trying to explain how idealistic young Levshin had fallen in love with Spain fighting for the International Brigade in the Civil War and survived the grey Arctic by dreaming of its sun.

'Oh, I see. Okay. I'll try to get it organised as quickly as I can – but the material will have to be worth it. And we'll need a name for the bank account.'

He hesitated. 'Anatoly Levshin.' He had thought of using a false name, but some latent pride stopped him. 'Dr Anatoly Levshin.' He hurried away into the dusk, wondering where he would be safe sleeping rough that night and whether Nadia Alexandrovna was in the slammer yet. The man sitting in a mud-spattered Volga by St Basil's spoke softly into his pocket radio. A woman in a fur hat moved into place ahead of Levshin, another man behind, two more about thirty feet to either side. When he reached the Metro, another team took over.

18

Karachi

Nazim thought it politic to take a Pakistan International Airways flight back to Karachi. As soon as the airliner landed, a jeep approached at high speed trailing a cloud of dust. The cabin crew seemed to know what to do; a gangway was lowered from the back of the aircraft and Nazim climbed down alone while two soldiers unloaded his travelling bag from the hold. An army officer saluted smartly and they sped away down the runway to a waiting executive jet. It had been standing under blazing sun and was stifling inside, but within minutes they were above the sprawling brown city and air was rushing from the ventilators to bring the temperature down. As they headed north, away from the ocean, a white-coated steward served chilled lime juice. Nazim winked at his reflection in the oval window: so this was how the rulers treated themselves.

At the airport between Rawalpindi and Islamabad the air was cooler, there were green trees and hills in the distance. The officer, who had sat in silence throughout the flight from Karachi, ushered Nazim into the back of a black Mercedes, then got into the front passenger seat himself, balancing a machine pistol on his knees. There was only a fine line between being protected as a VIP or being under arrest. Nazim hoped to God he was still in the former category. Despite the ego-massaging deference and unaccustomed luxury, for a moment he almost envied the beggars squatting by the road, white sores callousing the bony limbs that stuck out from their rags.

Although the airfield served the modern capital, images of the past were all around him: two bullocks drawing a wooden plough across a dry field, bells tinkling on their yokes; men drinking tea in a circle outside a mosque; an old woman grinning at the passing car with toothless gums, mechanically working a loom under the straw awning in front of her house. Nazim stared at it all sightlessly, his mind still oppressed by the fateful meeting a week ago.

The man had said his name was Kay. Nazim had never discovered his nationality – he had been expecting an Australian, but there had been the hint of a Scottish accent – and he knew that Kay would be a cover name, but that was to be expected. They had talked for several hours, going through most of Nazim's life to date, and that Kay had been clever: gentle, subtle, but damned clever. It had been hard to hide anything from him. At first he had refused to believe that Nazim did not know about a weapons programme in his country. 'But look at the stuff you have been purchasing – equipment that can only be for the enrichment of uranium to bomb grade?'

'I know the specifications well enough but, believe me, I have been denied knowledge of the end use. I suspect they are building these weapons – but it is as well concealed from me as it is from you.'

'How can you expect me to believe that, Dr Khan? You have been highly educated in nuclear science at your state's expense, trusted to be a student in America, to be a diplomat in Vienna. You travel all over Europe secretly purchasing machinery for an enrichment plant. People who have pried into it have been killed to protect you.'

'I was very shaken when I learnt that – I knew nothing of it at the time.' Nazim had studied the row of silver trophies on a shelf in the little clubhouse, noticing that they had been arranged so that the inscriptions were hidden. He still did not know what country they were in. 'For the rest, I have my suspicions – that is why I spoke to Mallaband – but I don't know anything concrete.'

'Why did you approach Mallaband?'

Nazim had hesitated. 'There's no simple answer – I don't think I can tell you without going through my whole life. Like many of us, I have grave doubts about the government I serve. Ever since I came back from San Francisco, I have tried to develop nuclear power in our country – purely for generating electricity, I can't stress that highly enough.'

'You could have made a fortune if you'd stayed in America. You must feel they've betrayed you by pressing ahead with weapons rather than power stations?'

'So I should betray them in return?' Nazim smiled wryly. 'Life is not so simple. But building the bomb can only bring us danger while Pakistan is full of unrest and surrounded by enemies. Apart from the Russians in Afghanistan, there is always India threatening from the east; we were born in the blood of partition – they say two million died, you know – and no one has forgotten that yet.'

'Go on, I am still waiting for your truly selfish motives – they are usually the most important.'

Nazim had looked away, then faced his interrogator squarely. 'I am a scientist and I want to work as a scientist again. If I go back to Rawalpindi, what happens when Benazir and the People's Party kick out Zia? I probably end up cleaning lavatories with the rest of those identified with him. Maybe I end up in jail or dead. Perhaps that sounds unpatriotic, but what's the point of being a patriot killed in the crossfire as the country falls apart? I have seen enough violence and poverty for one man's life. Is that selfish enough for you?'

'And you believe Zia *will* be kicked out?'

'Sooner or later, yes.'

'And you'd want to settle in Australia, or America, or Britain? Under an assumed name, I imagine, but following your profession?'

'That is what I want, yes.'

'Are you *sure*, Dr Khan? There can be no going back.'

'It's not a sudden decision – I'm sure enough.'

The man with the Scottish accent had poured more drinks and lit a pipe, puffing clouds of blue smoke for several minutes before he spoke again. 'Okay, it's a deal – but the price is every last detail you can get of your weapons programme.' He paused and searched Nazim's face before adding quietly, 'And I agree with you – it won't damage your country one iota for us to know. Pakistan is surrounded by enemies, but we are your friends and it is better for us to know how strong, or weak, your defences really are.'

'My government would see it as treason.'

'No doubt they would, which is why you are a brave man, Nazim, and I respect you for it. But we shall take care to protect you.'

'If I do it, what would happen afterwards?'

'Afterwards? It would be best if you continued as a top man in your government for many years, keeping in touch with us and using your influence wisely.'

'I wouldn't have the nerve. If I help you, sooner or later that will be discovered. I would find out all I could, but I'd want to cash in my cheque with you damn soon.'

'That would be a pity.' Kay held up his hand as Nazim opened his mouth in protest. 'But if you were in danger, however soon that might be, we should get you out, offer you that new identity and a home in the West. In any case, *after* you have provided the material we need,' Kay had smiled benignly and puffed his pipe, but the message was clear. 'Then we'll pull you out whenever you want. We'd prefer you to stay, but it'd be up to you.'

'And my family too?'

'Of course. Believe me, Dr Khan, we should owe you a great deal – and we are generous to our friends.'

'I still hesitate.'

'He who hesitates is lost.'

'How much do you need to know?'

'Everything, Dr Khan. Hard data on everything. Is your enrichment plant at Kahuta producing weapons grade uranium? If so, are warheads being manufactured? Where, how many, where are they stored? Are they for missiles or to be delivered by aircraft? Above all, are there usable weapons already in place? Is their deployment a distant possibility, far in the future, or a military reality *now*?'

In the early hours, when his resistance had been at its lowest, the pact had been made. Even at the moment of final agreement, he could not have given a single plain reason for taking the Westerner's hand. The risk was enormous. Yet in his heart he knew he was doing it willingly enough, that he *wanted* to do it. Somewhere deep in his mind was a corner that hated them, the rich and powerful who had humiliated him when he was the street urchin sent to a toffee-nosed school by the Khans, but then been glad enough to use his brain and grudgingly allowed him to join the ruling circle, even to marry one of its daughters. Nazim Khan did not belong in Islamabad, however grand he might have become. It was unfinished business, twenty years old; yet in a distant way, as if looking at someone else from outside, he was still shocked at where his bitterness and anger were leading.

They had flown him back to a disused airfield near the Hungarian border. As they drove him into Vienna, the car had passed through a small town where posters were advertising an amateur production of *Faust*. Now he knew how that poor bastard had felt. Sarah was away on some kind of training course, so he had not seen her before the telegram arrived summoning him home to discuss his new job. Perhaps it was as well, for he had to resist any temptation to confide in her – or in anyone. He was on his own.

The drive to the nuclear plant at Kahuta took about twenty minutes. Passing through the heavily guarded gate, Nazim noted several new buildings since his last visit over a year ago. One was still under construction, sweating men carrying baskets of bricks on their heads, watched by a cordon of soldiers with sub-machine-guns. The low centrifuge hall, the size of five football pitches, was still the centre of the site. He would check that the long rows of black tubes were still whirling to enrich their uranium, but that alone would tell him nothing. Were they enriching to three per cent, for reactor fuel, or over ninety, weapons grade? Given the sensitivity of the inverters he had purchased in Europe to control them, it surely had to be over ninety.

Outside the administration block, a clerk met him with an obsequious bow. 'I will show you to your office, Director.' It was a large room on the upper floor, furnished with a Western-style desk, conference table and sofas. Sliding glass doors gave on to a verandah overlooking the site and a cheese plant stood in the corner. Syed had spent years working at Almelo in Holland – that was where he had perfected his knowledge of enrichment – and he had made his office just like one on a Dutch industrial estate.

The old man bowed again. 'My name is Ranjit, Director. I sent Dr Syed's photographs and personal things to his wife, but his books are still here. I thought he might wish his successor to have them?' Nazim nodded curtly as Ranjit went into the outer office, took his place at the typewriter and picked up a phone; to be a secretary was still an honourable profession for a grandfather here.

Hamid Ibrahim appeared a few minutes later, all smiles, and clapped him on the back. 'How good to see you again, Nazim!' He sat on one of the white sofas and grinned with the sincerity of a crocodile. 'I thought it would be appropriate to brief you here, on your own territory, so to speak.'

'I appreciate that.' Nazim refrained from adding that since Ibrahim was now junior to him in the Commission, he could have ordered him to his office had he wished; but Hamid must have craved Syed's job for himself, so he would be quite bitter enough already.

'I expect you are anxious to get home to Farah and the children?'

'Later. First I must get the measure of this new job.'

'Of course.' Ibrahim smiled again. 'Don't mind me mentioning it, old man, but is everything all right? You seem jumpy, not quite the gay dog I knew in Stanford.'

'I'm okay, thanks. It's just been a long journey and I'm bloody tired. So what do you want to tell me?'

'First, the Chairman will see you tomorrow morning at eight; that will be your main briefing, of course. But he has appointed me as head of his private office, so he has asked me to show you round the site.'

'Let's start at once, then.' Nazim pulled on the white lab coat hanging behind the door and ten minutes later they stood on a metal balcony overlooking the floor of the enrichment plant. The long rows of centrifuges, joined by complex piping, were not in operation. 'When is the next run?' He asked the question casually, concealed in a list of other technical points.

'I think in three days. I will check – I take it you want it to go ahead?'

'Of course.' They moved on to a manufacturing area for reactor fuel rods and a storage building. Here it was necessary for security passes to be checked, even though the four guards armed with machine-pistols instantly recognised their visitors. Through a steel door opened by two keys and a combination lock, they entered a corridor lined floor to ceiling with metal safes, like lockers in a changing room, but spaced out with criss-crossed angle-iron separating them, so that their contents could not get too close and go critical. Despite the sun outside it was cold and there was the hiss of air-conditioning.

On each safe, a card in a slot showed its contents: some contained plutonium pellets, some uranium marked at ninety per cent or above. It was not conclusive, for there would be a little high-enriched material even if the plant was innocent, but Nazim filed the details mentally. He made a point of listening to everything Ibrahim said, saying little and asking no questions that might point to military applications. Sooner or later he would have to be taken into the charmed circle; until then he was not giving his old enemy a stick to beat him with.

Later he stood at the wide window, watching Ibrahim drive off in his Morris Oxford. Once his closest friend, the man had been his rival for twenty years, using all his resources of back-stabbing and gossip to belittle Nazim and do him down. The vendetta had not been of Nazim's making and it had taken him a long time to understand why Ibrahim hated him so much – the power of simple jealousy, the resentment of the boy who came from nothing but rose so effortlessly. But Nazim felt a quiet satisfaction that his enemy had failed. The pleasure it gave him almost made him regret that his tenancy at Kahuta would be so short – perhaps Ibrahim would succeed him. Nazim smiled to himself. It would be fitting if Ibrahim were director when the Islamic mob smashed down the gates and destroyed the advanced technology with rocks and fire.

He sorted papers into a briefcase and ordered a car to take him home. For years he had forgotten the encounter at Carmel, by the rolling Pacific, more than two decades ago, but now he could not get it out of his mind. It had been dusk on a summer evening. Robin had gone into San Francisco to meet a visiting aunt – she seemed to have a never-ending stream of relatives passing through – and he found himself at a loose end. He had driven down the coast road alone, intending to have a drink by the sea, walk a bit and drive back.

Pushing through the bushes in the moonlight, under the pines to the beach, he almost stumbled over them. She was kneeling in the sand, dark head bobbing, bending forward in invitation, the pale ovals of her buttocks parting slowly as she arched her spine. She laughed as Ibrahim's arms encircled her to caress her breasts and she felt the hair of his legs rough against the smooth backs of her thighs. Nazim had stepped back into the shadows, shamed, devastated as he saw the life he thought they had planned crumbling to dust, then furious at the deceit. He had always cherished the way Robin cried out with pleasure as her tanned body shuddered through its easy orgasms; now it sounded grotesque as he hesitated, smouldering with anger, then hurried away.

19

Rawalpindi

Nazim was driven home in a Mercedes, across the scrubland that separated the twin cities. Waiting in the car, his driver was listening to a wailing sitar on the radio, but he turned it off sharply when Nazim appeared. In Rawalpindi the traffic was heavy, blue Lambretta three-wheelers and old Austin trucks picking their way through the bullock carts and bicycles.

Farah was waiting in the long white bungalow on Plantation Road. He had not been there for a year and was shocked to see the high chain-link fence that had been erected round the garden, capped by rolls of razor wire. Two armed soldiers with guard dogs were patrolling inside it. 'As-Salaam O alaikum.' She pressed her hands together and made the traditional gesture of peace, smiling up at him in the brown cotton blouse and baggy pantaloons of her *shalwarkameez*, a jewel glinting in her nose.

'*Namaste.*' Nazim took her dutifully in his arms, then gestured at the fence. 'What the hell's all this? It's like a prison.'

'They said the fence was necessary for security, Nazim – there has been much violence lately. The communists and beggars make it difficult to go out on the streets.'

'But soldiers and guard dogs? At our home? It's horrible.'

'They say it is for our safety, my husband – I thought you would wish it.' It was only six months since she had left Vienna, but she had put on a lot of weight since then. The Farah he had married had been twenty, a lissom girl with shining eyes and soft brown skin. Still only thirty, she had become dowdy and unattractive; the long black hair still glistened, but there was no light in her face. He felt a wave of guilt as she took him to meet the children. At first they greeted him warily, then Noor, chubby and only five, smothered him with kisses and burst into tears. 'I thought you would never come back,' she sobbed in Urdu.

He had brought them both small presents of mechanical toys and Mahmoud proudly displayed his school exercise books. Farah had prepared a banquet for two and they chatted together awkwardly after the children had gone to bed. Walking under the trees in the garden, the silence was broken by an explosion, then police sirens and the rattle of shots down in the city. A blazing building glowed in the darkness. 'That will be a car-bomb,' said Farah matter-of-factly.

'Good God, does this happen every night?'

She nodded beside him. 'Not always here in the capital, but there are many demonstrations in other places.'

'You should have told me – I had no idea things were so bad.'

'I thought somebody in the Commission would tell you.'

He took her hand in the dark. 'I missed you all very much.'

'Did you?' There was an unspoken bitterness, a knowledge that he did not love her any more, if ever he had. 'It will be better when you are back here all the time. I am pleased that you will be so important.'

'But I'm not back yet. I have to wind up my work in Vienna and it will take at least another month. I don't like leaving you all in danger here, Farah.' She said nothing. 'In fact . . .'

'Yes, my husband?'

'I want you all to return to Vienna with me.'

'But the children must go to school and you will be back here all the time soon.'

'Not soon enough. This place is dangerous. When I return, we will risk it together, but until then I want you with me. Come for a last fling in Vienna, a holiday away from all this tension. We will go to the lakes before I come back to this new job.' It was the only way out. If he had to leave them here when he fled and his treachery was discovered, he would never see Noor and Mahmoud again; he could already feel the pain of bereavement and knew he could never bear it. And if they stayed here as the children of a traitor, what terrors awaited them?

'I have seen quite enough of Vienna, thank you – and there is no point, when you will be back so soon.'

'I wish it, Farah.' He tried to sound like the firm head of a Muslim family. 'In our marriage contract you promised to obey me in all things – now you will do so. I insist.' Once he had them in Europe, he could find excuses to keep them there until it was too late to return.

She gripped his hand more tightly. 'In our marriage contract you also promised to whip me only within the limits of Islamic family law, yet you have never struck me or the children.'

'We are not peasants, Farah.' He chuckled and put his arm round her. 'But I could always start.'

Her body stiffened. *'Insh'allah.* If you did I should not protest. A wife must submit. What I am trying to say is that I would obey you if I could.' She pulled away from his hand. 'But I know it will not be allowed.'

'Who will forbid it?'

'Before Syed died, I wanted to return to you in Vienna next spring. I wanted to be with you and the children, to make us a family again, but when I told Ibrahim he said it was not possible.'

'Ibrahim?' Today he could not get away from the bastard. 'What the devil has Ibrahim got to do with it?'

'He is the Chairman's assistant – he would authorise our travel.'

'And what reason did he give for refusing?'

'None. I am a woman, why should he give a reason?' Suddenly she clung to him. 'But I am afraid. Afraid to be here, afraid for you, afraid for the children.'

He held her tightly, staring into the darkness, suddenly brutally aware of the reality of his situation. The constant movement – the meeting with the Westerner, the summons to Kahuta – had masked it before. Now he faced it coldly for the first time. He had placed Farah and the children in overwhelming danger. He had to get them out, but how? Was Kay misjudging the obstacles, or deliberately lulling him into a false sense of security? And he was already in too deeply if they blackmailed him to go on; he cursed himself for his stupidity. Later he made love mechanically to Farah, thinking all the time of Sarah, racked by guilt. Afterwards he lay awake until dawn, the faces of Mahmoud and little Noor haunting him in the dark. For the first time in twenty years, Nazim Rashid Khan wept.

20

Kabul

Kirov had left Moscow a week before. She had done all that she wanted, sleeping in the office which was guarded by KGB troops not under the control of the army. She dared not return to her apartment. Then she had slipped away on a routine flight to Kabul – it was not difficult to pull rank as a Major-General. The old Ilyushin was full of shaven-headed conscripts who regarded her warily as she was shown to an empty row of seats at the back. Poor little bastards, she thought, as an NCO bawled down the cabin and resigned eighteen-year-old voices joined in a marching song.

A phone call from the airfield brought Nikolai to drive her back to the house. The city was quiet and nothing had changed under the Islamuddin regime, except that a number of his enemies had been arrested at night. The prison out at Pul-i-Charkhi was even more crowded than usual, said Nikolai, as the black Volga nosed through a crowded bazaar, and there had been a number of executions.

'What happened to the Zil?' asked Kirov.

'The Ambassador is using it. His own car was damaged by a Mujahedin rocket.'

'I hear there have been military reinforcements?'

'Some more troops and tanks, they say, comrade Minister, but they are keeping well out of sight.'

'Do they say why, when we are supposed to be leaving the country?'

'I only hear mess gossip, but I gather Grigorenko wants greater strength on the ground because the Mujahedin have so many ground-to-air missiles now and our air superiority is no longer decisive.'

At the house, there were urgent files on her desk, brought from the Embassy, and a number of telephone messages. Fresh flowers had been placed in the main rooms, which felt light and cool. Kirov told Nikolai to arrange a roster for the guards to be on duty round the clock and started to go through her papers. Everything seemed quite normal, so normal that Kirov wondered whether she had been imagining things in Moscow. But then she remembered the hatred in Malinovsky's eyes.

Anatoly Levshin sat in the restaurant car as the train rocked southwards, enjoying the plate of cold meat and smoked fish, accompanied by black bread and washed down with mineral water. The absence of alcohol was an irritant, for which the tiresome Gorbachev was responsible. His plans had changed after the third meeting with Sandie, the wholesome girl from the American Embassy. Good sources, she assured him, said there was no warrant out for his arrest. Some individual security officer might have wanted to question him about something – or even just to frighten him after a few months of freedom – but he could travel safely if he had the necessary permits. These the Embassy would supply.

So Levshin had booked his cruise and set out for Odessa under his own name. The wad of roubles had enabled him to buy some decent clothes for the first time in nearly a quarter of a century. Apart from the blue lightweight suit, his badge of respectability for the journey – for it was vital not to arouse suspicion that might lead to close checking of his permits – they were in a cheap fibre suitcase in his sleeping compartment. The dollars in Spain were in two separate accounts, both operated by a passbook. One passbook was now sewn, as neatly as he could manage, into the lining of his suit, the other in the lining of his overcoat.

He lit a small cigar, one of a box of Havanas he had bought before leaving Moscow, and relaxed. Calling on Nadia Alexandrovna was one of the best moves he had ever made.

Nazim announced his return with a midnight phone call and met Sarah at lunchtime next day. They went to the Donaupark, close to the UN building, and walked hand-in-hand along a path in the woods. 'I have only another ten days here,' he said sombrely. 'Then back to take charge of Kahuta. You have no idea how much I shall miss you, Sarah.'

'I'll miss you too, Nazim, but I guess I'll come to Pakistan now it's on my patch. I could be coming quite soon, in fact.'

He nodded gloomily. 'We must make every moment count when you do.'

'God, you sound so bloody miserable – what on earth happened out there?'

'Not a lot. I went over the plant, met the Chairman of the Commission, went home.' He shrugged and his tone was casual, but she sensed the tension beneath it. 'That's it.'

'I don't believe you.' The agent-runner in Sarah said give him a chance to unburden if he needs it; the woman just wanted to break down the invisible barrier she still felt between them, to be truly close to him.

'Well – things are a little complicated, but it's good to be back.'

'Something's wrong, darling, that's so obvious – for God's sake, can't you tell me?'

'I wish I could – I *do* trust you, Cable, but this is my problem and no one else can solve it.' He looked so wretched that she flung her arms round his neck and kissed him. 'Oh, Sarah.' Suddenly he was hugging her, so tight that it took her breath away, and the tension was going. 'Let's go to the flat and forget it all – I'll get something for us to eat from Julius Meini.'

'Bugger Julius Meini.' She seized his hand and ran back towards the car.

When they reached the apartment she undressed without speaking and sprawled back on the bed, smiling up at him provocatively. In the park there had been a vulnerable, tormented look in his eyes that made her ache to show him he was not alone, to empty his mind of everything but the warmth and closeness his body could feel. But now he reared over her with powerful shoulders, his arms seemed crushing and she responded fiercely, tongue flashing into his throat until she rolled backwards, legs dancing in the air then flexed around him as her spine arched sharply and her body soared through a series of violent contractions. She clutched at him, gasping his name over and over again.

In the sudden calm they clung together, her head pressed against his chest, legs entwined, hers smooth and pale, his muscular and dark. 'Hold me tight, darling.' She lifted her face to kiss him. 'Oh, how I wish we could stay like this for ever.' She stretched dreamily and turned on her stomach, listening to the silence outside. Somewhere in the distance a dog was barking. That first time she had taken the lead, but now she wanted him to dominate, to overwhelm her with his strength and gentleness. He had amazingly sensitive hands and she wriggled with pleasure as he began to caress her, all the way down from her neck to her ankles, spreading her thighs when she felt his fingers deep between them. This time it would be slow and luxurious, precious in a way she thought she had forgotten; hips rising again, she was surprised to find that she was trembling.

21

Obertraun

Nazim Khan's second meeting with Nairn was that night, although Sarah was unaware of it. At six in the evening he walked from his apartment, down into the centre of Grinzing, crowded as ever with tourists and Viennese out for an evening of new wine. By the tram terminus he turned into an alley, then up the long flight of steps that led into the vineyards. At the top he emerged into an empty lane in which a green van was parked, shielded by hedges and shadowy in the dusk. There was no one to see as the rear door opened silently and he climbed in. He did not know where they were going, but they had said it would take about twenty minutes. Although it was a small van, there was a camp bed for him to lie on and he was comfortable enough listening to the Austrian radio news through a flap in the steel bulkhead that shut off the cab.

After a quarter of an hour, a voice spoke to him through the flap, 'Sorry, a small change of plan, we have to go a bit further than expected. Would you like some music on now?' Before Nazim could protest, he was drowned in a Beethoven symphony and the van speeded up; plainly they had joined an autobahn. Twice he felt the van leave the motorway and bump along country roads as the driver checked that they had not been followed.

It took over an hour to reach the wooden house by the lake. By now it was dark, but he could hear a lapping of water as a heavily built man beckoned him out and into a room furnished with cheap vinyl armchairs. The gaunt man he knew as Kay was waiting by a cassette recorder emitting a low rushing noise that rose and fell in waves. 'White sound,' grunted Kay. 'Supposed to baffle any bugs we haven't found.'

Heavy curtains had been drawn across the windows. Kay poured coffee and lit his pipe. 'Sorry we had to come out here, but I thought it was safer than meeting in Vienna. Wasn't time to let you know in advance. When did you get back?'

'Late last night.'

'How was your family?'

Nazim looked up sharply: this hard man was soft enough to know where his agent was vulnerable. 'To be honest I'm very scared for them – I almost didn't come tonight. We can talk about my visit to Pakistan, but after that I think all bets are off . . .'

Kay did not react, but smiled reassuringly. 'Okay, first tell me what happened.'

Two hours later Mr Munster had filled nearly three tapes, crouched in the loft above the living room, listening as Nairn gently drew information out of Nazim Khan. Not for the first time, he thought that the boss could have made a decent living as a psychiatrist – and rumour had it that he had been a volunteer with the Samaritans in his younger days, before he had become too senior to have a life outside the service. Munster disturbed a patch of dust and stifled a sneeze as Nairn started to sum up. 'So you're pretty sure the plant is enriching weapons-grade uranium?'

'I can't see any other reason for building the bloody thing in the first place and there's far more material going through than we need for any peaceful purpose.'

'But we have yet to pinpoint the assembly plant and find out where the bombs are being stored?'

'I believe that could be done quite quickly from inside Pakistan.'

'Easily? Without risk?'

'No, there would be a lot of risk.'

Kay went out through a door and reappeared with two glasses of beer. 'Worthington White Shield, poured them myself to avoid getting the sediment in – hope you like it. What I need to know, Nazim, is what your government plans to do with the hardware?'

There was a long silence. In the end Nazim shook his head. 'I'm sorry, but I can't do any more for you. People have already died – it's become too dangerous.'

'It's important, Nazim.' Kay sank back in the armchair and puffed his pipe reflectively, as if conducting an academic seminar. 'Let's assume, for a moment, that all these riots lead to an armed rising against Zia – a rising of disunited left-wing groups but financed by Moscow.'

'Which is quite possible.'

'Now if it's overwhelmingly successful, there's a new government and the Russians are its best friends. We get Soviet warships in your Indian Ocean ports, Soviet land forces can march down to the Indian border if they feel like it, the Mujahedin are really in the shit. It's bad news, but not the worst?'

'No, not the worst.'

'But what happens if your rebels meet heavy resistance from the army? There's a deadlock? Then the Russians or the Afghans bomb the hell out of some more refugee camps, send arms and advisers to your rebels, maybe even cross the border from Afghanistan to maintain order?' Nazim looked away awkwardly, the answer unspoken. 'So you see I really do need hard intelligence on whether they're in a position to drop a bomb on *anyone* – and if they're organising themselves to do it, converting planes or missiles to carry nuclear warheads?'

'I don't like the situation any more than you, Kay,' snapped Nazim. 'But what about my family? My bungalow in Rawalpindi is guarded by the army, for God's sake.' His mouth twisted with a flash of bitter humour. 'My new job might put me in a position to help you, but it has turned my wife and children into hostages. When I go back we shall all be prisoners.'

'It would only be for a short time. Afterwards we would provide you and your family with a new identity, a new life – isn't that still what you want?'

'Of course it is, but it – can't – be – done, Kay.' Nazim's voice was rising and he emphasised each word, smashing his fist into his open palm in anger. 'You'll never be able to get us out and that changes everything.'

Kay did not reply directly, but poured two more beers. 'Why not bring your wife and the children back to Vienna, then leave them here for a few months when you start work in Kahuta? Say it is for the boy's education? They'd be safe enough and we could spirit them away when the time comes.'

'Not a hope. I've tried but I'm forbidden to take them out of Pakistan.'

'Nazim – it's my problem to find a way. Won't you just *trust* me? My government has an Embassy only miles from your home and I'm sure we can devise something. Will your wife co-operate?'

'No she won't. Farah has no idea that I am doing this and I can't possibly tell her. She might well betray me.'

'Should I plan to bring her unwillingly – or do I confine myself to the children?'

'Didn't you hear what I said? Just forget it!'

Kay poured more beer before replying. 'If you are determined to break our bargain, you place me in some difficulty, Nazim. I need an agent in Kahuta and you are ideally placed.'

Abruptly Nazim slammed his drink down on the small table at his side, so violently that it shattered, shards of glass exploding, beer dripping on the carpet. 'I said no. No! For God's sake don't push me any further. I've risked my life for you, risked my children, do you want my soul as well?' He leapt up and turned for the door, his hand dripping blood from a cut. 'I've had enough, just take me back to Vienna.'

Nairn stood up too, gaunt and stooped, towering over the younger man, sunken eyes commanding. 'Sit down, you bloody fool, and listen to me.'

'Why the hell should I?'

'Because you've committed treason against a government that would flay you alive if it caught you.' The man roared like a Scottish revivalist preacher threatening eternal damnation. 'And you're having a decidedly non-Islamic affair with a rangy white girl – how do you think that would go down with your mullahs, eh?'

Nazim jerked and shouted, 'How do you know about that? Don't bring her into it!'

'I didn't – you did. You picked her up when your wife was safely away in Islamabad. Treason and adultery! Whatever happens now, friend, you're in too deep and you'll need my protection for the rest of your life.'

'Don't try and blackmail me.'

'I'm not blackmailing you, Nazim. But one day your government will discover that you tried to betray them.'

'You bastard!'

'I'm offering to *help* you, Nazim, to protect you, to get you out of this mess you've got yourself into. The only way out is to go through with it. Sit *down*, Nazim, I haven't finished with you yet.'

They drove Nazim back to Vienna at five in the morning, asleep in the back of the van and unaware of the sedative that had laced his final coffee. Dropped in the woods above Grinzing, he staggered down to the apartment. On the corner of Rudolf Kassnergasse he passed a tram driver cycling to work; the man recoiled from the foreigner's wild eyes, concluding that he was either a madman or drunk.

22

Hallstatt

Next morning the summons to Hallstatt caught Sarah unawares. It came in a dawn telephone call on a day when she was due to leave Vienna anyway, for a short training course at a German fuel plant. 'Sarah?' The voice was Munster's, but as ever he gave no name. 'Your flight to Frankfurt has been cancelled. You are to go by car. Take the autobahn to Salzburg and turn off for Hallstatt, where you will be met by the lake at eleven hundred hours. Ring Germany from a petrol station on the autobahn and say you'll be a day late for the course. Okay?'

The village clung to a narrow strip of land between the towering rock of the Dachstein and a lake with waters that looked black and cold. It clustered round the solid tower of the Catholic church and the narrow steeple of the Protestant, yellow houses with steep tiled roofs. A grey Volkswagen Golf was parked where the road ran close to the shore: it had a Salzburg number plate and a sticker saying it was hired from Avis. She drew up behind it and a man got out. There were no recognition phrases. 'Cable?' he asked curtly.

'Yes.'

'Go into the village, park and take the ferry across the lake. Walk along southwards, close to the railway. There is a ferry going in twenty minutes.' He handed her a fishing rod and a small metal box about the size of a cigarette packet.

The small boat had a cabin and open stern deck, with only a handful of passengers, dressed in heavy boots and thick red socks for walking. The valley sides were so steep that it felt suddenly cold as they passed from the sun shining on the village, to the shadow opposite. Sarah wandered along a path between the railway, winding along the rock face, and the lake. Nairn was half-hidden by a tree, holding a fishing rod and eyeing the red float bobbing out on the water. She stopped a hundred yards away and drew a tiny ear-piece from the metal box, pushing the wire inside her anorak, and plugged

111

another short lead into the handle of the fishing rod. She cast the line and heard a crackle in her ear. The radio signal would be confined to the water, so it could be intercepted only by someone with similar equipment. Nairn would have three or four watchers around the lake to check that they were unobserved.

Eventually she heard his voice through the ear-piece. 'Okay, the fishing's good down here.' She wound in her line and strolled round to him.

'Have a sandwich?' He pointed to a plastic container. 'Corned beef and mustard.'

'No thanks.' Sarah smiled at the great man's aggressively proletarian tastes, in a country with some of the best salami and cheese in Europe. 'What's up? Has something gone wrong?'

'Not at all. I talked to your friend Ali Baba about a week ago, before he went back to Pakistan. I met him again last night.'

Sarah bridled. 'Where? Why wasn't I told?'

'You're being told now, Sarah, and I came myself to tell you.' She blushed at the reproof, resenting the way he always made her feel like an insecure teenager. The float vanished and he reeled in the line to reveal an empty hook. 'Devilish clever these Kraut fish.' He cast the line again. 'The first time we picked him up and flew him to a private flying club near Salzburg. Last night I met him a few miles from here.'

'What happened?'

'I thought he might tell us to bugger off when we put the pressure on, but he agreed to co-operate when he gets back to Kahuta. He's got guts, I'll say that for him.'

There was a long silence and Sarah stared at him curiously. It was rare for Nairn to express admiration for an agent. Finally she said, 'And where does all that leave me?'

'He's got no idea you're one of us.'

'Are you absolutely *sure* about that?'

'Well – he didn't mention it, nor did I. There's no reason why he should connect you, he thinks he's dealing with the Australians. He likes the Aussies – he once had an Australian girlfriend.'

'Is he really willing to do it or are you blackmailing him?'

'No, he wants to get out and settle in the West under a new identity with plenty of money. We're providing that in exchange for some intelligence. It's all perfectly simple.'

Sarah sensed that she was not being told everything and felt a flash of irritation. 'Simple? He must have a death-wish.'

Nairn nodded thoughtfully. 'Ah – you may have a point, Sarah; it's not unusual for those who come from nothing to fear being cast down again. Ali Baba isn't quite like that, but I have a feeling that in some curious way he's waiting for his bubble to burst, putting himself in danger as a challenge to fate. He's not a gambler, yet he's gambling everything he has.'

'I hope he's going to win.'

'So do I.' But Nairn's tone said that Nazim Khan was, in fact, eminently expendable.

Sarah had seen this ruthless streak before and it still had the power to horrify her. 'David,' she said quietly, trying to master the surge of emotion welling up inside. 'I don't believe you.' She wanted to scream at him when he just went on fishing, biting her lip in frustration. 'I don't believe you!' Her voice was rising. 'I think you've planned everything that's happened. You've conned me! You're using Nazim like a pawn on your fucking chessboard and me like . . . like bait for those bloody fish.'

Nairn faced her abruptly, the deep-set eyes uncharacteristically cold. 'You know pair-fectly well,' he sounded so Scottish when he was irritated, 'that one never tells a field agent more than he or she needs to know. That's elementary, Sarah – it doesn't mean I don't think highly of you.'

'So highly that you got me here under false pretences? Just a little help, you said, to trap this shitty Pakistani, but he wasn't like that at all and you damn well knew from the beginning that Syed was going to be assassinated, didn't you? I bet you or the CIA arranged it. Then you got me appointed as a safeguards inspector for India and Pakistan, along with a bloke from Poland, but surprise, surprise, he's suddenly gone back to Warsaw.' She was shouting and checked herself, shaking with anger. 'I don't know how you fixed it, but I'm going to be in Pakistan every few weeks now, aren't I? And Nazim will be working there as director of Kahuta. For Christ's sake, David, you *planned* all this, didn't you?'

He turned and put his arm around her shoulders. 'You're an intelligence officer, Sarah, what the hell did you expect?'

She shook his arm off and stared at him in astonishment, suddenly empty after the burst of fury. 'Expect? I don't know, but I did *not* think you'd treat me like this.'

'Why not? If you're serious about the service, you'd better get used to it. You may think I'm being a complete bastard, but that's how it is. For God's sake, girl, I wouldn't be here at all if I hadn't been a friend of your father's and recruited you myself.' The concern in his eyes belied the curt words. 'Am I really asking too much?'

She met his gaze resentfully. 'What do you mean?'

'You can drop out now – I'd understand – but if you go on, you carry out orders, no more nonsense like this.'

'It's not bloody nonsense!'

'It *is* bloody nonsense, Sarah.'

Her eyes flashed with anger, but she blushed awkwardly. She had always felt attracted to Nairn, even though he was nearly sixty, and suspected that, despite Alison and the baby, he could be more than a little in love with her. The reproof wounded her in a way that she knew was ridiculous. Afterwards she marvelled that she had not seized his offer to drop out, but at the time it never crossed her mind. 'Okay,' she lowered her eyes passively. 'But from now on I must know *exactly* what I'm supposed to be doing. We're coming to the crunch. For God's sake trust me.'

Nairn reeled in the line and sat down on the bank, gesturing her to sit beside him. 'That's quite enough cover for the time being. You've done a good job as his girlfriend, Sarah, but the plan's changed because we're so close to confrontation out there – I need some results quickly.' Sarah said nothing. 'I'm afraid I was being economical with the truth about Ali Baba – he lost his nerve when we pressed him, so he's acting under duress now.'

Suddenly she understood the tormented man she had held in her arms only yesterday. 'You're blackmailing him?'

'No, I wouldn't say that. The deal hasn't changed, but I've had to lean on him heavily to get him to go on.'

Sarah saw the reality all too clearly. 'The poor bastard.'

Nairn shrugged and lit his pipe, shielding the flame of his gas lighter with cupped hands. 'And I've decided to change your role too, now that you'll be in Pakistan every few weeks.'

Her heart sank. 'You mean that you want me to act as his courier?'

'Yes. Islamabad is a suspicious, back-stabbing place and I don't want him to be seen to have too much contact with the Embassy. Nor to use drops – he's going to be too visible, always chauffeured around, guarded, hardly ever on his own. You'll be passing through and visiting Kahuta in the normal course of work. His colleagues will know you met him in Vienna and probably suspect that you had an affair, so you'll quickly become part of the woodwork.'

Sarah eyed him bitterly. 'You planned that too from the beginning, didn't you? But he thinks he's in love with me – he doesn't know I'm anything to do with you.'

'He still won't. Soon after he returns to Kahuta, he's going to Delhi to give a scientific paper at some kind of conference, in place of Syed, the fellow who was assassinated. Alan Mountford-White at the High Commission will contrive a meeting and put it to him that we want to use you as his courier.'

'Won't that give the game away?'

114

'I don't see why. We'll just explain that your relationship has been noticed and that we trust you because your father was once in the navy and the diplomatic service.'

'He'll still be furious.'

'It's a risk. If he goes through the roof and never wants to see you again, we'll have a few days to get on with finding an alternative.' He eyed her cold-bloodedly. 'But we'll threaten to use our influence in Vienna to get you moved off duties in Pakistan and I don't think he'll want never to see you again.'

Sarah felt sick inside. 'Just how long do you expect me to keep this up?'

'If there *is* a weapons programme, they'll have to indoctrinate him into it as soon as he becomes director of Kahuta. How else can he do the job if they're manufacturing the warheads there? But we may not have too long, so I want to siphon off everything he can get as quickly as possible.'

She flinched. 'You mean he's under suspicion?'

'Not that I know of. They've given him Kahuta so they must have complete confidence in him at the moment. But he has an old enemy who's head of his Chairman's office in Islamabad and they're paranoid about leaks and penetration – he might cast doubts on Ali Baba just to pay off old scores. So find out where those bloody bombs are stored, Sarah, as fast as you can. That's all I need.'

'I hope I can handle it.'

'You'll do fine.' He was reeling in again, his Scots accent marked when he used words like *fine*. 'But take this with you when you go out there.' He gave her an envelope with a bump inside. She opened it to find a small bottle containing six blue and green capsules.

'What are these?'

'The label says a well-known brand of anti-depressants. In fact any one of them is lethal.'

Sarah felt a cold fist clench in her stomach. 'Why?' Her voice was almost inaudible. Now she knew why Nairn had come to Austria himself.

'In case it goes wrong. If it does, we'll move heaven and earth to get you both out. I hope we could get you, at least, into the Embassy or the Consulate-General in Karachi.' Sarah stared at him silently; it was impossible to imagine the reality of what Nairn was saying, sitting there by the lake, looking across at the fairy-tale village. 'We might not be able to do anything for him – and he wants us to get his wife and kids out as well. It won't be possible.'

It felt colder in the shadow of the rock and Sarah pulled her anorak round her. 'So what are the pills for, David?' She didn't need to ask, but horrified disbelief made her want to hear it spelt out. An orange electric locomotive whined slowly along the railway pulling three passenger coaches.

'If he and the family can't escape, they may need a quick way out. It's all we can do for them.'

For God's sake, she wanted to scream, *I've grown close to him, I respect him, I was naked with him only a few hours ago. I love him!* 'Okay.' It was as if someone else were speaking. 'If someone's got to do it, it had better be me.'

Nairn looked relieved. 'I shouldn't think about it too much. I hope it won't be necessary.' *He might hope*, she thought, *but he certainly didn't believe*. 'It's just that if things go wrong you'd be saving him from a great deal of unpleasantness. And it would be better if he didn't confess that he was working for the West rather than the East. I'm sure you understand.'

'Oh yes, I understand.' Sarah was desperate to walk away, back into the real world and the sun. She almost cried out with relief when Nairn nodded her dismissal. 'You won't be seeing me again until it's all over, Sarah, but keep in touch with Ken Payling. If you walk on beside the railway you'll come to another jetty where the ferry calls in about half an hour.' He was about to say something else, but seemed to change his mind.

A few yards down the path she turned back. 'David?' Suddenly she sounded very young and vulnerable. 'What if I lose my nerve?' But he had already vanished.

23

Vienna

The next ten days passed quickly. Nazim was occupied in packing, emptying his apartment for the new man at the Embassy, and a round of farewell calls on other missions. He visited the Director General of Sarah's agency to confirm that she was acceptable to his government as a regular inspector of their nuclear sites. The boss summoned Sarah to pass this on. He was a dour Swede, but sounded almost pleased as he congratulated her in his lilting Scandinavian intonation. 'It is difficult inspectors to place in Pakistan, Miss Cable; to win their confidence you have done well.' She wondered how he would feel if he knew the real reason. Within days she had been accepted by India as well and given a programme of inspections that would take her to the sub-continent every few weeks. Nairn's plan was beginning to make sense. It would not take long for her to be accepted as a regular visitor to Islamabad and Karachi and, as a junior UN official, she would not be suspect in the same way as a diplomat from an Embassy.

Two farewell parties were given for Nazim, one by the Pakistan Ambassador at his residence, the other by a group of friends in the agency at Feuerwehr Wagner's *Heurigen* in Grinzing. Sarah was asked to that one and went along in a bright Hungarian blouse and swirling black skirt, a little uncertain how to behave towards Nazim. The proprietor had shut off the back of the building for the people from the outfit every Viennese knew as *Atombehörde* and lit the old-fashioned beehive stove, covered in green tiles and reaching to the ceiling. It gave off a steady heat like a giant radiator.

When Sarah arrived the new wine was already flowing by the *Viertel*, served in little quarter-litre tankards. She walked through a room with whitewashed walls and smoke-blackened beams – where a buffet of salad and cheese, with hot joints of pork and beef, bread and pickles, had been laid out on a long wooden table – into the other which was plainly where the action was. It was barrel-vaulted in stone, like a cellar, dim and smoky. A mixed nationality group

117

of agency staff was playing sultrily in a corner – a guitar, trumpet, violin and balalaika, occasionally joined by an Indian on a sitar. The effect was mesmerising when not actually painful. There were about fifty people, some dancing, some chatting or necking at the rough oak tables.

Johan was there and Sarah danced with him. 'I miss you,' he said.

'You dropped me, you bastard.'

'You dropped *me*.'

'It doesn't matter any more.' She kissed him on the cheek and moved on to dance with a small Vietnamese lawyer from the agency: there was something incredibly sexy about Nguyen's wiry body, spiced with that look of downright lust and cruelty in his eyes. Waving her body at him was like dicing with death. By midnight the noise was deafening and the alcohol fumes from the wine mingled with tobacco smoke and the sweet smell of marijuana.

She danced a little with Nazim, enough to be polite, not enough to look suspicious, touching him only when she held his hand. 'I must stay to the end,' he whispered. 'Or at least until one. Would you like to go back to the apartment first?' He smiled and slipped a latchkey into her hand, kissing her chastely and turning to dance with the wife of the Russian Deputy Director General, a huge woman whose heaving bosom swayed before a figure like a heap of cement sacks wrapped in a tarpaulin.

After socialising some more, Sarah left and turned into the path that led up through a vineyard to Rudolf Kassnergasse, walking slowly in the dark. Glancing over her shoulder at the sound of footsteps, she thought she saw a figure vanish into the shadow of the vines, but it was probably her imagination. When she paused outside the apartment block, the street seemed empty.

Neither of them felt like going to bed when Nazim returned soon after one, so they drove up the Leopoldsberg, leaving the Mercedes near the monastery and walking to the very edge of the crag towering above the Danube, moonlight glinting silver on the frost. They huddled together for warmth, staring down at the lights of the city. 'I'm glad you'll be coming to Pakistan so often, Cable. That's the best news I've had for weeks.' She could not see his face in the darkness, but he kissed her as his hands unzipped her anorak and cupped her breasts under the blouse. 'Are my hands too cold?'

She shook her head: his fingers were icy, but she pressed them to her, wriggling closer. 'No, I like them there – and this is a beautifully romantic place to come for our last night in Vienna. Thank you.'

'I have great respect for you, Cable.' Sarah smiled: it was such a strange thing to say, although she thought she knew what he meant.

'And I love you.' He kissed her again in a lingering way that made her shiver despite the warmth of his body, feeling his hands explore delightfully lower.

'I love you too, Nazim.' She stroked his face tenderly, suddenly hating the whole business. It wasn't just that, against the rules and all common sense, she really was more than half in love with him; she respected him too and hated seeing him used like this. *No!* she wanted to cry out. *Don't go back. You've taken too many risks already. You've done enough. Don't go back or they'll kill you!* Instead she gripped his hand, hiding her face in her hood, close to tears as they walked slowly along the path back to the car.

He stopped, sensing that she was weeping, and looked into her face, his eyes kind and questioning in the moonlight. 'What is it, Cable? Why are you crying?'

'Because I'm a sentimental bloody idiot.' She buried her head in his chest. 'Don't take any notice. I don't want to think or talk any more, just screw me. Quickly.' She wanted to make love to him there and then, on the lonely hillside, but the temperature was sub-zero so they hurried back to the car, where in seconds she was laughing at herself, naked except for her blouse like a half-peeled banana, wincing as her bottom touched the cold leather. She crouched on the huge back seat, throwing her arms around his hips as he rolled beside her, kissing his body, taking the taut salt-tasting penis in her mouth, no longer tearful but looking up at him with wicked eyes.

'You're beautiful, Cable. I don't deserve anyone as lovely as you.'

She gave a dreamy sigh, smiling at the muscles of his body in the silver light from the moon. 'You deserve someone much better than me, darling, but I'm so glad you haven't found her.'

Nazim left for Pakistan the following morning. An Embassy car took him to the airport, but Sarah met him there for a farewell coffee in the departure hall. From that first night out at *Le Salut* they had both been discreet, but a few of Nazim's Embassy colleagues had heard of the affair. Now that Nazim's appointment to Kahuta had been confirmed, Munster had decided it was safe for them to be a little more open. Islamic puritanism must not be offended, but it would help if Nazim's more Westernised compatriots suspected that he and Sarah were more than friends – then her cover when she visited Pakistan would be complete.

She stood alone on the cold balcony, watching the Austrian Airlines DC9 climb steeply into the cloud. It would take him to Frankfurt, where he would join a PIA flight to Karachi. Her own journey would start in another ten days, first to Bombay where she would visit the Bhabha Research Centre at Trombay, then on to Delhi. She felt horrible inside, hating herself yet emotionally anaesthetised; she could not explain why or how, but she would go through with it.

There was a queue at the dock gates in Odessa, with frontier guards scrutinising all vehicles and pedestrians. The liner looked bigger than Levshin had expected, but probably that was because it towered above him, moored by long wire hawsers to the cobbled quay. *Sea of Azov* it said on its stern, in both Latin script and Cyrillic; the superstructure was a faded white, pitted by flecks of rust, topped by a red funnel with its gold hammer and sickle.

When he reached the head of the line, Levshin pushed his passport and ticket under the sheet of glass. A woman examined them, her neat white blouse and uniform skirt separated by belt and holster carrying a pistol; a man in a peaked cap was looking over her shoulder. They checked a loose-leaf index of names and photographs; then tapped something into a computer terminal and waited for a reply. Levshin's hands were sweating and his mouth dry.

PART FOUR

24

Delhi

The middle-aged man, who had been trailing Sarah since she arrived in Delhi the previous afternoon, stood awkwardly in a pair of hired trunks on the edge of the swimming pool. It was a hot afternoon and the old-fashioned Ashoka hotel was asleep. His quarry was alone in the pool covering her sixth length at a fast crawl. She pulled herself out and walked slowly towards the spring-board. He sprawled in a canvas chair, half-hidden by a bush, and ran his eye appreciatively over her body and legs; the white bikini made her tan look darker than it was. Powerful muscles swelled in the back of her thighs as she bent forward, toes gripping the end of the board, and dived off with a splash.

Satisfied that she was there only for a swim, he returned to the changing room, casting a last lustful glance back at the fair-haired girl curving through clear water. He would wait for her in the car park where she had left her hired Fiat.

Sarah had not seen Nazim since he had left Vienna a fortnight before. She had arrived from Trombay yesterday and taken a taxi down to Raj Ghat, where she left the crumbling walls and teeming bicycles of the old city behind her and set off down the slope to the river about a mile away. She crossed the neat park around the site of Gandhi's cremation, a slab of black marble strewn with marigolds, flames flickering in a brazier beside it. An Indian couple stood there barefoot in prayer, the man in traditional long coat and tight trousers, the woman in a green sari.

Avoiding a beggar squatting in the dust, she walked on downhill towards the Yamuna and stepped over a sagging wire fence into a wood of plane trees, creaking in the slight breeze. Soon she was lost in a wilderness of brown grass and bushes, criss-crossed by dry ditches. Every few minutes she stopped to listen, but there was no crackle of feet on the brittle undergrowth.

When the wood cleared she was looking down the mud flats, dry and cracked in the sun, to the sluggish brown river: a desolate spot, not a soul in sight except a man ploughing with two water buffalo half a mile away. Alan Mountford-White was waiting in the shadows, elegant in a fawn tropical suit. He reported briskly that he had confronted Nazim. At first Nazim had been angry and refused to accept that Sarah should act as courier, but in the end he had recognised that he had no choice if he was to see her again. He had stalked off furious that they had approached Sarah 'behind my back' – but there had been no sign that he suspected her of any prior complicity.

Now she drove south under a black sky in torrential rain. The monsoon had arrived without warning, as it always did. On the way out of the city, the rickety bazaars by the road were empty and the potholes already full of muddy water. She reached Tughlakabad about five, parking the Fiat out of sight in a grove of trees.

On one side of the track towered the massive sandstone ramparts of the ruined fortress. On the other stood a small white building with battlemented walls and a white dome. It was the only place in the ruins with a roof to keep off the downpour and she ran towards it, slashes of rain stinging her face. In the shelter of the gateway, she looked back at the drenched plain, stretching away under low grey clouds. There wasn't a house, a car, anything, as far as the eye could see. No beggars. No filth. Nothing but a pair of monkeys cowering in the gateway with her. It was as if the monsoon were washing away the dark side of India.

Under the dome, rain drummed on the marble roof and she sat down on one of the stone tombs, shirt and jeans steaming in the wet heat. The walls were open on three sides, but it was dry inside. She did not hear Nazim's car drive up. Suddenly she heard feet splashing outside and he was standing there, grim-faced, shaking the water from his hair.

'Well – I found it.' He gestured at the carved marble. 'The tomb of Lord Tughlag, six hundred years old. I bet he was a nasty bit of work. Have you noticed how all the historic buildings in India are forts or tombs? There's the occasional temple, but it's forts and tombs they were really into, especially tombs.' He was talking too fast and she sensed his tension as he peered out at the dripping walls of the courtyard. In a corner, three monkeys stared gloomily at the rain. He picked up a handful of nuts from the floor and threw it at them. 'Cheer up, chaps. We who are about to die salute you.'

She motioned him to sit beside her on the stone sarcophagus, but he remained standing, holding her shoulders at arm's length, searching her face. 'Now then, Cable, how the devil did you get mixed up with all these spooks?' His eyes cut straight through her with concern – or was it suspicion?

'They just came and asked me to help, Nazim. They said you would want to get some documents and film out of Pakistan and it would be dangerous for you to have contact with an Embassy. That's all I know. I don't mind doing it – it's really quite exciting.' She hated lying to him, but there was no hint that he suspected her.

'I'm absolutely furious. Who approached you? Was it a man calling himself Kay?'

'I don't know any names.'

'They've no bloody right to involve you. Why the hell can't they use someone from their Embassy?'

'They said that would make it more dangerous for you.'

'But what about *you* for God's sake? I love you, Cable. I really can't let you go through with this – have you any idea what they'll do to you if we're caught?'

Sarah wanted to say that she knew in sickening detail. Instead she took his hand. 'I don't believe we *will* be caught. Anyway, I'll only have the stuff for a few days. You're the one taking the risks – are you doing it willingly?'

His expression was unreadable, but there was an atmosphere of suppressed violence. 'I'm doing this for my own reasons, Cable, and I'm not ashamed of them. But it's dangerous and I don't want you mixed up in it.'

'I want to share it,' she said firmly. 'And it's too late to change – I'm flying to Karachi in a couple of hours. I'll be at the Paradise Point power station for a few days and then I'll see you in Islamabad. It's all fixed.'

He sighed and kissed her. 'You are being very brave, Cable. Since you're so determined, we'll do what they want the first time if I have anything to pass on – but it will be only the once. When you come to Pakistan in future, there must be no more of this.'

'Let's just give it a try, Nazim.'

'And what happens if it all goes wrong? Do we both get a posthumous CBE? I don't find that much comfort.'

She laughed, 'They don't give CBEs posthumously,' and launched into practicalities. 'I've brought the camera and a lot of film.' She handed him the tiny Minox. 'Do you know how to use it?' He nodded. 'Good. Then we must arrange a way of meeting in Islamabad that won't attract suspicion.'

'That's quite easy. Your movements will be reported to me as a matter of routine, like those of any foreign visitor to the Commission – I'll get in touch when you arrive in the capital, probably at your hotel. I'll do my best to protect you, Cable.' There was a sudden silence. The rain storm had stopped, as if a tap had been turned off, the sun came out and the paving stones began to steam. Nazim was holding her in his arms, no longer angry. 'I wish I knew what will happen to us when all this is over.'

Sarah hated herself and looked away. Did he imagine that by some miracle he would be with her in that mythical new home in America or Australia? Had he forgotten about Farah and the children, about Zia's security police, about the reality of living in fear for year after year even if he survived? It could never happen, but she was determined not to lie to him any more, not to make the ache inside even worse. She took his face in her hands and kissed him gently, suddenly aroused by the imminent danger, or the strange thrill of knowing that they were about to make love in a place of the dead; and that it might be for the last time.

25

Odessa

Levshin had joined the ship without difficulty and thoroughly enjoyed the cruise. His cabin was simple, but a great improvement on both the freezing apartment and the labour camp. The food was excellent and drink could be bought at the bar. He wasn't much impressed by the company, but had decided at the beginning to keep his head down, so the more boring they looked the better. His fellow passengers were mostly *apparatchiks* with overfed wives, sunning acres of white skin that rapidly burnt a painful red. A few had daughters, one or two stunning in their bikinis after his years of deprivation, but Levshin confined himself to a benevolent smile. He was not there to enjoy himself.

They sailed through the Bosporus without stopping – the liner was due to visit Istanbul on the way back – so the first port of call was Piraeus. Levshin was tempted to jump ship then, but held to his original plan. There would be a large KGB presence in Athens and they might well pick him up when the ship's captain reported that he had gone. He had paid for a fortnight of luxury – albeit only Soviet-style luxury – and would enjoy a little more of it.

The report from GCHQ took several weeks to surface again and travel with thousands of others in the daily green pantechnicon to London. It arrived on the desk of the case officer in Century House, an hour after he had received the package of photocopies by hand from the CIA annexe near Grosvenor Square. Hesitantly he rang Nairn's office, only to be told the Chief was chairing a selection board in Whitehall. Eventually he got him on a secure line. 'What's up then, Hugh?' Nairn sounded irritated. He did not like being interrupted in his visits to the Old Admiralty Building, with its cool tiled corridors and high corniced rooms overlooking Horseguards, a relic from more gracious times when spies were gentlemen and there was no radio to intercept.

The young man explained. 'I thought you should know, sir, since you've been taking a personal interest in the case.' He paused awkwardly, aware that Nairn had recruited Sarah Cable himself and retained a soft spot for the girl.

'How the hell did the Cousins get hold of these files?'

'They say they came from a walk-in about three weeks ago. It was a one-off – he was a dissident who'd recently been released from the camps, visited a childhood sweetheart who happens to be a senior KGB officer, and pinched the stuff.'

'Why?'

'To trade for a ticket and forged papers to get out of the country.'

'Sounds bloody unlikely to me. Does the stuff look genuine?'

'Yes. It came from the flat of General Kirova, one of their most effective people, and has handwriting identified two years ago as hers on it. I've got complete photocopies. The files deal with a whole collection of things – this is only one, but it suggests they have someone high up in Islamabad. The intercept confirms that.'

Nairn groaned. 'Not in the AEC?'

'No – seems to be in the army, with AEC links.'

'And he was on to our man *three weeks* ago? Then why the devil is Ali Baba still walking about free?'

'I suppose their agent is waiting until his masters see some tactical advantage in denouncing him. At which point Cable will be arrested, the UN will be screaming like a raped virgin that we've been using it for espionage and HMG will have egg all over its face. It'll be a disaster.'

Nairn watched a line of Life Guards, breastplates glinting over red tunics as their horses trotted through the arch from Whitehall. A military band was playing in the distance. 'What are you suggesting, Hugh?'

'I think we should abort the whole operation, sir. Get Cable to scrub her visit to Pakistan – she could feign sickness and go back to Vienna. Then warn Ali Baba, offer him sanctuary if he wants it.'

'Have you checked any of this with Islamabad?'

'Not yet. Look, there just isn't time – Cable is already in Delhi and we may have only hours to stop her flying to Karachi. If Zia's boys arrest her, she'll have a very rough time. They'd put her on trial – she has no diplomatic protection – and they usually hang spies in Pakistan . . .'

Nairn hesitated and the other man lost his temper. 'For Christ's sake, we must pull her out *now* or it'll be too bloody late.'

Suddenly Nairn felt his age and for the first time acknowledged inwardly that he could have got it all wrong. 'Okay, tell them to hold Cable in Delhi until we decide what to do.' His face was grey as he put down the phone.

26

Karachi

Sarah had never been further east than the Mediterranean before, so both India and Pakistan were new to her. She arrived at Karachi late in the evening; the airport buildings were shabby and pools of light from the windows showed armoured cars patrolling and numerous soldiers carrying rifles or machine-pistols. She was met by a young man from the AEC and ushered through customs to a rusting car of a make she had never seen before. As it drove off, they passed a Ford Cortina speeding in the opposite direction, as if late to meet a plane. The figure hunched over the steering wheel was unmistakably English and the car looked like one of those issued to British Consulates.

She could see little of the sprawling city in the dark. They stopped at a railway crossing while a steam locomotive rattled by, a man in a turban shovelling coal on the footplate in the glow from the firebox. The train was carrying field guns, lashed down to flat wagons. But after that the streets were empty as if under curfew. In India the roadside bazaars had been crowded at night, when the heat subsided and people came out: rough straw awnings silhouetted against the yellow flames of braziers, the smell of sizzling lamb and chicken, the cries of bartering and wailing sitar from transistors. Here the bazaars were empty as they drove through ghost villages in a ghost country. 'There were two car-bombs today,' said her escort. 'Almost fifty people killed – we have a terrorist problem. Not as bad as in Northern Ireland, of course.' The brown baby-face smirked, shining in the glow from the lamp outside a ramshackle cinema, doors closed with padlock and chain.

That night she slept in a government guest house by the sea, in a comfortable room with its own bathroom. But she noted that both the french doors to the balcony and the door to the corridor were locked from the outside when she woke at five and checked them. Breakfast of rolls and tea was brought in by a white-coated steward and at six thirty the young man appeared. 'If we start now, we can make the most of the cooler part of the day. Later it will be very hot.'

SECRET

GR 50
CYPHER CAT X
FM DELHI
SECRET
PRIORITY FLASH

TO FCO LONDON

FOLLOWING FOR CLAYTON

1. CABLE FLEW KARACHI BEFORE URTEL 576 OF 3 NOVEMBER ARRIVED.
2. ALERTED CONSULATE-GEN KARACHI, BUT CABLE ALREADY EN ROUTE TO PARADISE POINT IN TRANSPORT PROVIDED BY PAKISTAN AEC. REGRET INTERCEPTION IMPOSSIBLE.

MOUNTFORD-WHITE

At the power station they gave Sarah a freshly laundered white coat and she went through the routine she had practised in Germany, checking lists of material in the reactor and in store, removing the seals from the cameras that surveyed sensitive areas such as the top of the reactor where fuel rods could be inserted or removed, taking photographs automatically in the months between inspections. She took out the spent film and put in fresh spools, then replaced the small metal seals with new ones. Her escort, whose name was Ali, followed her everywhere, watching with suspicion and making no effort to be friendly. His skin was smooth and greasy.

At the end of the day she was escorted back to the car, noting the soldiers in green berets who guarded the gates of the power station with Armalites. She passed more soldiers on the road, dug in on the verge, the barrel of a machine-gun pointing through a barrier of sandbags.

Sarah spent three days at Paradise Point, eating all her meals alone in the bedroom overlooking the sea. After several requests, Ali unlocked the doors of the balcony for her, and she sat out there in the evening, completing her report forms and watching waves break on the yellow sand. The comfort of the place contrasted eerily with the squalor and poverty she knew to be only miles inland. As the time to leave for Rawalpindi drew nearer, she felt increasingly nervous. She would only be a courier, and then only if Nazim had material for her to deliver, but if she screwed it up she felt sick when she imagined what they would do to him. And to her.

In Kabul Kirov stood on the Embassy roof, watching the stream of Antonovs take off from the airport a few miles away. She had been back nearly three weeks, but Grigorenko had refused to speak to her, even on the phone. Despite demands, she had been shown no papers about the military situation, although she knew from Nikolai's mess sources that the Antonovs contained *Spetsnaz* who were to be dropped near the border with Pakistan. What they were to do there, she could only speculate.

Inwardly she was fuming – it was infuriating to spend a lifetime getting to the top in intelligence, only to be shut out by the Red Army, *her* army, as if she did not exist. She feared the outcome of what they were doing, she feared for herself, but she was still unmolested, able to move freely between her house and the Embassy. The house remained guarded by a section of twelve troops, under the command of a corporal, but Grigorenko could remove them with a single phone call. At the Embassy her desk was empty, no telegrams came from Moscow and she knew that if she enciphered one herself it would never leave the machine room in the basement. The Ambassador, an experienced time-server, already averted his eyes when he met her in the corridor, avoiding meeting the gaze of the condemned. How much longer would Malinovsky leave her free? Not long, she guessed, once his hold on the Politburo was firm.

In London Nairn cursed silently and thrust the pink sheet of another telegram from Karachi into the burn-bag beside his desk. He walked to the window and stared down at the commuter trains grinding out of Waterloo station, then picked up the intercom. When Clayton answered, Nairn gave him no time to say anything. 'I gather that Cable is still floating about in Pakistan and hasn't a clue how much danger she's in. You got us into this mess, Clayton, and you'd better take some effective action to get us out!' There was a spluttering at the other end of the line. 'She's on her way to Islamabad – for Christ's sake get someone from our station to contact her. Pull her into the Embassy for safety if necessary.'

'How the devil are they supposed to find her in Islamabad? If they contact Ali Baba it'll blow the whole thing.'

'Then find out some other way. Just do it.'

On Thursday afternoon Sarah was driven back to the airport and flown in an old DC3 to the capital. Although she was still apprehensive about her role as courier, she was glad to leave the south. For seventy-two hours she had been treated with a calculated coldness, with no opportunity to speak normally to anyone. She could not even phone a friend; she had only one in the whole country and a single overheard call to him would land both of them in jail. She had no doubt that any phone call she made would be monitored. No wonder it had not been difficult to get her on this patch as an inspector – no one in their right mind would want to do it.

At the airport there was another smooth-faced young man in a grey suit to meet her. He drove her in an old-fashioned Ambassador to a hotel in Rawalpindi, where a tall Sikh in a red turban opened the car door with a flourish. As the Sikh carried her small case inside, the escort spoke for the first time. 'Tonight you are invited to dinner by Dr Khan, the director of our national research centre. It is a great honour. The car will collect you at eight o'clock.'

Sarah froze. She had not been expecting such an open approach but, when her heartbeat slowed again, she saw that it made sense. 'Thank you, I shall be very pleased to accept.'

'Perhaps you knew Dr Khan when he was at our Embassy in Vienna?' Was there a hint of suspicion?

'Oh, I think *everyone* knew Dr Khan, he was an important man in the diplomatic community.'

'I am hoping to go to Vienna, either to our Embassy or to a job in the agency where you work.'

'Are you?' They stood facing each other awkwardly in the lobby, Sarah wishing he would clear off. 'I expect you'd like it, but it's not all cakes and ale you know.'

'Cakes and ale? I am not understanding.'

'Sorry, it's an old English expression – I mean it may look attractive, particularly from a developing country, but there are drawbacks too.' She almost bit off her tongue when she realised how tactless that must have sounded.

'I am proud to work in what you call a developing country. We are not being beggars, you know.'

'No, of course not. Sorry, but I *am* rather tired. Could you leave me to have a rest before I go to meet Dr Khan?'

He eyed her stiffly. 'You are not wanting to see Islamabad? They told me to take you for a drive and this is a fine city.'

'I'll be here a day or two, could we put that off till tomorrow?'

Sarah lay on her bed, exhausted although she had done nothing but travel all day, feeling ambivalent about the prospect for the evening. Plainly it would simplify matters later if she had been seen to meet Nazim officially, and it was more or less natural for the director of Kahuta to entertain a visiting agency official. Equally, in a deeply hierarchic society she was too junior for that sort of treatment. It might lead to raised eyebrows – and it was going to be horrible being in the same room with him, treating him as a stranger, unable to touch him.

For that much was clear. She would go through with it now to the end, she had no choice. It was just sod's law that, once she had found his wavelength, Nazim had turned out to be the most intriguing man and exciting lover she had ever known. She felt empty and incomplete without him; it was as simple – and as complicated – as that. She clenched her fists as she turned to look at her travelling clock in its red leather case. Play it by the book. Her task had been to make Nazim fall in love with her; it simply wasn't in the script that she should fall for him too. Deep inside she knew that she could have no future in which Nazim figured, that she was a bloody fool to let her emotions get into this kind of turmoil; but she was still weeping into the pillow when the time came to throw on her dress, scrub her face with cold water to hide the marks of tears and go downstairs. As a talisman she had brought the piece of jade on a gold chain that he had given her; she kissed it and hung it round her neck.

The same black Ambassador drove her through crowded streets – there was no curfew here – and she noticed the political slogans flyposted on walls. She wound down the car window to let in the cooler evening air, but closed it again when she saw the hatred in faces staring at the official car, sensed the suppressed violence just feet away. Policemen in blue helmets were patrolling in jeeps, carrying machine-pistols and long wicked-looking staves.

Nazim's bungalow was in a residential area with tree-lined streets. The car halted at a gate guarded by soldiers, then they were through the wire fence and stopping under a porch. A servant in white turban and long blue coat bowed her into the hall, highly polished wooden floor scattered with white rugs, then Nazim was coming towards her, followed by a woman in *shalwar kameez* of shimmering dark-green silk. They raised their hands, palms together, and bowed their heads in greeting. Sarah clumsily did the same. 'Miss Cable, welcome to Rawalpindi.' Nazim's face betrayed nothing. 'This is my wife, Farah.'

Although she was getting plump, the woman was dark-eyed and beautiful: *that one could be sensuous if she felt like it,* thought Sarah, *and how.* Their eyes met. *God, did she suspect anything?* But there was no sign of unease or anger. 'Thank you for asking me to your house,' she said.

Farah bowed her head again formally. 'It is an honour to receive you and I look forward so much to talking about Vienna.' The three of them turned into a long room where two other men in dark suits were waiting with their wives, one wearing a brilliant orange sari with jewelled bangles at her wrists. There was an awkward silence, broken as Nazim introduced Sarah to the men, then the women, and another liveried servant offered a silver tray of fruit juice. One of the men bowed slightly in Sarah's direction. 'I hear you are being educated at Oxford, Miss Cable? I went to the other place myself.'

'No – I was at Liverpool University.'

The atmosphere remained tense. It was plainly going to be a riotous evening.

27

Rawalpindi

Sarah had a bad night. She slept fitfully for a few hours, tossing and turning, unable to forget the stiff little dinner party, constantly imagining the loveless wife eyeing her with suspicion, the opaque faces of the two officials he had invited, their cold distance telling Sarah that her unbeliever's life was as expendable as that of the lowest peasant in the fields. To make it worse there had been no cushioning of alcohol but now she woke several times drenched in sweat as if she had taken a skinful, tormented by the trusting faces of Nazim's children who had been brought in for five minutes by a maid. In the end she just lay there, naked under a single sheet, staring at the pattern on the wall made by moonlight filtering through the slatted blind.

She must have fallen into the sleep of exhaustion about four in the morning, for when the hammering on the door woke her, at first she could not remember where she was. Then she leapt up in confusion, pulling the sheet around her like a shroud. 'Who is it?' she called, noting that the hotel's chain was still in place under the lock.

There was a muttering in Urdu, then a deep voice began to speak uncertainly in English. 'Military security. Kindly open door or we are breaking it down.' In emphasis a heavy kick followed, then the sound of cracking wood. Sarah felt a wave of panic. Had Nazim decided to save his neck by turning her in?

'Okay, wait a moment.' Her fingers trembled as she unlocked the door, without freeing the chain, so that it opened about six inches. A brown face under a green beret glared at her through the gap. 'What do you want?' Her voice shook.

'You will be opening this door!' roared the sweating face. For a few seconds they stared each other out, then there was another kick, a crash and the door swung inwards, hinges torn from its splintered frame. Sarah sprang aside as the heavy baulk of wood toppled to the floor, but it caught her on the back of the ankle and she yelped in pain. Three men in khaki shirts and trousers stamped into the room: two privates with machine-pistols and a sergeant waving a swagger stick, the old-fashioned leather holster on his belt still closed but his eyes blazing. The hotel manager hovered outside the doorway, looking terrified.

'You will be coming with us,' bellowed the sergeant.

'Why?' Sarah fumbled for her light-blue United Nations *Laissez-Passer*. 'You have no right to smash down my bedroom door like this, nor to arrest me!'

He whipped the short cane down on the bed with a crack like a pistol shot and Sarah sensed that she was seconds away from feeling it herself. 'You will be coming with us!' he shouted again, gesturing to the other men who seized her arms. As they did so the sheet slipped to the floor and one soldier looked away in embarrassment. The other leered at Sarah's body until the sergeant snapped something in Urdu and they released her. 'Get dressed, woman.' The cane tapped her sharply on the tender flesh at the side of her hip: not a real blow, but sharp enough to sting and demand obedience. The two young soldiers turned their backs as the sergeant snapped another order, but he continued to watch as Sarah pulled on her shirt and jeans. Wherever she might be going, a cotton dress was unlikely to be convenient.

They marched her downstairs and stopped at the reception desk. 'You will be paying bill,' shouted the sergeant. In other circumstances Sarah would have laughed at the incongruity; now she just pulled a book of travellers' cheques from her pocket and paid the clerk in US dollars, two gun barrels trained on her spine.

When they opened the glass door to the street, she was deafened by the noise. In her hotel room she had been protected by double-glazing and air-conditioning – but now she could hear shouting and gunfire not far away. A hundred yards down the street a mob was being broken up by police in blue helmets, after setting a row of wooden shops ablaze. She stopped and turned to the sergeant. 'What the hell has happened?'

'Hurry, move!' He waved his swagger stick, swishing it threateningly through the air, and she started to run between the soldiers towards an armoured car. As black smoke drifted towards them, and screaming figures came closer, she was pushed into the vehicle, a dim metal space smelling of oil, and a steel door clanged shut behind her.

In Kabul, Kirov heard of the coup on the news from the Red Army radio station. She had been expecting it, but it was still a shock. *In Pakistan the tyrannical President Zia has been assassinated by free-*

*dom fighters who destroyed his aircraft as it took off from Bahawalpur.
Power has been seized by a Revolutionary Council after a night of
popular demonstrations in which hundreds have been killed. The
pent-up fury of the newly liberated masses is expected to turn on the
Afghan rebels camped in the north of the country, where their presence
has ruined the economy and brought terror to the population . . .*

She was in her office in the secure wing of the Embassy, the
intelligence section shut off behind its combination locks and steel
doors. The window was barred against intruders and Nikolai had
just brought in a sealed pouch of documents from Moscow. Kirov
looked up at him with a wry smile. 'No, Nikolai,' she shook her
head. 'I did *not* know this was going to happen.'

'But it must be good news, comrade Minister?'

'We shall see.'

'But isn't this a Marxist coup, backed by our own government?'

'If it is, no one bothered to tell me we were promoting it.'

Nikolai looked confused. 'But, Minister, I thought . . .'

'Just what did you think, Nikolai?'

'I imagined that was why you went to Moscow. There has been
gossip in the mess whenever I have been down to the barracks,
about a *Spetsnaz* team in Pakistan – I imagined to assassinate Zia –
about a build-up of arms for the rebels . . .'

'Which rebels?'

The young man shook his head miserably. 'People's Party,
National Party, Awami? I'm sorry – I just don't know. I thought
you must know and could not tell me for security reasons.'

'What else did you think I was keeping back?'

'I hear that we are sending *Spetsnaz* across the frontier to harass
the Mujahedin in the North-West Frontier Province of Pakistan, so
that they cannot interfere in the coup.'

'You hear that, do you? Get me Grigorenko on the phone.'

'I'll try, Minister, but they tell me he is in the command post with
his senior officers and will not talk to anyone.'

Kirov gazed out of the window at the brown mud walls of the
slum opposite, the lines of washing flapping across the alleys, the
mountains in the distance. She imagined the highly trained special
troops dropping by parachute to the east, desperately trying to assess
the situation, plan her next move. 'Very well, leave it until I've gone
through the pouch. Is there anything important?'

'Just some intercepts, a few requests for clarification on our
intelligence reports – and a sealed letter marked *Personal* for you.'
He handed her the white envelope and Kirov waved him to sit down
while she opened it. Long practice kept her face expressionless as
she read the short note ordering her to return to Moscow at once

137

for consultations, with the hint of a possible promotion. A classic gambit – once there she would be in Malinovsky's power, on the way to retirement in disgrace or the Gulag or the execution cellar. She considered the situation calmly. If she wanted to survive the only way was to get out of the Soviet bloc altogether, before they moved on from polite notes to coming for her with a squad of armed men.

'Can I do anything, Minister?' He had been with her for five years and his voice was full of concern.

'No, Nikolai. I think I shall hold my hand for twenty-four hours. Call the car and I'll go back to the house.' Twenty-four hours. They'd leave her that long to make arrangements to travel, but not much longer, and then Grigorenko would thoroughly enjoy arresting her. There was nowhere to go unless she could get a plane to India – and no one would welcome her there except the Americans, and then only if she came as a defector with valuable material. Twenty-four hours to betray everything she had fought for, over nearly fifty years – or to wait for it to betray her.

Nairn had just arrived home in Chiswick when the phone rang, holding hands with Alison as they looked down at their daughter asleep cuddling her teddy. It was the direct line from the office and he answered instinctively. 'Nairn.'

'Duty clerk, sir. I have an urgent telegram from Islamabad.'

'Hold on, I'm going over.' He flicked the switch to secure. 'Ay, I'm listening.'

'President Zia has been killed, sir. His plane blew up just after taking off from a town near the Indian border. It was a Hercules with the American Ambassador and a lot of other brass on board, about thirty people – they're all dead too.'

'Assassination?'

'Almost certainly. Either a bomb or shot down by a ground to air missile. A fuller report is coming.'

'What's been the reaction?'

'Violent demonstrations all over the country – seems to be an attempt at some sort of coup, but the situation's very confused.'

'Any idea who did it?'

'Islamabad suggests the Afghans or the Russians.'

'That makes sense. Anything else?'

'No, sir.'

'Thanks then. Keep me in touch.'

He put the receiver down with a clatter. 'Oh Christ.'

Alison smiled at him. 'What's up, love?'

'Trouble in Pakistan. Someone's blown up their President and all hell's let loose.' He ran his fingers through thinning iron-grey hair. 'Remember young Sarah Cable?'

'The pretty girl with fair hair and legs that start just under her shoulders? Of course I do, you're fond of her, aren't you?' His wife spoke without rancour, secure in the knowledge that her capture of him was long since complete.

'She's in a bloody awful mess out there and I should never have sent her. I wouldn't have let it happen five years ago – I'm getting too damned old, Alison. I just hope to God I can get her out. I'll never forgive myself if I don't.'

28

Rawalpindi

The armoured car drove for twenty minutes. Its oily fumes made Sarah feel sick and there were no windows, but she could hear chanting crowds, explosions and gunfire outside. Several times they stopped and the vehicle swayed as it was kicked and buffeted, animal baying reverberating all around them. When they finally stopped and the steel door opened, she staggered out into a courtyard surrounded by high stone walls and the soldiers led her into a building with the unmistakable smell of prison. She pulled back. 'I'm not going in there! I'm a UN diplomat and I demand that you take me to a responsible official at once!'

The sergeant spat on the ground and struck her viciously across the shoulders with his baton. As she swayed in pain, two pairs of iron hands gripped her arms and hustled her down a long flagstoned corridor; one of her shoes came off but they did not stop. She was thrown into a low cell already crowded with twenty or thirty women. Some wore the tunic and baggy trousers of *shalwar kameez*, others nightdresses, others rags. A few were whispering to each other fearfully and the place stank of sweat and urine.

When Sarah staggered in the whispering stopped and brown eyes stared at her curiously as she pushed her way to a wall and leant against it; there was no room for anyone to sit on the floor. A girl smiled shyly at Sarah. She was about sixteen, naked to the waist, her back criss-crossed with weals that were congealed with blood and turning black. Forcing herself to be calm, Sarah smiled back and put her arm round the child, wishing that she could comfort her in Urdu, then started to examine her own situation. If Nazim was not responsible for her being here, what could have happened to him – and how the hell was she ever going to get out?

SECRET

GR 100
CYPHER CAT X
FM ISLAMABAD
SECRET
TO PRIORITY FCO

FOLLOWING FOR C/SIS

REFERENCE URTEL 984056 CABLE ARRESTED, WHERE-
ABOUTS UNKNOWN. NEW REVOLUTIONARY COUNCIL
NOT IN FULL CONTROL AND IGNORES REQUESTS FOR
INFORMATION. TELECOM BREAKDOWN AND CON-
TINUED STREET-FIGHTING MAKE COMMUNICATION
DIFFICULT. WILL PURSUE CAUTIOUSLY AS DEMANDS
FOR RELEASE OF FRENCH NATIONAL BY HIS EMBASSY
YESTERDAY LED TO EXECUTION TO CONCEAL MAL-
TREATMENT. CABLE IS UNITED NATIONS OFFICIAL,
CANNOT UN SEEK RELEASE?

TOMKINS

In Kabul Kirov had come to a decision. Alone in her office, she put
on a civilian overcoat and pulled a floppy chitrali cap – like an
enlarged wool beret – from a drawer. Fortunately her section was
shut off from the rest of the Embassy by a permanently locked door:
to gain admission it was necessary to ring a bell and identify yourself
to the guard. But following normal practice there was also a back
way, a narrow spiral staircase to the ground floor, through a steel
grille to a lobby where another locked door led to an alley and the
street: a secret entrance for willing or unwilling visitors. Only Kirov
had the keys.

She paused in her doorway, but the corridor was empty. No one
saw her take the seven steps to the door which led to the stairway
and she locked it silently behind her. Once outside Kirov pulled her
cap down and pushed through the brown-skinned crowd into a
bazaar. Although it was a cold October day, the shop fronts were
open, with piles of vegetables, sacks of flour and galvanised buckets
cascading out on the beaten earth. A porter staggered by, two huge
bales of straw swinging from a pole cutting into his shoulders. At
the other end of the alley, she paused in a wider street and hailed a
taxi weaving through the bicycles. It was a rusty Volga and she
ordered the driver to an area a mile away, where she vanished into
another alley, black, menacing, occasionally lit by a slanting burst

of sunlight through a gap in the tenements. Flies hovered over open drains running with thick, brown water. From the shadow of the doorways, dark faces stared at her with suspicion as she strode past. The alley twisted and at the last corner she stopped and turned, waiting for several minutes, but it remained empty.

The car was waiting as promised, by a square cistern sunk below street level, its stone walls green with slime. At the bottom of the steps a woman was filling a brass jar from a spout, while children played in the mud. It was a Moskvitch, with no diplomatic number plates, and the rear door opened silently as she approached. He was sitting in the back seat; they had never met, but she knew his life story from a file, as no doubt he knew hers. 'Good afternoon, General Kirova.'

'Good afternoon.' She sat beside him and closed the door. 'You do understand that I am not prepared to enter your Embassy?'

'Yes, I understand that.' He had a curious mid-Atlantic accent: perhaps that came from going to both Yale and Cambridge.

'I am armed.'

A bleak smile. 'So is my driver, but you have my word on your safety. I suggest we just drive around and talk?'

'Are you wired for sound?'

'No.'

'Show me.'

He slipped off his jacket and raised his arms while she ran her fingers over his shirt feeling for sound equipment. 'If you prefer we can talk in the open air – there is a quiet cemetery I know not far from here?'

'I should prefer that.' They drove off in silence.

Sarah's legs began to ache after an hour or two, first her ankles, then her knees and the muscles in her thighs. She wanted desperately to sit on the floor, but it was physically impossible with so many other women already collapsed on the filthy straw. One had plainly been tortured, from the dead look in her eyes and the bloodstains on the rags around her hips, but none of the others attempted to look after her. Sarah was torn between wanting to comfort and despising them all for their weakness, each one alone with her terror. But she began to understand as the stench made her head swim and her own fear shut out all other thoughts. She still had her arms around the frail sixteen-year-old, whose body was now burning with fever, but she could not speak her language and it was too hot and crowded to do anything practical.

At one point the door opened and a bucket of water was thrust in. The women fought to get at it, spilling most of the contents on

142

the floor, where it was absorbed by the excrement-covered straw. Apart from the thirst, Sarah badly needed a pee, but it was not until the sky darkened outside – for the only light in the cell came from the barred window – that she could face relieving herself in a fetid corner. She knew from the luminous dial of her watch that she had been there more than twenty hours, when the door opened again and she felt eyes turn on her as she was dazzled by a flashlight searching out her face. Blinking against the glare from the doorway, she saw the two soldiers who had brought her there, pointing her out to a man in civilian clothes.

Kirov strolled among the gravestones, some bearing phrases from the Koran, others the framed photographs, stark names and dates of post-revolutionary times. The pleasant young man with the red beard walked beside her. He was one of only two diplomats left at the white Palladian villa built sixty years ago to be the finest Embassy in Asia, the ballroom and orangery in its bullet-scarred walls now echoing and empty. 'You say there are already *Spetsnaz* in place, General, across the border in Pakistan?'

Kirov nodded. 'They are ordered to use the diversion of the coup to take out as many Mujahedin as possible.'

'That makes sense. How will your people evacuate them afterwards?'

'With the new government in place in Islamabad, it should be possible to use troop-carrying helicopters. Hips covered by Hind gunships.'

'And there are back-up forces too, for use further across the frontier if necessary?'

'So far as I can tell the paratroops are on full alert and transports fuelled at the airfield, but they will not move unless Moscow orders it. If the change of power takes place smoothly, they will not move at all. If they do, the situation will be very dangerous. That is why I am here.'

'Your people must be aware that there is a large American naval force just off Karachi? Carriers with aircraft that can reach this city?'

'Of course. The high command is taking a deliberate risk to oust Gorbachev.'

'But have they succeeded?'

'He's been out of sight ever since his heart attack – if he really had one.'

'And Malinovsky will take over?'

'I'm sure that's what he intends.'

'What a bloody awful mess. I will report all this to London,

143

General, and I am exceedingly grateful.' He met her eyes searchingly. 'And I can say now that if you decide to come over to us, you will be welcome, but I think you would have to get to India under your own steam.' He smiled ruefully. 'Our Embassy here is down to a skeleton and I just don't have the resources to guarantee your safety. I'm very sorry.'

29

Rawalpindi

Sarah left the prison in a state of terrified confusion. 'Where are you taking me?' The three escorts ignored her and she shouted the question again, but their only response was to seize her arms and drag her out into the blackness of the yard; she was still barefoot and the gravel cut her feet. Thrust into the back of a car, she sat jammed between two soldiers as they drove in silence through alleys that would normally have been busy in the cool of the night but now were silent and empty.

'There is a curfew,' said the civilian in the front by way of explanation. 'Anyone caught on the streets will be shot.'

'How jolly. Exactly *why* is there a curfew?' Again they ignored her. They had left the city and were driving between stone walls and fields, their headlights flickering across the beam of a pumping-engine rocking in the darkness. After twenty minutes the car stopped at the gates of a large compound, guarded by soldiers with SMGs, where the escort showed a clutch of papers to the sentries. As the gates opened to admit them, Sarah could make out two flags hanging in the floodlights above the gates: the green of Pakistan and another that was plain red.

Six hours earlier, late in the evening in Kabul, Kirov's mood had changed to black despair. She knew that she was facing defeat. Malinovsky was in control, the Gorbachev era was over, units of the Red Army were in Pakistan, even though operating as guerillas and not in uniform. She did not know what the outcome would be and no longer much cared, for it seemed increasingly unlikely that she would be around to see it. Her walk through the cemetery had ended on a friendly note, but in her heart she knew that defection was not for her. Even if she could get across the border and on into India – which was far from certain – what then? The long debriefing in a house outside Washington, denying everything that had guided her for fifty years? The false identity, the new existence somewhere in the Mid-West or Australia, living on the margins of a society she despised? The dreary wait for the assassin to find her? For find her they would – no one of her seniority would be allowed to go without retribution.

Equally she could not stay. Nadia Alexandrovna Kirov had made the most serious mistake of her career: she had backed the wrong horse. She could not face the degradation of being taken by her lifelong enemies, so the inevitable bullet might as well be her own. Her mind was confused, she felt desperately alone, she had made no clear decision; but an ice-cold corner of her brain said that she would simply put a round through her head when they came for her. The revolver was ready loaded and hung at her side. As a young woman she would have wept with the frustration of it all, but now she felt surprisingly calm. Damn Malinovsky for his ambition and stupidity. Damn Mikhail Sergeyevitch for his weakness and failure.

At midnight she was still awake, afraid to sleep because she knew they would come in the early hours. If she was in bed they might manage to take her, so she would not sleep. Nikolai had placed the guard on full alert. All twelve of them were patrolling the grounds or in the gatehouse, but she could not order them to fire on their comrades when they came; and if she did they would disobey. Their presence would just give her time to pull on her tunic and take the soldier's way out. She sat on a hard chair by her desk, to stop herself dozing off. Her thoughts drifted to the past and, with a flash of bitterness, she thought of her days in the swamps of Vietnam when she fought with the Viet Minh after the war, of the marks still on her body from her imprisonment under Stalin, of recent triumphs. After all that, what a rotten, squalid end. But most of the time she was not going over her life, just struggling to keep awake.

Twenty miles off Karachi, the bridge of the massive aircraft carrier rolled slowly in the swell. A dozen seamen, a third of them black, sat at the flickering screens of computer consoles, their captain peering out at the dim lights of the battleship and accompanying frigates, spread out over a distance of several miles. He was in command of the most modern carrier in the world, a floating airfield that had never seen a shot fired in anger. He turned to his executive officer, jerking a thumb down at the dark flight deck. 'All fuelled and ready?'

'Sir.'

'How many of these boys seen combat before?' The lazy Mid-Western drawl did not quite conceal his anxiety.

'The pilots, sir?'

'The pilots, Abbadessa.'

'About twenty, sir.' He followed the captain out through a sliding door and they both leant on the rail.

'Guess that could be worse – ah just hope to Christ we don't get beyond patrollin' up and down this goddam coast.'

The two men contemplated the long line of shaded blue lights, occasionally broken by the flickering white of a signal lamp. The land was out of sight and there was a clean, salty smell as the sea dashed spray against the hull below them. 'Ten ships of the US Navy – lot of firepower out there, sir.'

There was a long silence before the captain spoke again, almost inaudibly. 'That's what bugs me, Abbadessa. Do those monkeys in the Pentagon have the slightest fuckin' idea what game they're playin'?'

'I hope so, sir.'

'So do I, Abbadessa, so do I. This is like Russian roulette with every darn chamber loaded.'

Nairn stared at Clayton across his cluttered desk, the lower half of his face lit by the old-fashioned green shaded lamp. 'This is incredible.' He fingered the report from Kabul, deciphered only ten minutes ago. 'Do you believe it?'

'On balance, yes. Kirova would be totally opposed to this strategy, so I can't see what possible motive she can have in leaking it, except to damp down our reaction.'

'Copy it to Washington Flash and send it round to Downing Street by despatch rider. I hope she survives this; I've always had a sneaking regard for her.' As Clayton rose, he added, 'And tell Kabul to get a message to her – if she comes over, pay and protection for the rest of her life in return for debriefing. We'll treat her well.'

Kirov jerked upright when she heard the commotion outside. It was one in the morning and her study was in darkness except for the shaded lamp on her desk, not unlike Nairn's, playing yellow on her hands. She peered through a slit in the curtains, straight down the drive to the modern gatehouse with its sliding steel gate, gleaming in the circle lit by floodlights. Two army trucks stood outside the gate and a man in a helmet was arguing with the corporal in charge of her guard. She sighed and pulled the revolver from its holster. Now that the moment had come, she felt no emotion, just a weary resignation. It would be like switching off a light, although she must take care to fire straight up into the roof of her mouth and she felt a certain distaste at putting the cold barrel between her teeth. She flicked open the chamber and checked the six gleaming brass cartridges. One would be enough.

*　　*　　*

Outside a two-storey building, the young man beckoned Sarah to follow him. 'We are very sorry that you were arrested, Miss Cable: it was a mistake and we shall be apologising to your agency.' She sensed that they were going to meet someone important and the man was nervous; perhaps it was his fault she had been arrested and he feared retribution. They mounted a flight of polished wood stairs and entered a long room with white walls and glass door giving on to a balcony. There was a white leather sofa and after the discomfort of the prison Sarah had an overwhelming urge to throw herself on it and sleep.

Nazim rose from a table covered in papers. 'Miss Cable, do come and sit down. I am most upset by the way you have been treated.' He looked different: unsmiling, with a gravity she had never seen before. He had an unmistakable air of authority and, even if the other man had not been there, she would have hesitated to throw her arms around him.

'I am glad to be released, Dr Khan,' she said coldly. 'Can you please tell me where I am and what is going on?' Nazim gestured and she heard the young civilian leave and close the door behind him.

'You are in the research centre at Kahuta and in no danger now. There has been a change of government here. General Zia has been assassinated and everything is under the control of the Revolutionary Council.'

The room was bound to be bugged, so she remained aloof and formal. 'I am a United Nations official under the protection of your government. You had no right to arrest me and I demand to be returned to Vienna immediately.'

'The Council is not bound by agreements reached by the régime we have overthrown – we shall decide what to do with you when we have seen your report to the agency.'

'But you've no right to do that! It's against all international law.'

'We make the law now.' He gestured to her to follow and they stepped out onto the dark balcony. 'I don't think we can be overheard here, but I won't say much.' He was speaking fast and in a whisper. 'I'm sorry about the mix-up.'

'Mix-up? Nazim – that place was *foul*, a hell-hole. Is that what your so-called revolution has achieved? Locking up a lot of terrified women in conditions where they'll get cholera?'

'Those women were imprisoned by the old government – they'll be released as soon as they can be questioned to identify those responsible, and when they have somewhere to go.'

'Perhaps you should tell *them* that. Some of them are dying and they all think they're going to be shot.'

'I didn't know – I'll speak to the governor of the prison. You must have been very frightened.' His eyes smiled into Sarah's. 'But I got you out as soon as I could, Cable.'

'Don't call me Cable. I don't trust you any more.' She met his gaze firmly and did not smile back. 'And don't look at me as if you expect me to be grateful, Nazim – I shouldn't have been arrested in the first place. Anyway, if there's been this great revolution, how come you're still sitting here? Why the blazes aren't *you* in jail?'

'I have thrown in my lot with the new government.'

Her eyes narrowed and red spots of anger that he had never seen before appeared on her cheeks. 'Thrown in your lot, have you, Nazim? Just like that? And where does that leave me and your mission? Are you going to get me out of this shit-house of a country alive?'

'Of course, Sarah. But, please, there's no need . . .'

'There's every need, Nazim. You're lying in your teeth – you must have been part of whatever's happened for months or years. For Christ's sake, Nazim – who's bloody side are you really on?'

30

Kabul

Switching off a light. Like switching off a light. The gate had been opened and Kirov stood watching the soldiers crowd into the drive, the floodlights glinting on their helmets and weapons. She had told Nikolai to stall them for five minutes. That young man had been remarkably concerned and loyal, so she had written a note to Grigorenko, making it clear that Nikolai was not involved in any crime of which she was accused and worth a good new posting. She gripped the revolver. Her hand was sweating. Somewhere the phone was ringing; she could hear it despite that roar of engines and crash of boots outside.

She realised that the ringing phone was in the room: not the military line, but the connection to the appalling Afghan network, the one she never used. She ignored it. Nikolai rushed in without knocking. 'There is an officer from General Grigorenko – I've told him to wait, but he is getting angry – and a phone call that the caller says is personal.'

'A call from where?'

'They will not say, but it is very faint.'

She hesitated – no doubt it was someone from Moscow to encourage her to return and put her head in the noose. *You will be quite safe, Nadia Alexandrovna, we need you in the new set-up.* They must think she was born yesterday. But she picked up the receiver, curious to see who was acting as the Marshal's hangman. The line crackled and the voice was almost inaudible. 'General Kirov?' It was a man's voice, clipped, like a soldier.

'Yes.' The line went hollow, lost in interference and crackling.

'General Kirov?' The voice sounded impatient. 'You are very faint. Is that General Kirov?'

'Yes, this is Kirov.'

'This is the Central Committee, comrade General. I have the General Secretary of the Party for you. Please hold the line.' Her lip curled. So Malinovsky had made it and couldn't resist twisting the knife. The bastard.

The line crackled and whined. Then it was his voice. 'Nadia? Mikhail Sergeyevitch speaking. This is a terrible connection. Can you hear me clearly?'

'Yes, well enough.' Her fingers trembled as she gripped the hand-set. The curtain was still pulled back a few inches and she could see a black prison van pulling into the drive; it must have been hidden outside. 'Is that *really* you? Where are you? *How* are you?'

His voice was lost in interference and she banged the receiver on her desk in frustration. Suddenly she could hear him again. 'Yes, it *is* me. I am out of hospital and back in charge.'

'I can't believe it.'

'You *must* believe it. The old guard thought I was going to die, but it was only a mild heart attack. I promise you, I'm phoning from my Party office on Staraya Square – it's been a close run thing but the nonsense is over.'

Her throat was dry. 'And not a moment too soon. What has happened to Malinovsky?'

'Marshal Malinovsky is under arrest for treason. The army has stayed loyal to me, at least most of it has. There will be a lot to talk about when things are back to normal, but for now just listen carefully.' He was speaking distinctly but very fast, like a man making a long series of calls under enormous pressure. 'I have sent a telegram to Grigorenko, copy to you. He is relieved of his command and replaced by Azamov, his number two. Azamov is ordered to get all Red Army units back out of Pakistan within twenty-four hours. You are ordered to arrest Grigorenko and return him to Moscow under guard.'

'How do you imagine I can do that? I have ten men – he has an army of thousands.'

'Azamov is now supreme commander and he'll know where his future lies. Just *do* it. Is that quite clear?'

Kirov felt weak at the knees, her head spinning, sensations she had not felt since her teenage days in the trenches outside Leningrad. She had been ready to die, reconciled, minutes from oblivion. She did not know whether she welcomed or resented the reprieve. 'Yes, quite clear.'

'Good. There's one piece of action instigated by Malinovsky that I don't want stopped; it can take its course . . .'

Kirov listened, making notes and nodding agreement, peering through the curtains at the score or more of heavily armed troops trampling the shrubs in the garden. As he was about to hang up she jumped in. 'Just one more thing, Mikhail Sergeyevitch, there is a squad of Grigorenko's troops outside – they've come to arrest me. Would you be willing to·speak to the officer in charge? It might help me to survive long enough to do what you want.'

The familiar baritone laughed, but the sound faded into the crackling. 'Yes, but be quick.'

Kirov turned round. Nikolai was standing in the doorway, unable to conceal his grin. He must have been listening on the extension. 'I'll bring him in, Minister. It'll be a pleasure.'

Seconds later a major in battle-dress stood by the desk clutching the phone, his helmet upside down on a chair, his face a mask of confusion as he listened to the unmistakable voice. At first he looked suspicious and Kirov thought he would not co-operate. But then suspicion changed to hesitancy and he started to sound positively scared. 'Yes, comrade General Secretary.' Kirov smiled to herself: the fellow was actually standing to attention as he held the phone. 'I fully understand your instructions.' He put the instrument down as if it were electrified and turned to Kirov. 'I am at your service, comrade General.'

'Then get your men back in the trucks – we are going to army headquarters.' She turned to her ADC. 'Nikolai, my greatcoat and helmet.'

She stood on the steps of the villa, flanked by the major who had come to make her a prisoner and faithful Nikolai, watching the soldiers shouldering their Kalashnikovs as they scrambled aboard. With the glare from the floodlights it was like a scene from an Eisenstein film of the revolution; and she would act her part well. Nadia Alexandrovna was back on automatic pilot. She strode down to the first truck outside the gate and climbed in beside the driver, while Nikolai attached her Major-General's pennant to the radio aerial, glancing at her through the windscreen with a distinctly unmilitary and conspiratorial grin. The engine roared and the convoy rocked down the mud track to the highway. At the bottom they turned towards the city and picked up speed.

Three hundred miles to the south, another military convoy was on the move. Carrying forty men of the Pakistan Army and three white technicians, it travelled fast up the new tarmac into the Sulaiman Range, three armoured personnel carriers climbing between the mountains. When the convoy reached the first floodlit gate in the ring of fences around the closed area, the officer, who was riding separately in a Land-Rover, waved a sheaf of papers at the guards. 'There is trouble in the capital.' He spoke crisply in educated English. 'I have orders to take control of the complex and strengthen its security.'

Although the place was supposed to be top secret, it was so remote that there had never been any trouble, bar the murder of Dr Syed a few weeks back. The sentries spent much of the day squatting in the sun, gazing at the distant ice-blue and white peaks if the air was clear, and playing cards. The sudden invasion caught them off balance; it was past midnight – and who was going to argue with the insignia of a full colonel? Hurriedly they opened the metal gates and pointed the way to the administration hut.

The hut stood on an area of gravel, also blazing with white light, just outside the entrance to the tunnel bored into the rock face of the mountain, large enough for an eight-wheeled missile carrier to drive down into the storage caves. The man in charge was a warrant officer, class two, who dashed out to salute the colonel and obey his instructions. He had already received a telex from Islamabad telling him to do so.

The colonel was driven into the hillside in his Land-Rover, through three sets of steel blast-proof doors, each guarded by machine-guns. Deep in the rock, he was shown the interconnecting caves, bright light from neon tubes glinting on rough walls and the grey metal of the bomb racks. One small cave had been turned into an office, where two young men in white coats sat before a battery of dials, monitoring conditions. The colonel shook hands and peered at their equipment. 'The radiation level looks quite low?'

'There are only ten warheads, sir, and the HEU is of high purity. The radiation level is higher than it would be outside, but mainly alpha, pretty harmless.'

'What would happen if you had an accident? Say a minor explosion caused by a vehicle catching fire?'

'There are sprinklers to put out any fire, sir, but the weapons are just scrap metal until they are armed with the detonation mechanism. Nothing would happen if we had an accident. Even if the roof fell in, nothing would happen.'

The officer seemed satisfied, nodded and marched back to his Land-Rover. 'Looks jolly efficient, sar'nt major. Good show. This tunnel the only way in?'

'Two other small ones, sir, for ventilation and emergencies, only big enough for a man crawling. They come out further up the mountain, closed off by steel gates. Would you like to see them?'

'No, I'll send one of the men up to check.' They bumped along the rock tunnel towards the circle of light at the entrance. A hundred yards inside, a group of soldiers was already at work with a whining electric drill. The WO2 looked at the colonel questioningly.

'Additional security precautions, sar'nt major. Top secret.' The officer rubbed his nose with his forefinger conspiratorially.

153

Two hours later the whole of the existing guard had been relieved and despatched down the valley. The Russian NCO reported that he was ready to place the charges and the colonel summoned the warrant officer and the two young scientists. 'Because of the disturbances in the capital, I have been ordered to conduct a short exercise to check the new security arrangements. Since these are secret and I have not yet been given authority to indoctrinate you, you will return to the hotel in Mina Bazar until I telephone you to return.' The sergeant major looked doubtful. 'It's okay. You will shortly receive a personal order from your GOC, confirming this. One cannot be too careful.'

It was three in the morning when twenty of the new guards also left, in one of the armoured troop carriers. The others were all in place underground. The colonel and his three technicians sat in the hut on canvas chairs, waiting for the helicopter. They had found several pint bottles of beer in a refrigerator and one of the Russians opened them with his pocket knife. 'I thought these blackarses were all teetotal.'

The Pakistani laughed. 'And I thought you blighters were, since your Lemonade Joe took over?'

The Hind gunship arrived right on time, clattering overhead, invisible in the darkness until two searchlights under its fuselage were switched on. It descended slowly, wary of air currents and the peaks all around, until it bumped on the ground a hundred yards away, huge rotors, fifty feet in diameter, swirling up clouds of dust in the white glare. When the twin turbos stopped, the air cleared and automatic steps came down from the steel and glass of the cabin. The colonel noticed that the munition pods under the stubby wings were armed with rockets, but the bomb racks were carrying extra fuel tanks.

One of the Russian technicians spoke with an officer from the Hind, then walked slowly back to the wooden case containing the detonation equipment. The explosions were over in five minutes. First the long rumble from deep in the mountain, as rock cascaded down to bury the caves and their contents; followed by the crash as flame and flints spurted from the mouth of the tunnel, and the crack of the smaller charges in the ventilation shafts. When the smoke cleared, billowing away into the darkness, the four men stood at the entrance to the tunnel. The lights in its roof had gone out, but those outside were still burning. With the beam of a flashlight, the men could see that the tunnel now ended after a few yards in a solid wall of boulders. 'It will take bloody years to dig that lot out.'

The colonel rounded on the Russian. 'I thought we were going to evacuate the men first – there were twenty young soldiers down there!'

The Russian shrugged. He was a hard-nosed *Spetsnaz* and knew his orders. Whoever was blamed for destroying the bunker, the deaths would give added spice; and at least half the world would blame America – or the Israelis.

The colonel said nothing but removed his insignia and tossed the scraps of metal into the rubble. If it was meant to be a significant gesture it fell flat, for the others were already walking towards the gunship. He hurried after them. 'We fly to Islamabad, yes? Then on to Kabul?'

The Russian shook his head. 'No, we've just received a message on the helicopter's radio. Things have changed – Zia's dead all right, but the army's on the streets everywhere. Islamabad isn't safe for us.'

'That is very bad news.'

The Russian gave a twisted grin. His job was almost complete and he didn't give a monkey's what these blackarses did to each other. He fell back a few yards behind the others and pulled out his Makarov, raising it silently to eye level. The first shot caught the Pakistani colonel in the small of the back and he collapsed with a stifled cry of surprise. The Russian placed two more shots carefully into his head, kneeling to check that he was dead. He glanced back over his shoulder at the man in flying kit. 'I trust you've got something decent to eat in that gin palace of yours.' He ripped off the colonel's identity disc. 'I've had enough filthy goat to last me a lifetime.'

31

Kahuta

Sarah reeled back, her cheek stinging. 'You hit me! You bastard!'

Nazim seized her by the shoulders and shook her violently. 'Shut up. Can't you see the danger we're in?' He gestured to her to put on a white coat hanging behind the office door and turned on his heel. She followed him in silence, still fingering her smarting cheek, down the stairs and across the yard to another building. Warm sun was already dispersing the mist of dawn. They stood on a steel balcony, looking down the centrifuge hall, its miles of black piping twisting like spaghetti.

'Now listen carefully.' He waved a clipboard as if explaining something technical to her, although the huge building seemed to be silent and empty. 'I hope we're alone here. I'm sorry you were arrested, but I came very close to it myself. I got you out as soon as I could.'

Sarah met his eyes grimly. 'This had better be good, Nazim.'

'A man came to the bungalow in the early hours, after the dinner party two nights ago.'

'How the hell did he get in, with all those dogs and guards?'

'He was a colonel in our army, in uniform with proper identity papers, and said he had an urgent message so they didn't turn him away. He made them get me out of bed.'

'Who was he? What did he want?'

'I had never seen him before, but I knew his name – he was at university with me. He had a reputation for being straight, not involved in politics. He said he had come to warn me that I was under suspicion and due to be arrested next morning.'

'Why were you under suspicion?'

'He said Zia had launched an investigation into leaks about the programme and a bastard called Ibrahim had denounced me. He's an old enemy – I don't believe he knew anything concrete, he just wanted to damage me.'

Sarah was still shaking with anger. 'Did you believe him?'

'Yes, I did – I'd had a sense of being watched ever since I got back to Pakistan and it made sense. So I told the guards there was an emergency and I had to go back to Kahuta. They were suspicious, but did not prevent me. Then I made Farah and the children lie on the floor in the back of our car, so that they could not be seen, and just drove out of the garage and out of the gate. There are no planes at night, so I took them to the station and put them on a train to Karachi in the early hours. Farah was difficult about it, but after an argument she saw the danger, took their passports and enough money to buy air tickets to Delhi from Karachi.'

'Why didn't you go, too?'

He took her shoulders and held her at arm's length in the familiar gesture. 'What an absurd question, Cable. I came back to get you.'

Sarah stared at him suspiciously. 'Why?'

He met her eyes in puzzlement. 'Because I love you. Just that. Hadn't you noticed?' He smiled. 'Unfortunately our colonel omitted to mention that the coup would break out the same night. Although there had been great tension for days, it was still a shock when I ran into rioters and street fighting on the way back from the station. The road to your hotel was blocked and I kept being turned back. I didn't know what to do.'

'Do you know what happened to Farah?'

'Most services have broken down, but she managed to get a phone call through from the airport at Karachi. They got one of the last planes to leave. I hope to God they're safe in Delhi by now.'

Sarah's expression remained grim. 'Did you *really* come back to rescue me?' But there was relief as well as anger and fear in her voice.

'Of course. You – and the children – matter more to me than anything.' She noticed that he did not mention Farah. 'If I was due to be picked up, I thought you must be too and I had to get to you first. In the end I made it to the hotel and they told me you'd already been arrested. The manager said he had no idea where you'd been taken – it was an awful moment – so I came out here and made hundreds of phone calls until I found you. The coup had saved me from being arrested, but I had to pledge support to the new régime to get the authority for your release.'

'So I should be grateful? The Embassy would have got me out in the end.'

'You might have been dead by then. People are being killed indiscriminately. A lot of blood is flowing.'

'I'm not sure what to believe any more, Nazim. I'm glad I'm not still in that filthy jail, but if it's not a daft question just how do you plan to get us out of *here*?' Her voice was drowned by a burst of shouting from outside, followed by several shots. She ran after him, into the blazing sun, then stepped back sharply to the shadow of the wall. The steel gates to the road had been locked but a mob was passing, several hundred people carrying banners, chanting, some waving swords and rifles. In many cases the white of their clothing was splashed with blood. A dozen men were rattling the gates in a frenzy, screaming at the four soldiers who stood in a line inside, levelling their SMGs but otherwise impassive. Stones started to come over the gates, followed by bottles and bricks. The soldiers ran ten yards further into the site, turned and fired a burst into the air.

'What are they shouting?' Sarah had to yell to make herself heard above the din.

'God knows. But this place won't be safe much longer. I was hoping the rioting wouldn't reach Kahuta – maybe they've heard the news about the destruction of the bomb store.'

'What bomb store?'

'There was an underground store in the mountains. A commando unit blew it up last night. No one knows where they came from but we suspect they were *Spetsnaz*.'

'So there *is* a programme.'

'Well – there *was*. The main outline was almost the first thing I was given when I took over running Kahuta, but plainly it's been set back many years now. Maybe it's been wrecked altogether.'

'Oh Nazim, what a bloody mess.' The screams and shouts were still filling the air, but after a long burst of automatic fire there was a lull. Sarah ran after him, crouching, back to the administration building. In his office they stood just inside the open window, watching the struggle at the gates. 'How did the Russians – if it was the Russians – know about the bomb store?'

Nazim's mouth twisted wryly. 'I don't know – they must have a source in the Commission or the General Staff.'

Sarah was pacing up and down. If the Russians were behind the coup, maybe this Ibrahim was their man, maybe he had denounced Nazim to cover his own tracks . . . if so their approach had been more subtle than Nairn's. It was all too difficult. She fell into an armchair. 'Jesus, I'm so worn out.'

'There's no time to rest, Cable.' During another lull in the chanting, she realized how quiet the site was. It had emptied – the hundreds of staff had vanished, to back the coup, flee from its wrath or simply save their property. Through the window she saw a figure in blue overalls and white turban flitting between two buildings, then Nazim drew the blinds against the sun. 'Stay there while I make some tea.' He went out to the small kitchen off the outer office.

Sarah peered out of the window again, trying to assess the extent of the violence and chaos outside. The soldiers were still standing ground inside the gate, their guns smoking. The crowd had drawn back, leaving several figures on the ground collapsed in puddles of blood. No one was tending them – presumably they were dead anyway – but the mob was plainly gathering momentum for a new assault. It looked very dangerous. She realised that a phone was ringing in the outer office and heard Nazim talking.

He came back a few minutes later, his face grim. 'That was a warning from our short-lived revolutionary council. The great rising is already over, Cable. We have been witnesses to one of the biggest cock-ups in recent history.'

'What do you mean?'

'Even with Zia blown to bits the army's still in control. They're smashing the opposition everywhere – the leaders of the coup are flying out to Kabul leaving a complete shambles and a lot of old scores to be paid off. I must get you to your Embassy – you'll be safe there until it's all over.'

'What about *you*, Nazim?'

'I'll stay here till nightfall, if the guards don't run away, then slip into the mountains. There is a Land-Rover on the site; I shall provision it, add some extra cans of petrol, and make for one of the frontiers. Maybe I shall be lucky, maybe not.' He spread his hands. '*Insh'allah.*'

Sarah gestured at the ugly scene by the gates. 'Never mind nightfall – that lot will smash the gates down any minute.' She shivered. 'Let's go now. I'm scared.'

He ducked as a bullet smashed the glass a foot from his head and she followed him down to a garage. The Land-Rover was dark blue, with a metal canopy over the space behind the cab. It was already loaded with jerry cans of petrol and water, plus some shovels and a plastic box containing snow chains. 'It must have been used for the journey to the site in the mountains,' said Nazim, hastily filling more cans with petrol from the pump while Sarah packed them aboard. 'That should be enough fuel, but we need some food and waterproof clothes.'

'Is there another way out of the site?'

'Yes. The perimeter is long and the mob will only be on the road side, so we should be able to leave by one of the back gates.' They found flat loaves of *nan* and some spicy cooked meat in a kitchen, army anoraks and rubber boots in a guard room, and loaded them into the back of the vehicle. Its door pockets contained maps of the whole country. Nazim took an old Browning machine-pistol from a dead guard, removing several magazines of ammunition from his belt.

By four o'clock, they were driving between the low buildings and the rear wall, until they stopped at a solid steel gate. Nazim climbed a ladder and looked over the wall. The stretch of brown scrub outside was empty and smoke was now pouring from a fire at the other corner of the site: that would be useful cover. He unlocked the gate with his master key, locking it again when the Land-Rover was outside, and bumped off towards the dirt road about half a mile away. 'We'll go to your Embassy first.'

'Thanks, Nazim.' Sarah gripped his hand on the steering wheel. 'But forget the Embassy. It's too risky.' She gestured towards the city, where smoke was rising and shots mingled with wailing sirens. 'We'll never get there. I'm coming with you.'

32

Kabul

The dead man lay on the floor. His eyes had the blank look that Kirov had seen so many times before; so expressive in life, they turned opaque as soon as life had gone. The top of his head was missing. Blood and brain tissue – a whitish-grey mess containing chips of bone – had stained the wall and carpet, which was a pity because it was a good Bokhara.

'Shot himself through the mouth,' said the army doctor. 'As you can see. Here is my death certificate.'

'There's no other copy?'

'No, comrade General. I shall be discreet – I understand that it may be necessary to issue some more seemly version of events.'

Kirov poked at the body with her boot. 'Yes, it may. Now for God's sake take this to the mortuary, it's already starting to smell.' Two medical orderlies loaded Grigorenko onto a stretcher and covered the smashed head with a blanket. As the corpse was carried out, Kirov sat down in one of the armchairs. She had sat in the same chair three hours ago, in the same panelled office with its carpets and hangings from the ancient cities of the Silk Road. Even with armed men outside, waiting to arrest him, Grigorenko had shown remarkable courage. He had sat impassive behind the desk, alone in defeat, just as she had been alone only a few hours before.

They had faced each other tensely as she conveyed her version of Mikhail Sergeyevitch's message, speaking abruptly, in a flat tone. 'If you return to Moscow you will face a military tribunal. There will be a fair trial but you are bound to be disgraced and sent to a camp. Your family will suffer – they will lose their privileges, the apartment and *dacha* of a Colonel-General, their future. If you prefer another way, you will be buried with full military honours and they will be cared for as the family of a hero. The choice is yours, Konstantin Ivanovitch, and it is a free choice; but make it quickly.' She had left without waiting for a response. The shot had echoed down the corridor five minutes later.

Now she had already had a long meeting with Azamov, a professional soldier with no interest in politics. Suddenly catapulted to Colonel-General at only forty-two, he was still in a state of shock; but she had no doubt that he was up to it and – more importantly – would do what he was told. She felt very tired. The last few days had taken her to the brink – she had peered into the abyss and stepped back at the last minute, not an experience she wished to repeat. Tomorrow she would fly to Moscow.

It took a week for the *Sea of Azov* to reach the Balearic Islands. Levshin was almost the only passenger on deck when the liner steamed into the long fjord of Mahon harbour between two rocky headlands, one topped by the fortress where he had been a Nationalist prisoner in 1938. He had seen a pilot join them from a small launch a mile or so out and the same man was up there on the bridge now, as the massive ship steered down the channel, past yachts and fishing boats flying the Spanish flag. The town rose up steeply on the left of the harbour; the other shore was barren, except for a few modern villas.

Menorca was not of great interest to Russian cruise passengers, most of whom were below getting ready for dinner, and they would be there only one night. Levshin watched as the liner's engines went astern, rumbling across the narrow stretch of water, and she bumped gently against the slimy wooden piles of the quay. There were a few other ships in the harbour – an American frigate, a four-masted Italian navy training schooner, several rusty freighters – but Menorca had the sleepy feeling that he was counting on.

Levshin slept badly that night. Next morning he forced himself to eat a leisurely breakfast, then returned to his cabin. He was planning to leave everything behind, except the jacket of his suit, which now had both bank passbooks sewn into its lining; he wore a sports shirt, light trousers and a sweater, for it was overcast, throwing the jacket over his shoulder. He let a few other passengers down the gangway first, then followed, strolling away casually into Mahon. No wall or gates contained the dock area, so within minutes he was climbing a long flight of steps, through gardens with palm trees, up to the narrow streets of the old town.

He had changed a few roubles for pesetas on the ship, so he was able to buy a coffee in the *Plaza de la Explanada*. There was a bus standing close by, almost full and plainly about to leave. Levshin climbed aboard and sat next to an old woman in black, nursing a basket of chickens. It did not matter where the bus was going.

33

Karakoram Highway

They drove across the strip of scrubland in tense silence, fearful that they might be seen by rioters or soldiers, but after five minutes Nazim nosed the Land-Rover down into a dry *nullah*, where they bumped along between its mud walls below ground level. Within twenty minutes they were mounting a rough track into the hills and Sarah rummaged through the maps in the door pocket. She pulled one out. 'How odd. This map is Russian.'

'All the most useful maps here are Russian – they've been interested in Afghanistan and what is now Pakistan for a very long time.'

'I suppose so. At least the place names are in English. Which way are we going, Nazim?'

'If we go due east we'll hit the frontier in about fifty miles, then cross the disputed border area in Kashmir, but after that we'd be safe in India. The drawback is that the army will be expecting a lot of people to flee that way, so it will certainly be blocked. They'll have a list of those marked for arrest – and photographs.'

'Is there an alternative?'

'We can't go south – that leads straight to Lahore which is stiff with soldiers. We'll have to take the Karakoram Highway to the north. Officially it's closed from the end of October, so I hope it's not blocked by snow.'

Sarah looked back at the twin towns below, Rawalpindi and the new capital. Columns of smoke hung over them, but they were too far away to hear more than the occasional explosion. Dust was rising over the road from the south. 'Is that a column of tanks?' she asked.

'Probably. This must have been the shortest coup in living memory – to the outside world it won't look more than an assassination and a few riots.'

'It pays to have the army on your side – even that collection of left-wing idiots ought to have known that.' Nazim grunted agreement, struggling with the steering wheel as the Land-Rover rocked

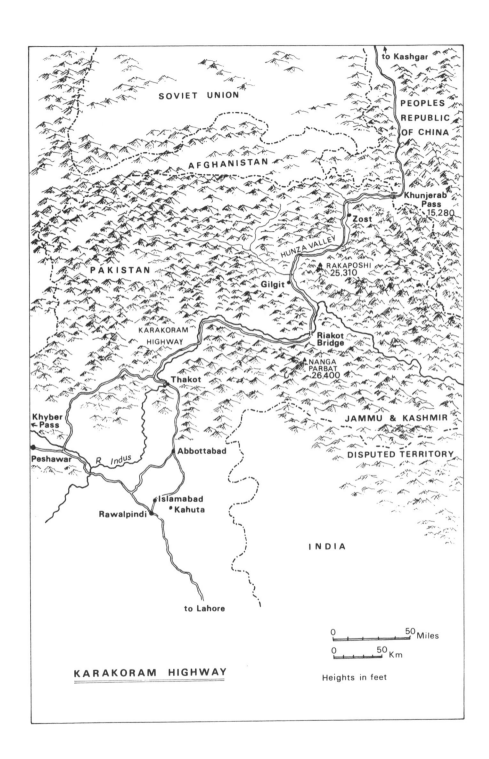

SOVIET UNION

PEOPLES
REPUBLIC
OF CHINA

to Kashgar

AFGHANISTAN

Khunjerab
Pass
15,280

Zost

HUNZA VALLEY

RAKAPOSHI
25,310

PAKISTAN

Gilgit

KARAKORAM
HIGHWAY

Riakot
Bridge

NANGA
PARBAT
26,400

Thakot

JAMMU & KASHMIR

Khyber
Pass

DISPUTED TERRITORY

Abbottabad

Peshawar   R Indus

Islamabad
Kahuta

Rawalpindi

INDIA

to Lahore

0   50 Miles

0   50 Km

KARAKORAM HIGHWAY

Heights in feet

164

from side to side, engine roaring as its wheels slipped on the loose shale. 'Tell me, Nazim – do you believe the Russians ever meant to support them?'

'I shouldn't think so.' He changed into a higher gear and the engine stopped screaming as they emerged into a wilderness of scrubby trees and rock, which went on for miles. They passed through a village, watched by men lounging on charpoys under awnings made of straw, a bullock endlessly turning a wheel to draw water from the well. Further on women were working in small fields cleared on the hillside. 'They seem to have missed the revolution,' muttered Sarah drily.

After two hours they were descending towards the waters of a lake, first down a slope strewn with boulders, then on a stretch of dirt track. The roadblock came as a shock. They ran into it just after rounding a corner: four soldiers facing them with rifles and a machine-gun mounted between sand-bags. A metal barrier had been placed across the road. Nazim hesitated, then pointed sharply to the machine-pistol and accelerated. Sarah scrambled into the back, buffeted by the collection of jerry cans and bruising a knee on the shovels, until she was lying prone with the barrel resting on the metal tail-board and the safety catch off.

She heard shouts and a shot outside. The Land-Rover was swaying wildly and moving very fast. There was a shuddering crash and the floor seemed to leap in the air. Then she could see the wreckage of the barrier and the machine-gun being turned to follow them. Sarah squeezed the trigger and felt the stock of the gun pounding into her shoulder as she sprayed a long burst of bullets from one side of the road to the other. It was the first time she had fired a gun since her training at Bovington six years ago. The explosions hurt her ear-drums, but she saw a soldier fall and the others ran for cover in a ditch. As Nazim accelerated away, the scene was hidden in a cloud of dust and she lay there panting, feeling her heart beating very fast.

They hit the tarmac surface of the Karakoram Highway about an hour later. It was dark and there was no one to challenge them. 'Any roadblocks would be nearer the city,' muttered Nazim. He turned onto the new road and soon they were moving along at a steady fifty miles an hour, stopping once to refill the fuel tank from the jerry cans.

'Will we have enough petrol?' asked Sarah anxiously.

'I hope so. How do you feel – you were magnificent with that machine pistol.'

'I was bloody terrified!'

'You're a better shot than me. Now we'll take turns and drive right through the night, try to get clear before they really start to mop up.'

Anatoly Levshin was relaxing on the terrace of a cafe in Menorca, overlooking the entrance to the long harbour and sipping a glass of *San Miguel* beer in the evening sun. He had spent the day curled up in a cave on a lonely beach and now he was watching the *Sea of Azov* gliding slowly out to sea. The rumble of engines drifted across the rippling water, passengers leaning over the rail as the Spanish flag was lowered and the hammer and sickle raised. He grinned broadly. They were going without him. He wanted to stand and wave, but thought better of it. Instead he raised his glass in a silent toast. 'Fuck Lenin,' he muttered. 'Fuck Stalin, fuck Malenkov, fuck Khrushchev, fuck Brezhnev, fuck Andropov, fuck Chernenko, fuck Gorbachev, fuck Malinovsky.' He would leave it for a day or two and then report to the police and ask for asylum. He had a hundred thousand dollars in the bank, so they wouldn't refuse him – and this island looked pleasant enough.

In London, Nairn was thumbing through the sheaf of telegrams that had arrived from Islamabad and Karachi. The telephone lines were dead and the airports closed to normal flights, so he had no other way of knowing what was happening in Pakistan. Plainly the attempted coup had failed, which was no great surprise. The unidentified sabotage squad had answered the questions he had put to Nazim Khan, who was no longer of much interest to him. There was still no sign of Sarah, but he assumed that she would be released by now and have the sense to take refuge in the Embassy.

Sarah was driving when they passed Gilgit. They had climbed thousands of feet into the foothills of the Karakorams, but the Land-Rover had kept going, grinding round hairpins, picking up a little speed on the flat stretches, slithering where the hard surface gave way to wet gravel. They had stopped again to refuel, then pressed on through the darkness, running into a rainstorm but feeling elated as the miles fell away. There were no more roadblocks, no sign of the army. 'What time is it?' Her eyes felt painful in their sockets as she peered through the screen, her teeth grating at the scrape of the wipers.

'About four in the morning,' he yawned. 'We'll soon be right up in the mountains.'

'Does that mean we're safe?'

'No. We're in danger until we hit the frontier – the army will be after us just as long as we're on Pakistani soil. Maybe longer.'

She shivered. 'Do you think they *are* still after us?' She wished that she could see his face in the dark.

'You bet they are. The Generals will want some scapegoats for losing their toy bomb.'

'They've got to find us first.'

'They may have identified us from that bloody roadblock – in which case they'll know we're on this road. But we'll make it, Cable, we'll make it.' He yawned again. 'You sound knackered – shall we stop for just a couple of hours? We could risk it. They can't search for us up here at night.'

Sarah parked under a rock face, towering above them like a cliff, and they both climbed into the back, making a space to curl up in the jumble of jerry cans and tools, wincing as metal corners cut into their limbs. Nazim put his arms around her and pulled the blanket over them. She was asleep in minutes.

34

Hunza Valley

The last village in the Hunza valley, before the road rises steeply, is Zost – 9,500 feet up, the air already thin and enervating. Sarah steered the Land-Rover between the low houses at speed, scattering chickens and goats, the back wheels slithering on a sheet of ice. Nazim expected a military post and clutched the Browning with both hands, but there was no challenge.

They began the long, slow climb to the pass, twisting around tight hairpins for hour after hour. At first the heater blasted hot air into the cab, but then it died with a rattle and the windscreen started to ice up. Nazim stopped and got out to scrape the ice away, huddling into his anorak against the flurries of snow. As they climbed higher, the patches of grass gave way to scrubby brown bushes on which thin goats grazed, then to rock and shale patched with snow. On one side of the road was a rock face, blasted jagged from the mountain, on the other a sheer drop with no barrier to mark the edge.

The jeep covered endless miles in low gear, its engine racing noisily with a lull for the change down at each corner, before it revved to pull them up the next incline. Shimmering air revealed the pinnacles of mountains in all directions, snow-capped, towering over the black ice of a glacier or the pink and green of a village deep in a valley. As suddenly as they had emerged into the sun, the sky darkened and they ran into cloud and heavy, penetrating rain. Sarah turned a corner and stamped on the brakes to avoid running into a heap of earth and boulders across the road. Nazim cursed. 'A bloody landslide.'

'What do we do?'

'We get out and shovel – that's what the tools in the back are for. I just hope it doesn't take for ever.'

They had both been wrapped in sweaters and anoraks against the cold, but soon he was stripped to the waist and Sarah to her tee-shirt, as they toiled to dig a track through, panting as they rolled boulders to the edge and watched them crash down the hillside, then shovelling at the wet shale. The rain stopped and their clothes began to steam in a burst of sun. Sarah mopped her head with a handkerchief. 'Christ it's sweaty. I hope we don't have to do this too often.'

'We can't afford to stop again. They must still be after us – and it's none too safe to be out of the vehicle.' He nodded down the slope to where a snow leopard was ripping at the carcase of an ibex it had killed.

Giving themselves no time to rest the Land-Rover whined on upwards, this time with Nazim driving. At one point they heard a helicopter clattering overhead, but he did not slacken speed. 'There's nowhere to hide – and nowhere much for them to land. We just have to keep going until we hit the border and hope to God they don't get there first.'

'The Chinese border?'

'Yes. Once we get over the pass we're in China.'

Sarah gripped the metal doorframe as they skidded round another hairpin, grey rock changing giddily to blue sky outside. 'If it's not a silly question, what happens then?'

He shrugged. 'We shall be safe, at least I hope so.'

'But how do we get out? We'll be thousands of miles from anywhere.'

'Let's get there before we start worrying about that. I hope there's a Chinese army post at the frontier, otherwise it's another two hundred miles to Kashgar.'

'They *will* let us in, won't they?'

'Sure, we're refugees.' She wondered why he sounded so confident. They drove on in companionable silence, taking turns to goad the Land-Rover ever higher until Sarah's arms and ankles were aching with the strain. When night fell Nazim went on driving, the yellow pencil beams of their headlights probing forward in the darkness. He slowed down with a curse as they illuminated the puzzled face of a yak, standing stupidly in the road in front of them. He revved the engine and hammered on the metal of the door until the animal loped off, its feet slithering on the loose shingle.

It was when he pressed the accelerator again that the engine coughed and died. After much whirring of the starter they drove on for several more miles, rain beating against the windows. One of the wipers stopped working, but the one in front of Nazim continued, though too slowly to clear the cascade of water on the screen. They passed a stone by the road showing they had reached 13,000 feet. 'Another two thousand to go. I think we're going to make it!'

169

A mile further and the engine died again, coughing back into life for a few seconds as the starter whirred, but stopping when he tried to put the Land-Rover into gear. 'Don't run the battery right down, love.' Sarah shivered when this happened for the third time, flinching at the dark wilderness outside. 'Please – we'll never get the thing going again.'

'I'd like to kill that yak. The jerk when we stopped must have disturbed some dirt in the carburettor. I'd better get out and have a look.' He rummaged in the toolbox between the hard leather seats. 'Oh shit.'

'What's up?'

'The Pakistan army has forgotten to include a torch, or someone has swiped the bloody thing.'

Sarah sank back into the corner, closing her eyes in exhaustion, listening to the sleet smashing against the windows. A trickle of water was running down the inside of the glass. 'I think I'm going to die anyway, it's so bitterly cold.'

'Let's rest for a bit. If I mess around with the engine now, I shan't be able to see anything and we'll get the electrics so wet it'll never start again. But it's already two in the morning – there'll be daylight in a few hours.'

The storm woke them about an hour later. Rain and sleet hammered on the metal roof, water poured in through the canvas back-flaps, howling wind started to rock the Land-Rover from side to side. 'Jesus Christ.' Sarah sat upright with a jerk. 'If it goes on like this we'll be blown over the edge.'

Nazim held her tightly, peering out through the streaming windscreen. Lightning lit up the hillside. 'Look, isn't that a hut over there?' He pointed to a patch of stones shaped like a beehive, a little way up the slope.

Outside he piled rocks around the wheels, hoping to save the jeep from going over the precipice, and they struggled towards the small building, leaning into the gale and drenched with rain. The refuge was derelict but dry, the lightning showing that it contained nothing but a heap of dry sticks piled in the corner. Crouching in the dark, Nazim found some matches in his pocket and managed to light a small fire, despite the wind gusting down the chimney. At first the smoke choked them, but then it cleared, the flames flickered weirdly on the rough walls and it smouldered comfortingly as they took off their boots and huddled together for warmth, entwined on the floor of beaten earth.

35

Karakoram

Sarah woke at about five. The storm had died and she felt a curious mixture of emotions, both protected and protective as she studied Nazim's face in the glow from the embers. Asleep he looked young, at peace, with a slight smile on his lips. She had a strong urge to make love, with a nagging fear that there might not be many more chances to do so, but it was too cold to remove any clothing. His arms were around her and she wanted to keep them there, but knew that they had to move; it would soon be dawn and they were still in danger. Gently she rearranged his limbs, so that he rolled on his back without waking, and stood up.

But before she could go outside to check the weather, he stirred and she turned back to see his eyes open. After the carnal thoughts of a few nights before, the best she could manage was to kneel and kiss his eyelids. He smiled and hugged her. 'I love you, Cable.'

She kissed him on the mouth. 'I love you too, Nazim.' But she was troubled by the exhaustion in his face and, asserting herself, she rested her knees on either side of him and lay astride his body, pressing herself to him. 'Even if I can never understand everything about you, I *love* you.'

They lay there silently for several minutes. He was still smiling, stroking her face, when a shadow appeared in the doorway. She turned and gasped. It was a man in a state of collapse, hair lank from the rain, khaki parka torn, hands bleeding where he had fallen.

'Ahmed Wazir!' Nazim sat up sharply. 'How the hell did *you* get here? I thought you'd all flown out to Kabul?'

The man sank to the floor in exhaustion. 'No, only a few. I was trying to escape in an army truck – there were hundreds trying to get away by this route, but the military put up a roadblock near Jalkot.' He was talking fast, nervously, trembling. 'I bluffed my way through because I was wearing army uniform; I guess most of the others were arrested, I haven't seen anyone else for hours. The bloody truck broke down after I'd passed Hunza and I've been walking through the rain all night.'

Sarah flinched as tension flashed between the two men: she could feel Nazim's humanity battling with an unexplained distaste. Then he stood and helped the other man sit up against the wall. 'Wazir was one of the Revolutionary Council,' he explained, helping him to drink from the water bottle. 'One of the great leaders of the coup . . .' there was a flash of contempt '. . . as it happens, the one who tried to prevent your release from prison.' Suddenly Nazim pulled the bottle away and his voice cut through the air like a whiplash. 'Still thirsty, Wazir? Remember this girl could have died if she'd been left in that jail. They were shooting prisoners at random – and you damn well knew it.'

'I'm sorry.' Wazir slumped against the wall shivering, eyes half closed. 'Does it matter any more? My feet are bleeding. Please help me! For God's sake help me.'

Nazim seemed to soften. 'Yes, Wazir, we'll help you so long as you can keep up with us. What's going on down there?'

'They've sworn in the Speaker of the Senate as acting President and restored martial law. I should think everything will be very quiet in Islamabad by now. They caught three of the Council, hanged them outside parliament, along with a few top civil servants who'd taken the wrong side . . .' His voice tailed away, his eyes staring at them opaque and empty.

'Any news of Kahuta?'

'A mob got in but the army threw them out. Not before they'd hacked some of your old colleagues to pieces and destroyed a lot of machinery.'

'I thought the place was empty when we left.'

'That little runt Ibrahim and some others went down there with a few soldiers – to defend it I suppose.'

'Ibrahim is dead?'

'They were all killed.' Wazir's eyes closed again.

'I'm not wasting much sympathy there – he tried to get me taken by the army just before your coup.' Nazim knelt and shook the man's shoulders. 'I know you're tired, Ahmed, but try to concentrate for a minute or two – I need to know if they're after us. If so, what's the road like? Do we stand a chance?'

Wazir nodded. 'They're after you, me and everyone else with the slightest involvement in the coup. But there've been a lot of land-slides lower down and one army convoy was swept away. Now they're trying helicopters.' He slumped back again and the atmosphere was too tense to bear. Sarah made for the door, leaving the two men alone. Outside there had been a fall of snow and the Land-Rover had gone, swept away in an avalanche. The temperature had dropped, the surface was icy and the wind cut through her clothes like a razor. She shivered and was turning back to the hut when Nazim appeared in the doorway; instinctively she started to run towards him, cursing as she slipped on the ice. The pain shot through her ankle as she fell and went on in sickening spasms as she tried to stand.

'Damn, damn, *damn*.' She stared up at him through tears of frustration. He sat her down and took the ankle in his hands carefully. 'It's not broken, is it?'

'I don't think so. Let's see if it's sprained. Try to put your weight on it.' He lifted her up, his gentleness contrasting so much with the moment of fury in the hut that for a wild moment she wondered whether he had killed the other man. She winced as she tried to stand. 'It's not too bad, Nazim. It hurts, but I'll be able to walk. How much further is it to the border?'

'It will take at least another day on foot.'

'What about this fellow Wazir?'

Nazim shrugged. 'We can't very well leave the bastard. The trouble is he's almost dead on his feet.' He removed his arm from Sarah's shoulders and watched her grimace of pain as she took a few steps. 'That foot looks bad, it's getting colder and we're both exhausted. Losing the Land-Rover is a bloody disaster – we need something to replace it.' He looked pensive. 'Look – I don't know exactly where we are any more, but I've still got the map and, if it's accurate, there ought to be a small hamlet an hour or two away. I've still got a wallet stuffed with rupees and I'm going to walk up there, see if I can buy a donkey. Okay? Then I'll walk, you ride, Wazir can crawl if he hasn't died of hypothermia.'

She clung to him. 'Don't leave me here, Nazim! What if you get lost? I'd be alone.' She shivered. 'I'm scared.'

'You'll be quite safe, Cable.' He stuck the Browning in his belt. 'And I shan't be gone long.'

She hobbled back to the hut, clutching him for support, and they had reached the doorway when they heard the helicopter again and hid inside, Nazim peering up at the black speck following the line of the road. 'Perhaps they'll see the wreckage of the Land-Rover and come looking to see if we're in it. We haven't got long – I'll be as quick as I can.'

When Nazim had been gone an hour, the sun vanished and again it became very cold. It was dim in the hut with the door closed against the wind and she sat with the Browning on her knees, eyeing Ahmed Wazir slumped against the other wall. Neither of them spoke. They both jerked at the crash of splintering wood, turning with frightened eyes to the oblong of light where the door had been kicked in.

After a long pause, a group of bearded men crowded in silently, each wearing a floppy woollen cap and shrouded in a rough brown cape. One took two steps into the hut, threatening them with his Kalashnikov, snarling in a dialect Sarah did not recognise. Wazir looked terrified. The man started to shout and there was plainly an argument going on. Sarah seized Wazir's arm. 'What's he saying? Who are they? Can't they help us?'

He pulled away roughly and she felt the tension in his body. 'These people are dangerous, for God's sake leave it to me.' He snapped out an angry sentence in the strange dialect, then turned back to her, talking very fast. 'They're Mujahedin or men from one of the mountain villages, guiding some soldiers. They're hunting Nazim and me. Keep quiet and I'll try to keep you out of it.'

Two of them pulled him to his feet and started to drag him outside. He screamed at them and Sarah leapt up to join in the struggle, but felt a sickening blow on her shoulder and fell to the floor. Giddily she watched the metal gun-butt whirl in space and flash down to strike her on the side of the head. She cried out at the pain and felt blood pouring down her cheek. Her legs were seized and they dragged her through the door, scraping her back and head on the stones.

Outside there were about twenty armed men, standing in a circle around Wazir, who was held between two of them. Some of them were soldiers – one was roaring at Wazir and he was shaking with terror. Several times she heard the name Rashid Khan in the furious babble. The helicopter stood a quarter of a mile away, but it was far too small to take the whole party, most of whom must have arrived on foot. Standing up painfully, she realised that Wazir was calling to her. 'They won't harm you if they see you're a woman, but they don't believe me. Show them!'

Suddenly she was pushed into the circle and became the focus of attention. She saw that Wazir's arms were tied behind him, but he kept gesturing at her with his head and shouting. He was struck in the face and his lip split but he went on shouting through the blood. Both her arms were held, but she aimed a kick at the man to her right. He relaxed his grip and she pulled her arm away, her hood falling back to let her hair fall free. A man who seemed to be the leader stared at her, then approached menacingly. His eyes were piercingly dark and his breath stank of rotting teeth as he searched her face. Without speaking, he zipped open her parka and gripped the sweater beneath. Shrinking back, she saw that his wrists were bony and covered in black hair.

He ripped the sweater, then her shirt, exposing her chest to the waist. His hands seized one of her breasts and twisted it painfully, then he seemed satisfied, struck her twice across the face and turned away. Cheeks stinging, Sarah was too shocked to speak as they dragged her back inside the hut, where she was thrown face down and felt her wrists tied tightly behind her, then her ankles roped together.

They left her alone. She rolled on her side and tried to wriggle towards the door, but found she was tethered by a rope joining her wrists and ankles that passed through an iron ring in the wall. Panting with the effort, she twisted to sit up, terrified that Nazim might come back. Outside she heard boots stamping on the rock, then a tense silence, broken by a sharp cry of pain. After some murmuring, she started in horror at the long, hideous scream, so loud that it echoed between the walls of the pass. There was another animal shriek, then another, smothered in jerking groans. A figure appeared in the doorway, spat in her direction and hurled something on the floor. It landed with a wet slap, like a fish on a marble slab. Sarah stared at it and choked on a surge of vomit. It was a hand, severed at the wrist and covered in blood.

The rope was long enough to let her reach the door and she peered out again cautiously. Most of the group was hidden, but she could see Wazir kneeling, half-naked and streaked in blood, one arm hanging uselessly at his side, his body jerking as a pistol fired. As he collapsed on the gravel, a man stepped forward unsheathing a knife and she turned away, choking again as she saw him start to hack off the head. There was a scrape of boots retreating on the hillside and she realised that they were leaving her behind. She heard the helicopter take off, closed her eyes and wept silently, praying that Nazim would come back, but not too soon.

Sarah did not know how many hours she spent huddled rigid against the stone wall. The hut had no windows and its half-darkness was comforting. She told herself to be practical, ease the knots, get free; but part of her mind was already numb, and after a few tugs she gave up. She had suppressed her terror while they butchered Wazir, but now she wept, lost in a wave of passive despair, shuddering with sobs of revulsion. Eventually the exhaustion of pain and misery began to spread through her and she became light-headed, sight blurred and head spinning. It was dusk outside, and she was wondering vaguely if she would die in the cold of the night, when she lost consciousness.

The hut was dark when the shaking woke her and she blinked, instinctively recognising the shape of his head. 'Wake up, Cable. It's me, Nazim. I've got a donkey.'

36

Karakoram Summit

That second night in the hut was long and cold. Nazim had run out of matches, so there was no fire, and Sarah's ankle and bruises throbbed painfully. She lay in his arms, sweating from a fever, haunted by nightmares whenever she fell into disturbed sleep: reliving the horror of the day, but with Nazim as victim. Several times she woke in terror, hearing his voice soothing her. 'It's all right, Cable, it's all right. You're safe now.'

At first light they set out along the snow-covered track, with more poised to fall from low grey clouds, Sarah astride the bony donkey led by Nazim. They both felt exhausted and light-headed, having eaten nothing for twenty-four hours, but he still had the water bottle from the jeep and filled it from a mountain stream. Sarah could not stop shivering. 'Christ, it's so cold.' She shifted on the donkey. 'And uncomfortable – how much did you pay for this clapped-out beast?'

'All the rupees I had left.'

'Do you think she'll last out to the border?'

'It's a he. I hope so.' Nazim looked up at the black zig-zag of the road, climbing for miles through the snow until it vanished behind the shoulder of a mountain. 'God, I hope so.'

They wound upwards between the sheer drop and the rock face, only the donkey sure-footed on the ice and loose shale. Sarah kept glancing anxiously at the sky for the black dot of a helicopter, haunted by the image of Wazir's death. 'Will Farah and the children be safe?' she asked suddenly.

'With luck they arrived in Delhi before we were forced to run.' He spoke casually but she could tell he was afraid for them.

They rounded another hairpin, the donkey stopping to devour a tuft of grass growing out of a patch of snow. Nazim jerked it back to the track. Snowflakes had turned his hair white and there were flecks of ice in his thick eyebrows, but he swung on like a machine. Sarah stared at him as she gasped for breath in the thin air, reassured by his strength but putting together all the little inconsistencies she had noticed since they left Kahuta. They were alone, cold, at the brink, and she was no longer interested in pretence. 'It was you that betrayed the bomb store so the *Spetsnaz* could destroy it, wasn't it, Nazim?' She spoke deliberately, just loud enough to be heard above the whine of the wind. 'All that stuff about midnight visitors was hokum?'

She waited for the explosion, but none came. He frowned at her, trudging on through the snow. 'They knew roughly where it was in the mountains, but I helped them pinpoint it. Why not?' His mouth twisted contemptuously. 'Didn't it solve the problem all those pillocks of society in their warm offices claimed to be so bothered about?'

'Why did you lie to me?'

'Did I lie to you, Cable? I suppose I was putting it off. I needed time to explain, that's all – we've had too much to do just to survive.' He sighed. 'Does it matter any more?'

'Of course it bloody matters.' The donkey paused and she kicked its flanks until it started moving again. 'And what was so difficult to explain – I don't understand.'

'I wasn't born in Pakistan, Cable. It never felt like home. I never felt that I belonged.'

'What the devil is that supposed to mean?'

They stumbled on as the sky blackened and sleet began to fall. The wind was rising, whipping frozen splinters against their faces. 'I believed that the weapons programme was dangerous – absurd when we can't even feed ourselves – and ought to be stopped before something insane happened. Just that. No more, no less. So I approached the Australians, not knowing quite what I expected to happen.'

'So how come you end up working for the Russians?'

He shot an angry glance over his shoulder. 'I told you – I wasn't working *for* anybody. I went to what seemed to be a friendly Western country for help, but they pushed me too hard. It got dangerous, I didn't like the way they tried to blackmail me – or the way they put you at risk.' He shrugged. 'And they wanted too much, they thought they could turn me into some kind of long-term agent – so I began to think I'd made the wrong choice. Then I was back in Pakistan and it was plain there was going to be a coup against Zia.'

'You must have been expecting that.'

He shook his head, dragging the donkey round a fallen boulder. 'Not so soon. I suppose I was out of touch. There was tension and unrest, but I was flabbergasted when they came to me a few days after I returned and asked me to join them.'

'Just like that?' Sarah chanced her arm. 'You mean you'd *never* been mixed up with them – whoever they were – before?' The suspicion in her voice was unmistakable.

He turned on her furiously. 'Don't piss me about, Cable.' He gestured at the bleak landscape, grey ice and rock under a black sky in every direction. 'This is no place for lies. If we don't trust each other we won't make it. Get one thing bloody clear – I've been my own man all my life. I almost stayed in America; I could have lived there quite easily. But I came back to Pakistan, gave them everything for twenty years and finally found I couldn't stomach Zia. Of course I knew the group that came to me was backed by Moscow. So what? I wanted to see a change and it didn't *matter* where our help came from. Can't you understand?'

'Sort of. But the Russians let you down, didn't they?'

He nodded sombrely. 'I'm puzzled about that. Something changed. They just slaughtered a few Mujahedin, blew up the store and withdrew; if they'd given the support they promised, we'd still be in Islamabad.' He stopped abruptly as they rounded a corner, then dragged the donkey back into the shadow of the rock face. 'Get off quickly, Cable.' He gripped her arm painfully. 'And if you want to stay alive for God's sake don't make a sound.'

Ahead of them the track dipped into a wide combe. Half a mile away the black shape of a helicopter stood on the snow; and a line of soldiers was advancing slowly towards them.

Nairn landed at Delhi airport at nine in the morning, nearly two hours late. It was sweltering in the arrival hall and he was deafened by the babble of English and Hindi. Mountford-White pushed through the crowd and guided him to the diplomatic channel. Outside, the sun was blinding on the peeling white walls of the terminal as old Ambassador taxis hooted their way through the sweating mass of porters and pedal rickshaws. Nairn settled into the back of the white Granada. 'I've only got two days, Alan, then I must get on to Singapore.'

'Thank you for stopping off, sir. I've been a bit overwhelmed lately.' Mountford-White crossed one elegant tropical-suited leg over the other as they passed a farm, an old man stretched on a charpoy outside his hut built entirely of woven straw. The car braked as the driver narrowly missed a cart pulled by two white bullocks, picking its way through a sea of street urchins naked except for cotton dhotis tucked around thin hips. A woman with a brass pot on her head carried on walking as if nothing had happened, long-necked, upright inside her sari. 'We'll go straight to the High Commission. Will you be okay staying in my house?'

'That'll do fine, Alan. What's happening in Pakistan?'

'The army's back in charge and the opposition parties want them to hold free elections – maybe they will, maybe it's the start of another military dictatorship.' He shrugged. 'God knows.'

'I don't suppose there's any news of Cable and Ali Baba?'

'No, I'm sorry – I hope there'll be something when we get back to the office – but you may not have seen this.' He handed Nairn a copy of *The Times of India*.

Nairn frowned at the headline. *Soviet Army Chiefs Killed in Air Crash.* 'Good Lord.' *Five top Russian Army generals were killed on Monday in an air crash.* Red Star, *the Defence Ministry newspaper, said five flag officers and two helicopter crewmen died in the crash. The newspaper gave no details about its cause or location.* He looked up. 'It just isn't believable. Malinovsky, Grigorenko and three others – all killed at a stroke? That's more than careless.'

'That's what I thought too, particularly as there's mounting evidence that they were all involved in Malinovsky's attempt to replace Gorbachev.'

Nairn shook his head wryly. 'Some things don't change over there.' He fumbled for his pipe. 'Any news of Kirov?'

'I don't think we'll be seeing her here now. Her man won.'

'A defection at that level was really too much to hope for.' Nairn drew on his pipe reflectively, tamping the tobacco down with a box of Swan Vestas. 'And for my money we're better off with that woman staying right where she is.'

Mountford-White nodded. 'She'll live and die a Marxist, but she's nobody's fool.'

'I believe she deliberately planted that fellow Levshin on us with his files – an insurance policy in case Malinovsky stuck her in the slammer.'

'You mean to warn us? Stop us over-reacting?'

'Something like that.' The big car was turning into the gateway of the High Commission, saluted by the Gurkha guards.

37

Khunjerab

Sarah shrank back against the rock, suddenly terrified, vividly picturing the death of Wazir. 'Oh God, no,' she whispered. 'Please don't let them find us.' She watched as the squad of soldiers fanned out across the snow, Armalites cradled in their arms. Another line of figures in rough mountain clothes appeared from behind the shoulder of a hill; with horror she recognised them and clung to Nazim, pulling his head down behind a boulder. If only the wind would turn into a gale and whip up the snow to block out all visibility. 'It's the men that killed Ahmed Wazir,' she said deliberately. 'Is there any chance they'll miss us?'

Nazim put his arm round her firmly, showing no sign of fear. 'I don't know.' He wrenched a clump of spiky grass from between two boulders and thrust it into the donkey's mouth. 'Keep quiet, you bugger.'

They crouched side by side, peering at the scene through a screen of rocks. Sarah felt sick with fear but tried to remain rational, in control. 'I'm so bloody scared for you, darling. What they did to Wazir was . . .' She gripped his arm and swallowed. 'Horrible. Quite awful. You mustn't let them take you.'

'I'm more afraid for you, Cable.' His body was tense, like an animal waiting to spring.

'But what if they spot us?' Her voice shook, despite clinging desperately to calm. The line of soldiers was zig-zagging across the snow under a black sky; sometimes the wind dropped and they could hear the men shouting to each other. The Mujahedin guides clustered in a group until an order was given and they spread out with the others. 'What do we do, Nazim?' She was trembling. 'For Christ's sake, what do we *do*?'

His arm was still round her shoulders, firm, comforting; he gripped her more tightly. 'If we make a break they'll catch us in minutes. There are too many of them – and that helicopter.' He pulled the Browning from his pocket and cocked it, the click lost in the howling wind. 'But there's a chance – the snow's drifting and our tracks are already covered.'

Fifteen minutes passed, the donkey munching silently on scraps of paper from Sarah's pocket. She sighed with relief when the soldiers seemed to give up and turned back to the helicopter. The rotor clattered into life and it took off, followed by a second machine that had been hidden behind a bluff. 'God, I can't go through that again.' Her hands were shaking. 'How much further is it?'

They climbed higher for another hour, the road clinging to the edge of the precipice, until they rounded a corner to find it blocked by another rock fall, leaving only a narrow ledge overlooking the chasm. Nazim made her dismount and tried to lead the donkey past the pile of rubble, but its feet slipped on the running water and it refused to budge, digging in its hoofs and braying in fear. A cascade of pebbles crashed down into the abyss. Sarah raised her foot, finding that her damaged ankle was no longer painful. 'Shall I kick his backside?'

'No. He's afraid because he knows it's loose and he'll slip. If we try to drag him along that ledge he'll go over and take one of us with him.'

Sarah peered over the edge and shivered. 'It's one hell of a long way down.'

'We'll have to leave him here.' Nazim looked up from his watch as if calculating something. 'It's still only ten in the morning – we can manage without him.'

'Leave him? But won't he die of starvation?'

He roared with laughter. 'Ye gods, only the British would start worrying about an animal at a time like this. That donkey's a survivor, Cable, and valuable – he'll wander down to a village and somebody will adopt him.'

Reluctantly Sarah followed Nazim along the ledge, crawling on all fours, fighting off vertigo by not looking down at the sheer drop. The rock was loose and crumbling; at one point she was poised on a loose slab that swayed under her weight and crashed down into the chasm just after she moved on. She lay rigid, panting with relief, listening to the sickeningly long pause before it struck the bottom. At the other side of the landslip they stood and looked back, Sarah supported by Nazim as she tested her ankle. The donkey had not moved, his eyes full of reproach at their desertion. Absurdly she felt close to tears as the animal stood there, braying wretchedly, before he turned and lumbered off.

Nazim put his arm round her. 'Can you walk, Cable? If it still hurts, I'll carry you.'

'It's okay now, thanks.' They started to tramp on in silence, leaning on each other, boots slipping on patches of ice. The sleet had stopped and the frozen road rounded a buttress of rock. Ahead there was a plain, pale sunlight playing on the unmarked snow, glinting on the spires of ice that rose to each side. They stood transfixed, holding hands. 'Oh Nazim, it's quite beautiful. Shangri-la.'

He kissed her. 'Journey's end, Cable, we don't have to walk any further.'

Mountford-White's office in the High Commission was large and air-conditioned, panelled in light oak as befitted one gazetted as a counsellor. Outside, although it was well into autumn, sun blazed down and sprinklers played on velvety green lawn. Nairn stood by the window, waiting for the Indian servant in knee-length white coat to take out the silver tray of tea things. When the man had gone, he waved Mountford-White to a chair at the long conference table.

'The file on Forty Thieves can be closed, Alan. Our *Spetsnaz* brothers have solved that problem for at least ten years.'

'You're certain the Sulaiman store was the only one?'

Nairn lit his pipe. 'Probably, but we'll need to verify. If it was, we'll still keep an eye on Kahuta, but it'll take them a very long time to start again. The problem now is what's happened to Sarah. I thought she'd take refuge in the Embassy – do you think she's still with Khan?'

The younger man hung his jacket on a wire hanger behind the door. 'Islamabad is certain they escaped together, up the Karakoram Highway. Nothing has been heard of them since.'

'Can we extract them easily if they get into China?'

'The Khunjerab is blocked by snow. There's no way they can ever reach China, David – they're still in Pakistan and if the cold doesn't get them the army will. There just isn't any other way out.'

Nairn looked haggard as he closed the file. 'It's a bugger. Is there *nothing* we can do? Would the Indians put in a helicopter to find them?'

'They say it's too dangerous, could stir up the border dispute with Islamabad.'

'Have you pressed them?'

'The High Commissioner made the request personally.'

Nairn opened his mouth then closed it again, as if changing his mind. His fingers drummed irritably on the highly polished table. 'What about Khan's family?'

'Something's gone wrong there, too, David. They were staying in a cheap and rather nasty guest house. His wife was managing on the money she'd brought with her – but it won't last long and she left everything else behind. Even if they don't catch him, they'll brand him a traitor and confiscate his property.'

'We must find a way of helping them. Have you made any contact?'

'Yes. To keep it low-key my wife went to see them first – sorry you've had to leave Pakistan, Britain had great respect for your husband in Vienna, anything we can do, that kind of thing? Mrs Khan was depressed, desperately worried, but the children seemed okay – the little girl was making beautiful paper butterflies for her father. They were looking forward to seeing him again.'

'So?'

'So I went myself yesterday. They'd vanished.'

'*Vanished?*'

'According to the owner of the boarding house, some men who looked like Pakistanis had turned up with a car. There was one hell of an argument with Mrs Khan, then she'd just packed up her bags, paid the bill – and gone.' He met Nairn's eyes grimly. 'They could be almost anywhere by now, but there's only one destination that makes sense to me.'

38

Khunjerab Pass

Sarah dropped Nazim's hand as if she had received an electric shock and stepped back. 'What the blazes do you mean, we aren't going any further?' Five minutes before she had been so unreasoningly happy, standing beside him in the sunlight; now she felt only a knot of icy fear in her stomach.

He gave the contemptuous smile she had not seen since that first evening in Vienna. 'We're just below the pass into China, but also only a few miles from the frontier with Afghanistan.'

She met his eyes coldly. 'What the hell do you *mean*, Nazim?'

He looked away, staring across the white plain. 'I'm sorry, Cable.' Suddenly he was speaking too fast, his tone a strange mixture of arrogance and apology, of distance and desire to cling to intimacy. 'You see, after it became clear that the Russians were not going to lift a finger to save the coup, they belatedly offered sanctuary to any of the leaders who could get out to Afghanistan. Since anyone crossing the Khyber would be cut to pieces by the Mujahedin, we were told the only way was to trek up to the summit of the Highway, where a Soviet helicopter would land to make a pick-up every day for a week.' His mouth twisted bitterly. 'After all, flying a few miles across the border this high in the Karakoram wasn't going to put our precious Russian friends at too much risk.'

Sarah stared at him, transfixed with horror. 'Why didn't you tell me this before?' She wanted to scream at him, but her voice was even, clinging desperately to calm.

He faltered. 'Didn't want to raise your hopes – it might all be a fairy tale like everything else they promised. If it is, we'll just have to carry on into China.'

'And if this bloody helicopter *does* turn up, where will it be going?'

'Kabul, I suppose.'

'And what the devil do you think is going to happen to *me* when we get there?' She raised her voice against the howling wind. 'You fuck off to a nice villa in Samarkand and wait for the second coming, while I go to a labour camp?'

He radiated confusion. 'I thought we could stay together, if you wanted that too . . .'

'Don't be bloody ridiculous.' The floodgates of Sarah's fury finally burst. 'What about Farah and the children? I take it they've been spirited to Kabul by now? What about me – I'm twenty-six and British. This isn't Vienna any more – did you really think I'd want to live in some flea-bitten corner of Central Asia for the rest of my life? And why all the deception?' He made to put his arm round her shoulders but she pushed it away violently, seized the gun from his belt while he was off balance and danced back across the snow until there was a boulder between them. 'Don't touch me, you bastard! I don't know what you were in America with your Australian whore, Nazim, but you've been a paid-up Marxist one hell of a lot longer than this last week. Ten years? Twenty? I've had a lot of time to think these last few days. You've been mixed up in planning this coup for years, haven't you? Is that why you had such contempt for Wazir – because he and the others weren't ruthless enough?'

Suddenly she was facing a total stranger, his face ravaged by hate and bitterness. 'Shut up, woman! You don't know what real life is about – you've never been starving, too poor to even cover your body.' He crouched to get a better footing on the ice, moving towards her menacingly with those powerful shoulders and outstretched strangler's hands. She ran further away.

'Don't come all high-minded with me, Nazim. What were you playing at with the Australians? It was part of some nasty little personal plan, wasn't it? Your commie pals don't know, do they? That's why you were scared when Wazir caught us up – you thought I'd drop you in it, didn't you?' He came closer and she retreated again. 'Let me guess. You knew all about the bomb programme, but pretended you didn't? Right? You knew the Russians would take out the bomb store – I suppose that was part of their price? So you weren't really offering that – it was just a sweetener, wasn't it? You went to the Australians, all brave and high-minded, so that when you ended up in this new left-wing government, you'd have your own private line to the West. Was that it?'

'Stop running away, Cable, and give me that gun before you hurt yourself.'

Sarah clutched the Browning tighter. 'Not bloody likely.' She picked her way through fallen boulders to a bluff of bare rock where there was a little shelter from the gale slicing across the snow. 'What was the long-term plan? It was something big, wasn't it? Nazim for God Almighty?'

'You couldn't begin to understand, Sarah. Are you telling me there's something wrong with trying to replace an Islamic tyranny by a decent government? You think it's right to stone terrified women to death in the market place? Politics is not about what's perfect – it's about what's possible.' But he was no longer confused or wheedling. She was facing a man who recognised a dangerous opponent, who would kill to survive.

Sarah turned and stood with her back to the rock face, legs taut and apart, gripping the pistol. 'Don't come any closer. No, Nazim, I could forgive your politics – even if there *was* more in it for you than you care to admit, you'd have done some good.' The wind had risen higher, whining eerily across the ice, and she had to shout at him, her whole body trembling with effort and emotion. 'But it's not that simple, you bastard. You *deceived* me. You let me fall in love with you, when you knew I could only end up destroyed.'

'You're wrong, Cable – I wanted you more than anyone in my whole life.'

'Some of the time maybe you *needed* me, but for the rest you just used me.' She was screaming, waving the gun at him wildly as the wind gusted with crashes like thunder. 'Love? For Christ's sake, you left me back there with Wazir, because you sensed the army was close, didn't you? We didn't need that bloody donkey – you just wanted to use Wazir as a decoy, let them cut him up instead of you. And you left me with him, Nazim.' Her face contorted with anger. 'When you knew they might easily do the same to *me*.'

'So?' He was standing about ten feet away and a yard below her, the gale whipping at his anorak. 'Don't come the innocent with me, Sarah. You were an intelligence officer on a job.' His roar of laughter was snatched away. 'I'd say we make a perfect couple.'

She was caught unawares. 'When did you guess?'

'From the start. What else could I do but play along – and then . . .' For a second his face seemed to soften.

'And then what? Don't pretend you fell in love with me, I couldn't bear it, and don't try to wriggle out like that. I hated myself for what I was doing, Nazim.' Her voice broke with wretchedness. 'I *hated* myself. I've been to hell and back – I was terrified of the outcome, terrified for you. But you *knew* what you were doing, every rotten bloody inch of the way. That's the difference between us, you bastard.'

Suddenly she felt empty, her anger spent, eyes blinded with tears. She reeled from the blow to her head as he sprang up the path, snarling like an animal. The gun clattered on the rock as she fell to her knees.

When she recovered he was standing over her, aiming the pistol straight at her chest. 'Now shut up – that's quite enough drama, Cable.' There was murder in his eyes as he gestured towards a cave a little higher up, about twenty feet above the plain. 'We're going to sit quietly in there, out of the wind, and wait for our nice warm Hind gunship to arrive.'

Sarah bit her lip, her breath sobbing in defeat, furious at herself for letting him overpower her. 'How long will it be?'

'Another six hours. It should come just before dusk so the return flight is under cover of darkness.' There was a flash of contempt. 'Does that suit you?'

Her shoulders slumped as she turned towards the cave. 'I don't seem to have any choice.'

39

Delhi

Nairn slammed the clutch of pink telegrams back on the table. 'What a bloody, *bloody* mess. But you were right, Alan – according to Hughes the Red Army's lifting off survivors of the coup from just below the Khunjerab. Quite a little émigré colony assembling in Kabul.'

'Assuming Khan has managed to get to the pass, will he take Cable with him to Afghanistan?'

'I don't think so.' The old man's eyes looked haunted in their deep sockets. 'No, of course not. How can he? He'll leave her there, either with a bullet or to freeze. Plainly Khan has been mixed up with this Soviet-backed group for years, but I'm sure he wasn't dealing with *us* on their behalf. It was a piece of private enterprise, an insurance policy for the future – *his* future – and the last thing he needs is Cable blowing the gaff on that.'

'I'm very sorry, David.'

'Not as sorry as I am, Alan. I sent her there.' Nairn groaned and stood up wearily. He studied the green lawns through the open window. An Indian driver was parking the white Granada, its tyres crunching on the gravel. 'Come on, the car's here – if there's nothing else to do we'd better get off to the airport.' He walked to the door, hunched like a very old man.

Sarah huddled in the back of the cave, deafened by the sound of tormented air screaming across the ice. Her eyes were unnaturally bright and fixed on Nazim crouched in the entrance, his form outlined as a blacker patch against the grey outside, the Browning cradled on his knees. They had been like that for three hours, never taking their gaze from each other, the atmosphere of tension and mistrust unbearable. She was terrified, relieved only that he had not killed her yet.

The fact that she was still alive showed a weakness – he had a tender side and something in his mind could not forget making love with her – but she knew that he could never risk taking her to Kabul. At the last minute his need to survive would prevail and he would shoot her; he had no alternative. She knew that, even if he had not yet faced it himself. Caught in the narrow space, surrounded by rock, she was trapped, impotent, light-headed from hunger and exhaustion, petrified by closeness to death. Every half hour he rose and went outside to scan the sky. Each time he was gone she inched a little closer to the light, gripping the rough splinter of rock that had been lying on the floor of the cave, jagged, heavy and twelve inches long. Now concealed beneath her anorak, she had no clear idea what she could do with it, but it made her feel slightly less sick inside.

It was mid-afternoon when there was a lull in the gale and she heard the steady beat of aero-engines growing outside. Nazim rose and gestured threateningly. 'Stay there, don't try to leave the cave or I'll kill you.' He stepped out into a flurry of snow as two huge helicopters swept out of the cloud. Under cover of the clatter from their rotors, Sarah scuttled to the opening and peered out cautiously. Nazim was about twelve feet away, leaping in the air and waving his arms to attract attention. One gunship hovered while the other came down, bucking in the squalls until its skids settled on the snow. Men in steel helmets and battledress leapt out.

Nazim was still waving at the soldiers, oblivious to her, hearing nothing but the din of the engines and shriek of the wind. Sarah crouched like a tigress, every muscle in her body taut, then sprang at him, raising the chunk of rock and smashing it against his head with all her strength. He cried out and stumbled, dropping the pistol. Before he could recover she followed through with a kick to his kidneys, aware of him jerking in pain as she stooped to seize the gun. He turned on her with a snarl of rage as she danced backwards, gripping the Browning with both hands, firing a burst near his feet. 'Keep back, you bastard,' she yelled, elated even though her hands were still trembling. 'Keep back! Turn round and walk towards that helicopter. Wherever you're going, I'm coming too.'

'Go to hell.' But she fired another burst and a splinter of rock ricocheted to sting his cheek. He flinched, hesitated, then turned reluctantly, slithering down the loose scree to the ice of the plain. He hesitated again, but she screamed at him, brandishing the pistol, and he started to walk slowly in front of her, two black figures stark against the white. The soldiers were coming closer and Nazim shouted something to them, but his voice was lost in the gale.

A shaft of sunlight broke through the clouds and Sarah screwed up her eyes against the glare from the snow. It was a large helicopter with two rotors and a curious orange, white and green device on its tail. A flight of steps had been lowered under its belly and a pair of legs in black trousers and boots was coming down them. Suddenly Nazim cried out in horror and Sarah identified the insignia. At the foot of the steps Nairn turned to face them, wrapped in a sheepskin coat too small for him, and slowly raised an arm in greeting.

Nazim whipped round, his face contorted with fury. 'That's not a Russian helicopter. It's Indian. You betrayed me – you bitch! You bloody bitch!'

'No, Nazim, you betrayed *me*.' As if in a trance Sarah raised the Browning and switched it to single shot. She held it with two hands, arms outstretched, bending her knees as they had taught her at Bovington. She could not bear to aim at his face and lined up the sights on his chest, the torn waterproof concealing the smooth brown skin she had caressed. But her fingers were no longer tender. There was a cry of disbelief as he paused in his rush towards her. She steadied the barrel and held her breath.

The wind had dropped and the shot cracked over the ice like a thunderclap. It went wide, but at the second Nazim staggered back, throwing up his arms, and collapsed. His body jerked violently as Sarah fired again and again until the magazine rattled empty. In the long silence she tossed the gun against some boulders and stepped round the corpse spreadeagled on the snow. She glanced down at Nazim's face staring upwards, twisted in death, crimson blood oozing through his sweater. Despite the numbness inside, her eyes were full of tears as she stumbled on to the others, suddenly overwhelmingly tired. At the foot of the steps, Nairn spread his arms to embrace her. 'Sarah my dear, dear girl. Thank God you're safe – but what in the world made you do that? He would have been invaluable to us.'

Gently Sarah pushed his arms away. 'Invaluable to *you*, David.' The tears had gone as she gripped the hand-rail and pulled herself up into the warm cabin. She did not look back.

Postscript

Several United Nations organisations have their headquarters in Vienna, including the International Atomic Energy Agency (IAEA), but none of these is intended to be portrayed in this novel. All characters, government agencies and events in FRONTIER OF FEAR are fictitious, with two obvious exceptions: at the time of writing Mikhail Sergeyevitch Gorbachev remains the General Secretary of the Communist Party of the Soviet Union, and President Zia ul-Haq of Pakistan died when his aircraft was destroyed, apparently by sabotage or a ground-to-air missile, on 17 August 1988.

Although FRONTIER OF FEAR was written in the expectation of political change in Pakistan and Afghanistan, President Zia's death occurred after the book had been completed. Despite some last minute editing it was decided to leave the action set in the late autumn, which is why his assassination is portrayed fictionally as taking place about two months later than, in fact, it did.